DARIA'S DAUGHTER

DARIA'S DAUGHTER

LINDA HUBER

This edition produced in Great Britain in 2021

by Hobeck Books Limited, Unit 14, Sugnall Business Centre, Sugnall, Stafford, Staffordshire, ST21 6NF

www.hobeck.net

Copyright © Linda Huber 2021

This book is entirely a work of fiction. The names, characters and incidents portrayed in this book are the work of the author's imagination. Any resemblance to actual persons (living or dead), events or localities is entirely coincidental.

Linda Huber has asserted her right under the Copyright, Design and Patents Act 1988 to be identified as the author of this work.

All rights reserved. No parts of this book may be used or reproduced by any means, graphic, electronic, or mechanical, including photocopying, recording, taping or by any information storage retrieval system without the written permission of the copyright holder.

A CIP catalogue for this book is available from the British Library.

ISBN 978-1-913-793-23-4 (pbk)

ISBN 978-1-913-793-22-7 (ebook)

Cover design by Jayne Mapp Design

Printed and bound in Great Britain

Created with Vellum

ARE YOU A THRILLER SEEKER?

Hobeck Books is an independent publisher of crime, thrillers and suspense fiction and we have one aim – to bring you the books you want to read.

For more details about our books, our authors and our plans, plus the chance to download free novellas, sign up for our newsletter at **www.hobeck.net**.

You can also find us on Twitter **@hobeckbooks** or on Facebook **www.facebook.com/hobeckbooks10**.

To Jim, and in loving memory of Helen

DAY ONE – FRIDAY 17TH APRIL

CHAPTER 1

They would miss their flight if the taxi didn't come in the next five minutes. Daria stood at her first-floor living room window, peering up the street. And, oh, glory, as if there wasn't enough to worry about – look at those clouds! Her shoulders slumped as the sun vanished abruptly and fat raindrops spattered across the window, transforming the dusty Glasgow street below into a slick dark stripe, punctuated by scattered hailstones that melted to join the torrents scudding along in the gutters. Daria rested her head on the windowpane. A rainstorm when she had to get her daughter, along with everything the two of them would need over the next two weeks, into a taxi, out again at the airport, into the terminal building and through departures – it was exactly what she didn't need.

'Where's Daddy?' Four-year-old Evie pushed in front of Daria's legs to see outside, her pink 'ready for the taxi' jacket matching the hot little face under her beloved bobble hat.

Daria held out her hand. 'Come on, we'll wait downstairs.

Daddy's at a conference in Stirling – remember he said 'bye-bye yesterday? Got your rucksack?'

Evie ran to fetch the pink elephant rucksack she'd left on the sofa. 'Daddy's in Stirling?'

They had been through it a million times, but what did Stirling mean to a child who'd never been there? Daria dredged up a calm-Mummy smile.

'That's right. And today we're going to visit Grandma and Grandpa in Spain, and Daddy's coming to join us next week.'

And how good it would be to escape the coldest spring on record for a little while. Daria pulled out her compact and checked her make-up. She would do. Okay – case, daughter, handbag, travel bag. Come on, Daria, you can do this.

Downstairs, they stood in the shelter of the doorway, Evie leaning out to catch stray raindrops on her tongue while Daria fumbled for her phone. She was still scrolling down her contacts for the minicab company when a blue-and-white taxi screeched around the corner and pulled up by the gate. At last. Thank heavens the airport was a mere fifteen minutes away; they would make it. Daria grasped Evie's hand and wheeled the case down the path to meet the taxi driver, who was standing beside his vehicle glowering at them. He heaved the luggage into the boot, and Daria opened the back door.

'In we get, Evie, love.' She fastened the child's seat belt, then her own. Evie was a slight little thing and it was never a good feeling being in a cab with no child seat. Another reason to be thankful the airport was so near. Daria sat tapping her fingertips together as the driver organised his meter and turned on the engine. Come on, come *on*, we have to go.

The rain intensified as they crawled along to the main road and joined a column of blurry red lights as every commuter in the city headed homewards for the weekend. A band of tension tightened around Daria's head. They had less than twenty minutes now and they were inching along at a speed she could have matched on foot.

'We'll take the back road.' The driver pulled into a side street, and Daria breathed out. Traffic was flowing here, albeit slowly, but they were on their way at last. She put an arm around Evie and the little girl beamed up at her, then reached across to take Daria's hand and, oh, it was so lovely to be travelling with her daughter. They were picking up speed all the time; it was going to be all right. The taxi cut round the back of the cemetery and came to a wider road. This was better.

Daria leaned over to kiss Evie's damp little forehead, then jerked back in horror as a long, deep horn blared and headlights from an approaching lorry swept through the cab. A single, sickening scream left Daria's soul as Evie's rucksack scratched across her face. The taxi skewed sideways, only to be hit from behind and flipped skywards. Daria's arms opened in search of her girl, but she was pitched across the car, twisting in the air as metal screeched and tore around her and—

She was flying. Daria clutched at empty air then crashed down, rolling over and over on something hard, more screams coming from a distance. Hers? Her leg, her arm... Oh, please, Evie.

Silence. Stillness. Pain. Daria sank into darkness, but far, far away, something was buzzing. Find Evie, you have to find Evie. Swirling grey shapes replaced the darkness. Breathing was agony and she couldn't move her leg. Darkness was hovering; God, no, she mustn't die here. Stinging rain was soaking through her hair, running down her cheeks, her neck. Far off voices screamed behind her, Evie's high-pitched wail the nearest.

Evie, oh, baby, Mummy's here.

Daria fought to call to her child, but black pain was all around now. No, no, she was going to pass out. Her fingers splayed and met wet plastic: Evie's rucksack. Howling sirens swooped closer as Daria fought to stay awake. Please, somebody, come…

The voices shouting in the background were still too far away to help when the choking smell of petrol reached her nose. And everything went black.

CHAPTER 2

Oh, for an umbrella. Margie pulled up her collar and stepped out of the food bank into driving rain, her bags of groceries banging against her legs as she scurried along. Dear Lord, she was going to be soaked through by the time she got home. This coat had stopped being waterproof years ago, but her pension went nowhere these days and the rent was due next week. The food bank at the main road was worth a wet walk, though – for one thing, you didn't need a voucher there, and they usually had the right cat food, too. She turned left at the corner and bent her head against the rain, now lashing ever more viciously from the new direction. Her hat was soaked through; she should have waited until the storm was over, but the kits needed their tea. Marmaduke and Tallulah would be prowling around the kitchen yowling by this time, and li'l Tabitha needed good square meals, now she had kitties on the way. Margie gripped her bags more firmly and squelched on.

A car sped past, throwing a wave of water over her legs.

Margie yelped, then moved under the dubious shelter of an over-large fir tree at the gates to the college grounds. Inconsiderate beggar, who did he think he was? Soaked through to her skin, she was, she—

Dear God in heaven—

Horns blared, and Margie shrieked as a lorry skewed across the wet road, slamming into an approaching taxi. Another car bumped up on the pavement behind her then skidded away to slam into the back of the pile up of lorry – no, it was a petrol tanker – and taxi. Margie fell to her knees, still clutching her precious bags, her head thudding against the tree trunk and then the ground as the taxi flipped into the air and smashed down again, slamming into the other vehicles and shuddering to a halt just yards away. Fog swirled through Margie's head. Oh, that hurt.

She put a hand up to touch warm wetness running down her face and mingling with cold rainwater. Her head, oh, her head. The world was swaying around her. She pushed herself up to her knees, rubbing her eyes and fighting to regain clarity. Where was this?

A speeding car... the screech of brakes... her own voice shrieking, 'Bridie, Bridie, where are you?'

Margie gaped wildly at the chaos in front of her. Someone should help – where was everybody? But apart from distant yells coming from the main road, there was no sign of life on the street.

Bridie, her baby, where was she?

A thin wail came from her left. Margie scrambled to her feet and stumbled over to the remains of the three vehicles. The back door of the taxi had been wrenched off, and piercing wails were coming from the floor behind the mangled passenger seat. On the other side of the car, the driver was slumped over the steering wheel. Oh, my, he wasn't of this world any more. God rest his soul.

Bridie's eyes were staring in terror, and Margie reached in for her. 'Come on, my lovey, let's get you out of here.' The moment she touched the child's shoulder, Bridie screamed. Margie pushed at the front passenger seat, but it was jammed, and the back seat was half-collapsed against it. She straightened up and looked back. There was no one nearby to help her, though people further along the road were running in this direction. Maybe she should wait until—

A pungent stench filled the air, and Margie's breath caught. Petrol. No. This was wrong. There was no time to wait.

'We need to go. Quick!' She gripped a handful of the child's jacket and pulled. Bridie tottered out onto the road, her face twisted in a silent scream, one arm cradling the other. Margie searched around for her bags, then lifted both in one hand and took hold of the child's sleeve. The smell was getting worse.

'Run! Across the road! We'll fix you up in a minute.'

Bridie tripped along beside her, a constant high-pitched keening leaving her throat all the time they were lurching across the street to the cemetery gates. Pain twisted through Margie's shoulder and back; this was too much. Sirens screamed behind them, and the rain was driving down, and oh, no, she had lost a shoe. This was as bad as anything had been since – but no, no. She was getting muddled. Bridie wasn't gone, she was here. Margie stopped to wipe warm and sticky wetness from her forehead, then dragged Bridie into the cemetery. On and further on. Under the big willow tree, quick. That would give them some shelter.

They weren't quite under the tree when a flash of orange from behind lit the skies, illuminating ancient gravestones in a snapshot of terror. The explosion roared through the air, and for a second, the ground shook. Margie dropped her bags and clung to Bridie, the child's scream cutting off abruptly as she gaped at the inferno beyond the cemetery gates.

Oh, my. Smoke was billowing towards them; it was time they weren't here. Margie gave her eyes a rub with a soaking sleeve and bent over Bridie again. Poor li'l soul she was, rain running down her face and her mouth half-open in an anguished wail.

'Come on, lovey. We'll get you home and fix you up. You'll be right as rain in no time.'

Bridie's blue eyes opened wide. 'Where's Mummy?' Her teeth were chattering.

'Mammy's right with you. Quick as we can, now. Is it just your arm, or does anything else hurt?'

More tears. 'My head. And my leg. And my face. I want Mummy!'

Margie wiped Bridie's face with her sleeve. Now they were both blood-smeared, but it was all in the family. More sirens were wailing behind them, and Margie lifted her bags. Time to go.

'Dangerous, those cars are. Listen, that's the fire brigade here to sort things out. Come on. Sooner we're home, sooner we'll get you fixed.'

'I feel sick.'

'A nice hot drink's what you need. Give me your good hand. We'll be home in five minutes.'

Five minutes was hopeful to say the least, but the rain was easing off and cracks of lighter sky were visible beyond the rainclouds as they hurried through the cemetery. Margie stopped at the east gate and checked right and left along Burn Street. She didn't want any nosy parkers staring at the state of them both. Bridie was flagging, eyes half-closed and legs staggering all over the pavement; they'd have come to a complete halt if Margie hadn't pulled her along. This was the last crossing, though, here was their street – and they were home. She led Bridie down the side of the house to the back door and into the kitchen, where all the cats were circling around yowling for food.

Margie abandoned her shopping by the sink and bent over Bridie. What a sorry little picture she was.

'Come on, my lovey. Let's get you into bed and I'll bring you a nice drink.'

'Mummy?'

Margie bent over, blood and rain dripping from her hair onto the floor. She pulled off Bridie's hat and eased the soaked jacket over the child's good arm, wincing as a shiver ran through the little body. 'Mammy's here, darlin'. Up we go.'

But Bridie's legs gave way, and Margie only just managed to back her onto a kitchen chair. Dear Lord, she would have to carry the maid upstairs. It didn't matter; she'd done it so often before. She took a firm grasp of Bridie's narrow shoulders and knees and straightened up, trying to ignore the pain that flashed through her back at every step. This didn't feel like carrying Bridie upstairs; this was – a marathon. A war. Because she'd banged her head?

She had to stop halfway up for a rest, but at last they were on the landing. Margie hesitated. Bridie's room? That was in here, wasn't it? Bridie and – where was Maeve? And the boys? But they were older, they'd still be at school, yes. She pushed the door open and staggered over to the bed by the window.

'Here we are, lovey, your nice bed.'

The pillow had vanished for some reason, but she'd sort that later. Margie laid her precious bundle on the mattress and pulled off damp little shoes and trousers, then searched around for the blankets. Those rascals had hidden everything again. Bridie was fast asleep already, bless her.

Margie tottered into her own room and rummaged in the cupboard until she found a blanket, then returned and covered the sleeping child. There. They'd had a fright, but they were home now and she could make everything better, couldn't she? Margie coughed and rubbed her temples as the room swayed. This headache was atrocious. A hot cup of tea and dry clothes, that was what she needed. And an early night.

Everything would be better in the morning.

CHAPTER 3

Liane Morton inched around the last customer in the shop – a fifty-something woman dithering between two cocktail dresses and delivering a monologue about the shortcomings of each – until the clock was in her line of vision. Hell's teeth, no. It was after closing time already, and for the third time this week she'd be late picking up Frith from the childminder's. Mrs Peterson was not going to be pleased, but short of interrupting one of their best customers in mid flow, there was nothing Liane could do about it. Staff in luxury fashion boutiques like *Paula's* were expected to bow and scrape until the last customer standing was satisfied, and tonight Liane was the only staff member here. Working until closing time every weekday was the pay-off for not having to work at the weekend.

The woman talked herself to a standstill and pursed her lips at the dresses, one black with sequins, the other red with a gold lamé swirl. Liane shifted her weight from one foot to the other, fighting to keep her expression neutral. For heaven's sake, pick one and go. They're both ostentatiously expensive and that's what you want, isn't it?

'I'll sleep on it. I'll call tomorrow and let you know.' The woman lifted her coat and bag from the chair and stalked off into Glasgow South Side.

The instant she was gone, Liane flipped the sign on the door to 'Closed', grabbed her things from the back room and left, pausing only to set the alarm and lock the door. Oh, for the days when she'd been head of acquisitions in *BB's*, one of the big city-centre stores. And blimey, the irony of it all. Back then, she'd earned enough to support a family. Now she actually had a child, she couldn't afford the time a job like that took up. The pay at *Paula's* was better than she'd get at a less posh place, but waiting hand and foot on customers who were paying more for a dress than Liane paid for a month's rent was soul-destroying. She'd started the job as soon as she was convinced Frith was one hundred per cent well again after her final operation, but four months down the line, working here was causing more aggro than the pay was worth. It was scary, how things were spiralling out of control. And heck, it was nearly seven now and this must be the worst cloudburst they'd had all century.

Rain stinging her face, Liane sprinted along Kilmarnock Road, clutching her umbrella and zigzagging through the first of the weekend revellers heading to the pub for a Friday night drink. Glasgow South Side had lots of little pockets like this one, a row of upmarket shops, bars and restaurants set within streets of staid and once-elegant sandstone buildings. Why, oh why hadn't she looked for a childminder nearer *Paula's*? Mrs P lived twenty yards round the corner from Liane's flat: great in the mornings when she was rushing to work, but useless when she was late leaving the shop. And a taxi was out of the question. She would have to find another job, a part-time one. Working full-time was taking her away from Frith for far too long every day.

A distant roar halted her in her tracks. Liane stared to the west, where an orange glow was seeping into the grey sky beyond the tenements on the other side of the road. Wow. That wasn't good; something had gone up big time over there. But she couldn't stand about gaping. Get on, woman.

Ten minutes later she was jogging along a deserted street of red sandstone terraced houses. Mrs P's curtains twitched as Liane swerved in at the gate and ran up the path. The door opened before Liane's finger hit the doorbell, and Mrs P, a comfortable, grandmotherly lady who'd been recommended by the nurse at the local baby clinic, edged out, pulling the door shut behind her. Liane caught a glimpse of her waiting daughter, sitting on the hall stairs already wearing her jacket.

Mrs P's face had never been stiffer. 'Ms Morton, this is not good enough.'

Liane's heart crashed to her boots. 'Oh, Mrs Peterson, I'm *so* sorry. I had a really difficult customer ten minutes before closing time and—'

Mrs P didn't stop talking. 'You'll understand I need the evenings free for my own family, and to rest. I make an exception for you as I know you can't be here before quarter to seven, but that's my limit and you repeatedly take advantage. I'll keep Frith until the end of the month as you've paid already, but after that I'm afraid you'll have to find a different place for her.' She opened the door again and Frith trooped out, a worried little frown between her eyebrows.

Liane gathered the child in for a hug. 'I'm sorry I'm late,

sweetie.' She straightened up and met Mrs P's eyes. 'I'm going to do something about my job, Mrs Peterson, and I hope we can come to another arrangement then. Frith loves being here.'

Frith kicked at the path. 'I don't. I want to go home.'

Liane shot a smile at the childminder and hurried off before her daughter did any more damage. Sirens were wailing in the background as they trooped along to James Avenue, where home was a two-bedroomed flat on the ground floor of a terraced house. Frith skipped on ahead, and in spite of the bad start to the weekend, Liane's spirits soared. Frithy could skip now without coughing and wheezing and turning blue and panicking, and oh, Liane could skip for the sheer joy of it too. She knew she'd never be able to say thank you enough to the heart surgeons who had transformed her sickly little girl into – she hardly dared think the words – a normal child. No matter how awkward life was right this minute, Frith's pink cheeks and energy made everything worthwhile.

The moment of positivity was short-lived.

'Daddy!' Frith ran in at their gate.

Liane closed her eyes for two steps. A visit from Tony at this time on a Friday evening meant one thing only – he wanted money. And although the month was barely half over, new clothes for a daughter on a growth spurt meant beans on toast or the like for tea every day until pay day. Okay, Tony was worse off in that he didn't have a regular job, but that was down to his own pig-headedness. Other would-be rock stars took on regular jobs to foot the bills. Tony thought that was beneath him. He was a moody teenager in a thirty-three-year-old body, and it wasn't an attractive look.

'Hi, Li. Wow, you're looking good. Super chic.'

Liane glared at him. Pity she couldn't return the compliment. He was wearing his usual six-day beard above jeans and parka, and that dark blond hair hadn't seen a comb for a fortnight at least.

'If you're talking about my make-up, Tony, it's part of my job to look like this. Did you want something?'

He swooped Frith up in his arms. 'To visit my girl. Daddy can come for tea, can't he, Frithy?'

Frith's face was one big beam, and Liane sighed inwardly. The poor kid adored her daddy and in a way, Liane could understand. She'd been pretty keen on Tony too, once upon a time. They'd lived together for a brief but heady year and they'd had fun, but while the unexpected pregnancy hadn't changed that, the arrival of a sickly baby had. They'd known before the birth there was a problem with the baby's heart, and Frith was whisked into an incubator in paediatric intensive care immediately after the Caesarean. Tony had taken one look at his child and literally left the building. 'He's had a shock. He'll be back,' the nurses tried to comfort Liane, and they were right in that Tony did appear at regular intervals to stare at the baby, but he made no pretence of supporting Liane, who was aching with love for the tiny creature she wasn't allowed to hold during those first few days. The terror that she might lose Frith had been as slow to abate as her sense of betrayal at Tony's behaviour. Even now the memory was enough to have her in tears at the unfairness of it all.

Liane unlocked the flat door. 'Let's get the show on the

road, then. Scrambled egg for three coming up.' And thanks be Mrs P gave Frith a proper meal at lunchtime, so something small at night was enough.

Tony's face fell a mile and a half. 'Gawd. Is there a choice on the menu?'

'Not unless you go shopping.' Liane led the way into the kitchen.

Tony followed and opened the fridge. 'Ah. Scrambled egg and bacon, then.

Liane snatched the packet of bacon from him and tossed it back into the fridge. Who did he think he was? 'Scrambled egg and cheese. The bacon's for tomorrow. And to clarify things before you ask, Tony, I'm broke too.'

His sigh was more of a groan. 'Got any wine?'

She pointed to the cupboard and he grabbed a bottle Liane's friend Suze had brought round on Wednesday evening.

'No food, but posh wine, huh? What would people think if they saw that?'

Liane bit back a retort. Suze had brought a couple of bottles for a goodbye drink before her upcoming holiday in Kenya, but what was the point of explaining? Tony sat at the table working his way down a brimming glass while Liane made the meal, ignoring him. At least Frith was having a good time, showing Daddy her library books. Look at those shining eyes. Liane dropped a kiss on the child's head on her way to the fridge for the cheese.

Afterwards, she cleared away while Tony bathed Frith, but the shrieks coming from the bathroom didn't bode well for Frithy getting off to sleep quickly. Liane's frustration mounted. She put her head into the bathroom.

'Can you switch to "quiet before bedtime", please? She needs her sleep.'

Tony scowled. 'It's Friday, she can sleep until lunchtime tomorrow if she wants to. And she's absolutely fine now. You overprotect her.'

'Every child needs quiet before bedtime. As you'd know if you were a regular part of her life.'

Tony swung Frith from the bath and wrapped her in the towel. 'Mummy's stopping the fun, sweetie. Let's get those jammies on.'

Demonstratively freezing her out, he took Frith through to her bedroom while Liane perched on a hard kitchen chair to leaf through the banknotes in her purse. Would he leave if she gave him twenty quid?

Tony appeared in the kitchen, and Liane went to say goodnight to her wide-awake daughter. Fortunately, Peppa Pig soon had Frith's eyelids drooping, and Liane stroked the wispy blonde hair away from the child's forehead. She wasn't overprotective, was she?

Back in the kitchen, Tony had emptied the wine bottle into their glasses. He disposed of half of his with one swallow.

'Any spare cash around? I'll pay you back – we have a concert tomorrow night.'

She'd heard that one before. Liane handed over the twenty pounds. 'It's the last time, Tony. I'm going to hand in my notice. I don't have enough time to take care of Frith properly, working for Paula.'

He crammed the note into his pocket. 'Millions of mothers juggle kids and jobs, Li. You're not managing very well, are you?'

Liane swallowed down the rage. Take the higher ground, Liane. 'Millions of fathers juggle jobs and kids too, Tony. You could try a little harder.'

'You should get in touch with Social Services if you can't cope. I'll see you around.'

He left the flat without looking at her. Liane locked the door behind him then fetched her wine glass and flopped onto the sofa in their tiny living room. A bit of mindless telly, that was what she needed.

She pressed the remote, and pictures of an accident near Pollok Road filled the screen. Liane gasped in horror. That must have been the explosion she'd heard on the way to Mrs P's. Three vehicles had crashed, including a petrol tanker, and the number of dead was unknown. They'd only got one person out before the emergency services had to retreat and the whole thing went up.

Liane snapped off the TV and sipped her wine, staring around the room. Truly, you had to live for each day, because you never knew when your world would change forever. It was time for her to get on top of her life, and a new – cheaper – flat might be the best way to start. They didn't need a living room – a roomy kitchen and two bedrooms would do. Not that a new home would solve the job and childminder problems. Tears welled up, but Liane forced them back. She'd managed before and she was damn' well going to manage again.

DAY TWO – SATURDAY 18TH APRIL

CHAPTER 4

Evie scrunched up her eyes. The sun was shining straight through the window and everything was too bright to look at; it was making her head hurt, but her arm hurt much worse and her face was all stiff and funny and that hurt too, and this wasn't her bed.

'Mummy,' she whimpered, then stopped because it made the pain in her head jab twice as hard. Mummy should come and make all this better. Hot tears welled up and now her throat was all sore and choky too.

A noise came from downstairs. Evie turned her head away from the sun and opened her eyes a tiny bit. Where was she? There was nothing in this room except for an old wooden chest of drawers and the bed. It was a big bed. And the blanket smelled all old and nasty. She lifted her head and tried to sit up, but oh! Oh! Oh! The room was going funny. Her arm… oh, no. A wail escaped from Evie's throat, and she lay still, eyes closed again.

'Awake, are you, darlin'? All better?'

The voice came from right beside her. Evie peeked up. An old lady was bending over her, the lady from yesterday, when – what had happened yesterday?

'I want Mummy.'

The lady sat down on the edge of the bed, and Evie started to cry. Her arm was so sore.

'Mammy's here. What hurts, darlin'?'

'My arm. And my head. Where's Mummy?'

The old lady touched her arm with gentle fingers, then stood up and left the room. Evie tried hard not to cry; it was too sore. Then the old lady was back with a bottle of pills and some water.

'This will make you better quick as you like.'

The old lady dropped one of the pills into the water. It fizzed up, and she held the glass to Evie's mouth. Evie drank. It wasn't nice, but it wasn't too nasty either, and she wanted to be better.

The old lady stroked her cheek. 'What a mucky pup you are, all scrapes and blood.'

The fingers moved over Evie's head, but it didn't make it hurt any worse.

'Where's Mummy? I want Mummy.'

'Right here, darlin'. We'll give your face a wipe, shall we? You'll feel better then.'

Evie pouted. Why wasn't Mummy coming, if she was here? Was she sick too? And the old lady was a mucky pup as well, she had blood in her hair and she smelled. Two fat tears ran down Evie's cheeks and her throat went all thick and hot again.

The old lady had gone again, but she soon came back with a damp face cloth. Evie allowed her face and even a little bit of her head to be wiped, but as soon as the flannel touched her arm, she pushed it away with her other hand.

'No! That hurts!'

The old lady bent over the arm. 'Show me where.'

Evie pointed to the place, all the bit between her elbow and her hand.

'Hmm. Reckon that might need a bandage. Let's get you some breakfast, then I'll go to the chemist's and get one, shall I? Toast as usual? You stay here and I'll make you some.'

Evie didn't reply because she usually had muesli for breakfast, but the old lady went downstairs to make toast anyway. Toast was okay, except she wasn't hungry. But maybe after breakfast she could go and see Mummy.

By the time the old lady was back with breakfast, Evie was sleepy, but she managed to eat some of the toast and drink half the glass of milk. The old lady helped her to a bathroom with a very old big bath in it, then tucked her back into bed.

'Have a good sleep, darlin'. You'll feel better soon.'

THE BEDROOM WASN'T sunny any longer when Evie woke up again, but the sun was still shining outside. White fluffy clouds were chasing across a big blue sky. Where was this? Mummy should come and tell her.

'Mummy!'

Footsteps came up the stairs but oh, no, it was the old lady again. She was coughing, but she gave Evie a big smile when she came in.

'Feeling better? Look, I've got you a lovely bandage for your arm, a green one. Shall we put it on now?'

Did she feel better? Her head didn't hurt so much, but her arm did and she was still woozy. Her fingers had gone all sausagey and stiff, too. Evie lay still as still as the old lady sat down on the bed and opened a new bandage and wound it around her arm, all the way from her hand up to her elbow, almost, then down again because they had a lot of bandage left. There was a spiky clip to keep it on nice and tight. Evie moved her arm with the new green bandage – it didn't hurt as much as before, but it wasn't better yet. And Mummy… oh, she wanted Mummy.

She was about to start crying when a great big orange cat walked into the room and came to sniff at her bed. He jumped up beside her and the old lady stroked him.

'Here's Marmaduke to see if you're better yet!'

Evie reached out her good hand and touched the cat's head. He lifted up his nose and she stroked the soft fur under his chin with one finger.

The old lady chuckled. 'Tell you what, Marmaduke can stay here with you and I'll make us some lunch.' Then she was gone, coughing all the way back down the stairs.

Evie pushed the nasty scratchy blanket away from her arm. She hadn't asked about Mummy, but she was sleepy again anyway. Mummy would be here next time she woke up. Yes. Evie put her hand on Marmaduke's furry back, and closed her eyes.

When she opened them again, the cat was gone and there was a plate beside the bed with a cheese sandwich on it. Evie sat up carefully. Her arm still hurt, but she wasn't as woozy now when she moved her head. She got up slowly and wobbled over to the door. Everything was quiet, so she went into the bathroom. There was green all around the plug hole in the bath and up to the taps, but the basin was better.

She was sitting on the loo when the old lady called. 'All right, darlin'? I've got you another visitor!'

Mummy! Evie almost fell as she pulled her knickers up – it was hard with one hand – and tried to run back to the bedroom. Her legs wouldn't run, though, so she walked the last part and – oh, no. It wasn't Mummy. The old lady was sitting on the bed again, but this time she had a black and white cat on her lap.

Evie burst into tears. 'I wanted Mummy to come!'

'Tsk. Back to bed with you. You mustn't get upset or you'll make yourself ill again.'

Evie clambered into bed and pressed her eyes shut tight to keep the tears in. This was all horrible. Why didn't Mummy come?

Something nudged her cheek, and Evie opened her eyes to see a black furry face right beside her own. She held up her good hand and stroked the cat's back. He purred.

The old lady stroked the cat too. 'He's come to make you better. Eat your sandwich and I'll fetch you a drink. You can have some magic medicine, too.'

Evie sniffed. 'What's magic medicine?'

'It makes everything better while you're asleep. You can have a wish, if you like.' The old lady put the plate beside Evie and grabbed the cat, who looked like he wanted the sandwich too. 'Socks! Leave that be!'

Evie chewed and swallowed. 'Why's he called Socks?'

The old lady held the cat up. 'Look at his legs.'

Evie stared, and – how funny! It really did look as if the

cat was wearing white socks at the ends of his black legs. She managed a smile.

The old lady patted her leg under the blanket. 'That's better. It's a long time since we've seen a smile, isn't it?'

Was it? 'What's your name?'

'It's Mammy to you boys and girls, me dear. Look, here's your new medicine. You can have some now and more before you go to sleep tonight. You'll be much better in the morning.'

She reached into a pocket in her cardigan and brought out a medicine bottle. Evie knew what it was because Mummy had the same pink medicine in the bathroom cupboard at home. Mammy poured out a spoonful and Evie swallowed it down. It was quite nice, but there was no sweetie afterwards like Mummy gave her. Why was Mammy looking after her, anyway?

'Can I have a wish now?'

'Yes, but you mustn't tell or it won't come true. Lie down and close your eyes.'

Evie screwed her eyes up tight. Mammy was kind and the cats were nice, but it was Mummy she wanted. Mammy–Mummy… how funny. Pink medicine always made you sleepy. Evie lay still, wishing as hard as hard could be for Mummy to be here when she woke up again.

CHAPTER 5

Saturday morning, woo-hoo. Liane rolled out of bed and stepped across to the window to see what the weather was doing. Wall-to-wall sunshine – brilliant. She stretched luxuriously. Let the weekend begin, two whole days to work out what the heck she was supposed to do with her life. Not to mention Frith's life. Oh, for some supportive family nearby, but she was an only child and her parents were long gone, and Tony's folks lived in Kent. Liane tiptoed through to the kitchen, avoiding the squeaky floorboard halfway up the hallway. If she was lucky, she'd have half an hour to do her own thing before a tousle-headed monster arrived demanding Coco Pops.

Her purse was still on the table, and she peered glumly at the lack of cash inside. No treats this week unless she used her card, and she'd done that too often recently. It wasn't a good idea to use her dwindling savings on day-to-day stuff, either. Damn Tony and his selfishness. Waiting for her coffee to burble through the machine, Liane drummed her fingers on the work surface. Okay, there was nothing she could do to change the father of her child, but she could – hopefully – change her job into something that met Frith's needs better. Situations Vacant, here she came.

Twenty minutes later, she was on to the second coffee and still wading through a selection of unsuitable jobs when a thump from Frith's room coincided with Liane's mobile blaring out from her bedroom. She leaped up to silence it.

'You monkey, you've been at my phone again, haven't you?' Liane shook a fist in pretend rage at the child giggling in the doorway. Frith liked nothing more than to attack defenceless mobiles and turn the volume all the way up. It wouldn't be long before she was changing the ring-tone, too; kids seem to soak up stuff like that. Liane flipped the phone open – bummer, it was Paula calling. This was either a complaint about yesterday's unwashed coffee mugs or—

'Liane, I'm sorry but I need you here. Marie has to go and help her mother.'

Liane's head reeled. Marie was the weekend sales assistant and this was the third time the wretched woman had cried off work on Liane's free day.

'I don't have anyone to take Frith, Paula.'

Paula's sigh nearly blew Liane's ear off. 'Bring her with you, then. And be quick – I have four customers here.' The line went dead.

Liane's fingers were squeezing her phone so tightly the case popped off. She clicked it back on, trying to stop steam from coming out of her ears. Who did Paula think she was, ordering her about like that?

Frith's eyes were wide. 'Mummy? You look scary.'

Wait until you see me in action with Paula, kid. Liane blew a kiss at the child.

'No need for you to be scared, love bug, but Auntie Paula's going to run a mile when she sees me. Come and have breakfast. We're going to work.' Liane smiled grimly. Paula had made the decision easy for her. She was going to work – to hand in her resignation.

She didn't rush Frith, so it was almost an hour later when they arrived at the shop, where Paula was serving the woman who'd been in yesterday evening while another customer was walking around with an armful of clothes and a miffed expression.

Paula gave her a look that could have killed her on the spot.

'At last! Liane will be with you straightaway, Mrs Cromarty. Thank you for being so patient. *Tout de suite, chérie.*'

Liane glowered right back. Oh, she wouldn't make a scene in front of the customers, but no way was she going to leave Frith standing in order to serve Mrs Too Much Money over there. Taking as long as possible, she steered her daughter through to the back of the shop and helped her out of her jacket, grinning wryly. She'd always had the suspicion she'd only been taken on because she could speak French, which allowed Paula to display a posh little sign on the counter: *Ici on parle Français*. A French grandmother had its advantages – or not, depending on how you thought about it.

By the time Mrs Cromarty left the shop, Paula was head first into her wretched laptop and smirking, and Frith was making an excellent job of colouring in Peppa Pig at the fairground. Liane grasped her courage in both hands. Do it, Liane. Things couldn't be worse than they were now. Different bad, okay, but not worse. She would apply for some of the least unsuitable jobs and cross her fingers hard. Her savings would see them through another month or two.

'Paula, I'm handing in my notice. And I'd like to leave immediately, in lieu of this month's pay.' Liane stood directly in front of Paula, arms folded, ready to fight it out.

Her boss's eyebrows jerked up. 'I'm not sure about the legality of that, Liane, but you can go. Marie's spending the weekend settling her mother into a care home, and then she wants to increase her hours to as many as I can give her, to help cover the costs.'

Liane smiled sweetly. 'In that case I'll just leave quietly, shall I? Come on, toots.'

'No, you—'

Leaving Paula wide-eyed and waving her arms, Liane bundled Frith back into her jacket as they ran down the road, Liane laughing because she'd done such a reckless, ridiculous thing and the look on Paula's face back there was to die for – and Frith laughing in sympathy.

'Are we going home already?'

'We are. And guess what – Mummy will never, ever be late picking you up from Mrs P's again.'

'Never ever ever?'

'Never ever ever and a day.'

Frith beamed, and Liane's heart melted. All she had to do now was find a new job that would fit in with the childminder's hours, and persuade Mrs P to keep Frith on. Not so easy but, hey, she was Supermum today, wasn't she?

Back home, she settled Frith down for her Saturday

cartoons on TV and went back to the job search. You never knew, something magnificent might have come in while she'd been at the shop; Saturday was supposed to be the best day for job ads. She should buy a local paper, too, there might be different stuff there. And – great idea – she would put up some Job Wanted cards in the newsagent's. She was about to click out of the website when a colourful ad swam into sight, and she clicked to enlarge it. O–kay. They were looking for an assistant playgroup supervisor at the children's hospital. The job was mainly admin, with the odd shift in the creche – creche work wasn't something she'd have searched for, but how hard could it be? The playgroup was part of childcare arrangements for the hospital staff, apparently. The pay was less than she'd earned at Paula's, but heck, it was the perfect solution – Frithy could come to work with her. Liane clicked through to the website and started to fill out the application form. Qualifications? Well, she didn't have any in childcare, but she had more than the administration credentials required, and thanks to Frith's numerous clinic visits and the friendships they had with staff there, she'd be able to produce a pretty impressive list of referees. Steve, the charge nurse at Accident and Emergency might help, and so might Janine on reception at the cardiac clinic. Would it be presumptuous to ask Mr Wilson, Frith's surgeon? But why not? Nothing ventured… She had all their phone numbers, too, but possibly midday on a Saturday wasn't the best time to call. Liane saved her application form and danced through to the living room.

'Lunchtime, honey pie – and fingers crossed, Mummy might have found the perfect new job!' She whirled Frith into her arms and waltzed back to the kitchen. Frith's heart clinic appointment card, stuck on the magnet board on the wall, came into sharp focus as they danced around the table, and Liane started planning. She would suss out the playgroup on Monday, after they'd seen the doctor. Sometimes things did happen for the best.

Frith shrieked in her arms. 'Mummy! You're silly!'

'We're allowed to be silly on Saturdays, didn't you know?' Liane sat the child on the work surface and opened the packet of bacon. Sometimes it was best to live in the optimism of the moment, and this job application had at least a fair shot at being successful. She'd have Paula to thank if it was. How ironic was that?

CHAPTER 6

Someone was touching her. Daria forced her eyes open and blinked at the nurse fiddling with the drip going into her left arm. Nurse. A hospital? What…? Dark memories flooded back. Oh, God, the accident. Evie? Daria struggled to sit up, then sank back on the pillow as the nurse's hand on her shoulder restrained her and a shaft of pain flared down her left leg.

The nurse gave her a brief smile. 'That's right, lie still. Do you know where you are?'

'Hospital.' Speaking was hard; her throat hurt. 'Where's my little girl?'

'You were in an accident yesterday – you have a broken leg and a lot of scrapes and bruises. They operated on your leg last night and pinned it, but it wasn't a serious break. You'll be up on crutches in a day or two.'

Last night? Daria's heart thudded. What time was it? 'My daughter?'

'This is the adult hospital, but your husband's here. He's

talking to the doctor – I'll let them know you're awake.' The nurse hurried from the room.

Daria tried again to sit up, but she was aching all over. She was in a single room, and – 'the adult hospital'? She'd never been here, but this would be the new South Side hospital. The new children's hospital was right next door – Evie must be there, surely? Or had she gone home already? Why hadn't the nurse said? Fear snaked into Daria's gut. The crash – headlights coming towards them, then, yes, she'd landed on the ground, hadn't she, and Evie was crying somewhere. A faint sense of relief replaced the fear. A crying child probably wasn't too horribly injured. Oh, please, let Evie be all right.

The nurse came back in with a full jug and a glass. 'Your husband will be here in a minute. Try a few sips of water.'

Daria sipped, then lay back. This nurse might not know about Evie, but Noah would. She lay still, taking stock of her injuries. She ached all over and her head was groggy. A drip was feeding into one arm and she had a dressing on her head; her left leg was in a splint from the knee down; she couldn't move her ankle and it hurt to try. When would they let her go to Evie?

The nurse left her again, and Daria closed her eyes. She had no memory of being brought here; she'd lost hours. Who had been there for Evie in those hours? Noah'd had to come from Stirling – had somebody contacted his parents to come and mind Evie?

The door opened and Daria stared as Noah came in. He was unshaven, and dark smudges surrounded his eyes. Had he been up all night? Oh, God – what had happened to Evie?

He pulled a chair over to the bed and sat down, grabbing

her hand and holding on speechlessly, his eyes never leaving hers.

Dread slammed into Daria. 'What is it? Tell me.'

He gripped her hand even more tightly, two tears coursing down his face, followed by more.

Heat flushed through Daria. 'No. No, no.'

'She didn't make it, love.' Sobs shook his body, and he laid his head on their clasped hands, a deep, growling moan from his throat filling the room with a sound she'd never heard before. *No.*

Daria jerked her hand away, clawing at the bedcovers – she had to go to Evie, she had to—

The drip tore from her arm, and Noah yelled for help. The nurse was back in seconds, followed by a doctor in green scrubs.

The nurse held her down on the bed. 'Daria, breathe! We've got you. I'm so sorry, Daria.'

The doctor was fixing the drip back into her arm. 'Steady. We'll tell you everything, but first lie still.'

She couldn't fight them. Nausea rose in her throat, and Daria gestured wildly. The nurse held a basin under her chin while she was sick, then wiped her face and held the water glass to her lips. Daria sipped because it was the easiest thing to do. She clutched her chest, gasping for air. Her heart was hammering away in there but Evie... Evie's heart would never beat again. That couldn't, it mustn't, be true.

Noah was crying quietly and now she knew why he looked like that. He'd been crying all night. And she would be crying for the rest of her life.

Another nurse arrived with tea, then a different, older

doctor in a suit came in and pulled up a chair, sitting on the opposite side of the bed from Noah.

He leaned forward. 'This is dreadful for you both. All I can say is, it would have been over in a second for Evie. She didn't suffer.'

Daria couldn't look at him – or Noah. Didn't suffer? She'd heard Evie crying. Or – maybe it wasn't Evie she'd heard? 'Over in a second' meant Evie had died instantly and a doctor would know, wouldn't he? Bleak reality sent a wave of blackness over Daria, pinning her to the bed. She would never hear her child cry again.

A shriek rang around the room, her shriek, as all the pain in the world crashed down, encapsulating her in a cocoon of grief and horror. Daria fought the restraining hands, Noah's sobs joining her cries and bouncing off the walls. Someone was working on her drip. No, please, she wanted to…

But blackness claimed her.

DAY THREE – SUNDAY 19TH APRIL

CHAPTER 7

The squeak of the cupboard door was enough to bring the whole family running in the morning. Margie reached for the box of cat food, Marmaduke and Demelza snaking around her ankles and miaowing, long tails waving in the air. Usually it was Tabitha who'd get here first, but she wasn't so quick on her feet now, poor love. It would be better when the kits arrived. Margie shook dried food into two of the bowls strewn around the kitchen floor, then refilled another two with water, wincing as a pain zipped into her head and out again when she bent down. She was fine and she was happy, not like Socks and Topsy there, spitting at each other over their breakfast. Bless their hearts, you'd think they went short of food. Not in this house. Which reminded her, human food should be on the menu too. Tea and toast for her, milk and toast for Bridie. Poor maid had still been asleep when Margie put her head around the door on the way downstairs, but she'd wake up soon. Bridie was never one for lying in bed all day, not like Aiden.

Happy children's voices rang in Margie's head, little ghost children, and she smiled, slotting two slices of bread into the toaster. The family all loved toast and honey. She gazed back inwardly over years of toast and honey – and sometimes toast without honey, too, it hadn't always been easy. Such times they'd had, especially when they were still at Bantry Bay.

A thud from above brought Margie back to here and now. A glass for Bridie's milk, that was what she needed, yes, here it was. She lifted the milk carton and poured, trying to ignore the shivery feeling she'd had all night. That soaking hadn't done her any good. Now to see to her maid.

Upstairs, Bridie was kneeling up on the bed to see out of the window. The little face was flushed and Margie put a hand on the child's forehead. Still hot. She'd been tossing and turning and talking in her sleep too, poor scrap that she was. That was what happened when you got wet through.

Margie frowned. Something else had happened to Bridie too, hadn't it?

'You said Mummy was here, I want her to come now. And my arm still hurts.'

The child's voice was a shaky whine, and Margie tutted. 'Enough of your nonsense. Mammy's here looking after you – eat your breakfast, then you can have some more medicine. That'll make you better.'

'And then I can go home?'

'And then you can go downstairs. Marmaduke and Socks and the rest are missing you. They're all playing in the garden.'

Bridie slid back under the covers and accepted a piece of toast. 'I don't want to stay here. I want my real bed.'

The child was delirious. Margie fetched the Calpol, then her legs gave out and she plumped down on the bed. 'This will make you better soon.' She poured a generous spoonful of pink medicine into Bridie's mouth. 'Close your eyes, darlin', and have a nice sleep.'

Love welled in her heart as she stroked the tousled dark curls from the child's face. Her Bridie, fast asleep in her own bed, just as it should be. All the way across the Irish Sea, they'd come, she and Ned and their little ones. Full of hope, they'd been. Ned's brother helped get them a nice place to live, and a job for Ned was on offer too. They'd never had a house like this before, with an upstairs and three bedrooms – rich as kings, they were. But it wasn't Ireland, was it?

Memories of days gone by surged into Margie's head. Going to the beach down Bantry Bay, her Ned teaching them all to swim and catch prawns – you didn't get good prawns in Glasgow, not like the ones in Ireland. And all for free they were, too, not that it helped when Ned broke his leg and couldn't fish any more. That was when they'd come here, and the first cats had arrived then too. Always enough for an extra mouth, she had. However many kits had been born in this house? And when Tabitha's little ones arrived, the family would expand again. Margie beamed. Now she'd have a lie-down on her bed too, all this running up and down stairs was wearing her out.

THE SUN WAS high when Margie woke. She sat on the edge of the bed and stretched – many a long day since she'd had a nap like that, but it had done her good. Now to see what the girls and boys were doing.

She lurched to her feet, swaying for a moment before catching her balance. Her head still wasn't right after that bang she'd given it. Her fingers strayed to the graze along her hairline; ooh, that hurt. Just as well she had the family; they kept her going, though money didn't stretch far these days and Marmaduke was a fussy eater, always had been. And Tabitha with her kits should have the best too.

She wandered across the landing, glancing into the other room – oh! It was empty. Bridie… where was Bridie?

Two steps more and she knew. Her bad child was sitting halfway down the stairs, playing with Ermintrude. Always up for a game of 'you pat me, I'll pat you', was Ermie. Bridie glanced up – good, the flush was gone, the medicine had worked. And so it should, for the money Margie'd paid for it. But sitting around half-naked wasn't good for Bridie, was it?

'Where are your trousers? Put them on and you can have some breakfast.'

Bridie's bottom lip trembled. 'I had breakfast before. I want to go home.' She scrambled upstairs and into her room.

Margie waited, but a wail had her hurrying to help. Bridie was sitting on the floor, her trousers half over one leg, tears streaming down her cheeks. 'My arm hurts. I can't get these on.'

'Let me help you. We'll put your bandage on again, shall we? It's come loose.'

Her back twinged as she helped Bridie to her feet and on with the trousers. Neither of them was a hundred per cent after that soaking. Downstairs, she made Bridie sit on the sofa while she reapplied the bandage.

'Better?'

Bridie sniffed. 'A bit. When can I—'

'You can sit here and play with the kits while I make lunch. Cheese on toast?'

Bridie nodded, and Margie went to shoo Ermie and Tabitha into the living room to keep the child company. The others were all outside, bless them. Back in the kitchen, she looked around for the cheese, and put two more slices of bread in the toaster. Lucky, they were. They had enough to eat. Hadn't always been like that, back in Ireland, but in spite of what you heard everywhere, times *were* better now.

Humming, Margie sliced some cheddar and put it on the toast when it popped up. Under the grill for a bit – there! She called for Bridie.

The child sat at the table, her eyes wide and the little face sombre. But she ate her meal, and Margie gloried in the empty plate and glass. What a darlin' she was.

'We'll have a rest on the sofa and I'll tell you a story. Come on.'

Bridie gaped around the kitchen again, but she allowed Margie to lead her through to the living room. Most of the kits were milling around too, always the way when there was food on the go. Marmaduke was still out, mind you – he was a bit of a loner. Tabitha was too, usually, but today she was at home.

Margie settled Bridie on the sofa with Ermintrude on her lap, then went to make a cup of tea. She took it through to the living room, eight pairs of eyes – everyone except Marmaduke – turning to look at her when she went back in. Margie pushed Socks to the floor and took his place beside Bridie. Miffed, he stalked into the hallway and settled down there. That was Socks for you. Margie leaned back, rubbing her chest, oh, it was good to sit down. She'd just close her eyes for a few minutes.

The living room grew distant as she sat there, lost in her memories. Ned and the family… walks along the beach…

A bang came from outside and Margie snapped back to the present day. A story, that was what they needed.

'Remember the beach at Bantry Bay? You loved running along the edge of the water, letting the waves chase your feet.'

Bridie's face was clouded. 'I was at the beach once. The water was cold.'

'It always is, darlin'. And we found lots of sea shells, didn't we, and put them all in your daddy's pockets.'

'Where are they now? And where's Daddy?'

'He's away doing business, isn't he?'

Bridie was staring. Margie coughed, then settled more comfortably into the sofa. It was good to rest, now and then. Life wasn't easy. Topsy jumped up and settled on Margie's lap. There, her and Bridie with cats on their laps, just as it should be. Sweet li'l Bridie. Margie bent sideways and kissed the dark curls beside her, pleased when Daisy jumped up too. All they needed was—

Margie laughed aloud. As if he'd heard her, Marmaduke set the kitchen window banging as he came inside and joined the family in the living room. Margie leaned back comfortably, crooning as she stroked the heads within reach. Her darlin's. And they were all safe right here at home.

CHAPTER 8

A clanking noise was coming from the corridor outside her room. Sleep vanished and for half a second, confusion filled Daria before reality hit home. She moaned. Evie. She would never stop saying it and Evie would never answer.

Noah's voice came from her left. 'Wha—? Oh, you're awake. Daria, I called your parents, love. They'll be here tomorrow.'

He was in the chair by her bed – had he been there all night? His fingers scratched audibly across a two-day beard, and his sunken eyes told Daria he'd slept in fits too, if at all. She pushed herself up on one elbow to take stock. She still had a drip, and – she lifted the bedclothes to see underneath – the splint was still there, some kind of boot. But none of that mattered. Not her parents, not her leg, not Noah. Evie was gone.

A nurse bustled in. 'Let's get you up in a chair, shall we? If you're drinking enough, we'll take the drip down later and the physio will show you how to use your crutches.'

Anything to get out of here. But first she needed more information. 'I want to talk to someone about Evie.'

Who'd been the last person to see her girl alive? A paramedic? Or had Evie died immediately? Daria rubbed her eyes. That little voice she'd heard… she knew her own child's voice.

Noah gripped her hand. 'Later, love.'

The nurse met his eyes, but didn't look at Daria. 'The doctor will be in to see you in an hour or two. They have rounds downstairs first, so it'll be sometime after ten.'

Noah lifted his phone from where it was charging on the locker. 'I'll nip home for a shower, Dar. Love you.'

He barely glanced at her, though, and the nurse was bustling around with her head down. Daria gritted her teeth. They hadn't told her everything yesterday; understandable when she was still groggy and ill from the anaesthetic. But today, she wanted answers.

It was nearer eleven when the senior doctor arrived, by which time Daria was ready to scream at him. Noah was back but had sunk into a depressed silence in his chair – not that she blamed him – communicating in grunts and monosyllables, wiping away tears every other minute. Daria's tears wouldn't come today. It was all too raw, too painful. Until she knew why and how Evie had died, she wouldn't be able to start grieving.

The doctor shook hands with her, and Daria sat up straight. 'Mr Evans', his name badge read, so he must be a surgeon.

He sat down on the chair Noah had placed ready for him,

one leg crossed over the other. 'Let's start with you, Daria. Your fibula – the thinner of the two bones in your lower leg – has been pinned. It was an uncomplicated break, you can be up on crutches straightaway, but you'll have to keep the boot on for six weeks. We'll check your wound tomorrow and if all's well you can go home then.'

'Thank you. I'd like to know about our daughter and – and what happened. No one has told me anything yet. Where is she? Can I see her?'

Mr Evans cleared his throat. 'I'm afraid not. She's not here. I'm sorry.'

'I—' Daria broke off. If Evie was with an undertaker already, that was all the more reason to get out of here and go and see her baby for the last time.

She gazed from one man to the other. Noah was hunched over his knees, shoulders shaking, and Mr Evans was grim-faced. They still weren't telling her something.

'Tell me what happened!' It was a scream from her soul.

Mr Evans took her hand. 'You were thrown clear and were taken away first. I'm so sorry, but it was a terrible crash and Evie was – too badly injured.'

What did that mean, 'too badly injured'? Daria pulled at Noah's arm. 'Did you see her?'

A shake of his head. Daria sat still, struggling to breathe. Nothing, nothing would ever hurt her again like this. Her baby had been so horribly injured they hadn't even let Evie's father see her. But it would be different at the undertaker's; she would insist on seeing her child. And as Evie wasn't in the hospital there was nothing more she could do here.

'I want to go home. Right now. I'm discharging myself.' She was *not* going to stay here with sympathetic eyes following her every move, eyes that had no idea what it was like to know that your child had been mutilated and disfigured…

Breathe, Daria.

THEY LEFT the ward shortly after half past two, Daria having spent the past hour learning how to use her crutches and waiting for an appointment to see a doctor at the clinic the following day. She didn't speak as they drove away from the hospital, and nor did Noah. What was there to say?

Their flat was in Albert Drive, in what had once been a lovely detached house and was now two roomy apartments. Millie and Roger, Noah's parents, were waiting at the flat door as Daria sweated and thumped her way up the stairs on her elbow crutches. Tomorrow, Mum and Dad would be here too. A family in grief.

Millie's eyes were red-rimmed as she hugged Daria. 'Oh, love. Come in and sit down.'

Daria wiped her damp palms on her pullover, then rocked along the roomy hallway. It was the same flat she and Evie had left to go off on their happy holiday in Spain, but it would never be home again, would it? She eased down on the sofa and gaped around dumbly. The photos on the bookshelves, the sideboard, the window ledge, family snapshots of a small girl enjoying life – they were all that was left. And the big studio portrait on the wall where a fireplace had once been, with the three of them laughing at the camera and looking slightly artificial in the usual way of posed photos – it was unbearable. Evie's little face was almost life-sized.

Roger perched on the edge of an armchair. 'It's true what

they say, Daria, you never lose the love. We all have to hold onto that.'

What could anyone answer to that? Never losing the love might be true, but it didn't help. 'I want to see her. Mum will, too. We can go to the undertaker's on Tuesday.'

Noah's expression was agonised. 'I – she – she's already cremated, Daria. I made a mistake, I'm sorry. I didn't think you'd want to... She was too – too injured.'

The world stopped turning. Daria could hardly breathe. This was unbelievable. 'You mean, you told them to go ahead and—'

He thumped the arm of his chair with one hand. 'No. I – didn't mean to.'

That look he gave Millie and Rog then – what did it mean? Daria closed her eyes. Whatever had happened, it changed nothing. Evie was gone, with no goodbyes said.

Millie sat down beside her and took her hand.

'Daria, love – what's your last memory of Evie? The last picture of her in your head?'

Daria's thoughts whirred through the taxi journey. Evie, excited to be going to Spain, that happy little face beaming up at her, those brightly shining eyes. Tears rose and escaped as Daria gripped the hand holding hers. Millie was right – this should be the last memory.

DAY FOUR – MONDAY 20TH APRIL

CHAPTER 9

Saturday's euphoria was still intact on Monday morning. Liane stretched luxuriously, glancing at the alarm on the bedside table. Twenty to eight – brilliant. Loads of time to have a leisurely ladies' breakfast with her daughter before they headed over to the hospital for Frith's eleven-thirty appointment. Life was good. Granted, pretty soon she would fall off this elation trip and start thinking, OMG what have I done? – but that day hadn't come yet, though it might if she didn't get an interview for the creche job. She'd managed to get hold of Steve, the A&E charge nurse, and Janine, the cardiac clinic receptionist, at the weekend, and both had promised her a glowing reference. The jury was still out about whether to ask Frith's surgeon, that might be a bit too cheeky. Another possibility was the nurse at the local baby clinic. Frith didn't go there any more, of course, but Sister Annie still took a keen interest and had made Liane promise to send clinic updates after each appointment.

The elation trip came to an early and abrupt end when she stepped into the shower and discovered it wasn't providing water today. Bummer. No hot water was a regular occurrence, but no water at all was a new low. Liane made do with a lick and a promise at the basin, vowing to find a new flat as well as a new job as soon as was humanly possible. She could do Superwoman at the same time as Supermum, couldn't she?

Frith was banging on the bathroom door. 'I have to go!'

'In you come. Toast or Coco Pops for breakfast?'

'Toast *and* Coco Pops!'

Rejoicing, Liane pulled on jeans and the posh sweater she'd found at the local charity shop after Christmas, and went to lay the table. It wasn't long since she'd had to bribe Frith into eating more than two mouthfuls of anything. Hearing her demand double rations was amazing.

'Clinic this morning,' she reminded her daughter when breakfast was over and the little girl was foraging around in her toy box. 'Do you want to go early and have extra time to play in the waiting room?'

'Uh-huh.' Frith gave her a tiny smile. 'And if other children have all the good toys, can I play with your phone?'

Liane pretended to think. Like most kids, Frith would spend all day glued to a screen if she was allowed. The problem was, Liane's phone had been the perfect distraction for a long time while Frith was poorly, and breaking the habit wasn't easy.

'All right. But no more than ten minutes. We'll take them from your TV time today, so think hard if that's what you really want.'

They set out at ten o'clock, Liane zipping her jacket –

another charity shop find – right up to her chin, and Frith jamming on her green woolly hat with the enormous pom-pom. It was chilly for April, and oh, for her nice warm Fiat to take them to the hospital. Liane sighed. Her car had been the first thing she'd given up when Frith was born and it became clear she wasn't going to be able to return to work any time soon. The second thing had been the West End flat. The third thing had been Tony.

The bus trundled across Glasgow South Side and deposited them right outside the Children's Hospital. Frith grasped Liane's hand as they walked to the entrance, craning her neck to get a better look at the high buildings.

'Can we go up on the roof one day?'

'Doubt it. We could go up to the top floor sometime and see what the view's like.' Liane dropped Frith's hand when they were inside the children's building. 'Give me your jacket, love bug, it's warm in here.'

Frith knew the way and skipped along in front to the cardiac clinic. Liane's heart melted at the sight. Would she ever get used to having a well child? It was the best feeling ever. Thank you, Mr Wilson, and thank you Glasgow for having such a lovely big new hospital for children. The place was light, bright, airy and colourful, none of which was vitally important, of course, but they were very pleasant extras when you had to be here anyway. She slowed down at the corridor leading to the staff creche, but no, she wouldn't look until she was sure she had an interview. No point tempting fate.

Janine was on duty at the clinic reception desk and waved when Liane and Frith appeared. 'You're well on time! We're running about fifteen minutes late. Have you sent in your application, Liane?'

'Not yet. I'm dithering about the third referee. I was wondering about asking Mr Wilson?'

Janine put her head on one side. 'Do you have an alternative?'

'Yes, the local baby clinic nurse.'

'Right – ask her, and I'll have a chat with Mr Wilson and see if he can put in an unofficial word for you. That way, you'd have four people.'

The perfect solution. Liane took Frith's clinic card and went to sit in the waiting area, where Frith was already setting out miniature cups and saucers at the play table. You could almost imagine you were at the kids' corner in a restaurant or shopping centre here. Almost. Liane rubbed her chest as a poor little boy with blue lips came in with a thin woman and a frowning man. That had been them, last year. Except Tony never came on clinic visits. She heaved a sigh, inhaling warm and heavy hospital air imbued with the peculiar sharpness that came from antiseptic or something and brought tears to your eyes. Get yourself a coffee, woman, and be happy. You have nothing to howl about today.

'Want a drink, Frithy?' Liane fished in her purse for coins for the machine.

Frith scrambled to her feet. 'Can I have cola?'

Blimey, she was going to have to be Bad Mummy again. What would it be like when Frith hit puberty?

'You can either have cola here or with your hamburger later. Come on, we'll see what the machine has.' Clinic days always included having dinner out, to make up for the blood tests and other less comfortable parts of the experience, and Frith usually chose McDonald's.

'Hot chocolate, then.' Frith ran over to the machine in the main hallway.

Liane handed over the coins and pointed out the correct buttons to press. She'd have hot chocolate too. It was better than the coffee.

Steve popped up beside her in biking gear. 'Hi there. I hoped I'd catch you before I started my shift. Applied yet?'

'I'll send it in today. Thanks for your help.'

'No probs. I'm on in ten – see you around.'

He gave her a wave as he strode off, and Liane waved back. He'd been staff nurse in children's cardiology before his promotion to head of A&E in the adult hospital next door. How many times had she dashed in with a blue and panicking Frith and found him there? A dozen at least, and he'd helped every time.

They started back to the waiting area, sipping, and a tall, thin woman on a chair further along the hall drifted into Liane's field of vision. She was staring at them – or more specifically, she was staring at Frith. Nothing like having a stranger ogle your child, was there? Liane treated her to a sniffy look – oh, wait. She knew this woman; they'd been in the same class for some subjects when they started secondary school, in fact they'd been pretty friendly for a while, but the friendship had petered out when Daria moved away two or three years later. Hot choc in hand, Liane made her way over, Frith following on.

'Hi there, Daria. It's been a while, hasn't it?' Liane tried not to stare. The other woman looked shocking, pale and drawn, though the splinted foot and crutches might be the reason why. But why was she here in Children's, all alone?

'Liane! Sorry, I didn't mean to be rude. Your little girl reminded me of someone, that's all.'

Daria's voice was gravelly and not quite steady, and Liane sat down beside her. Frith was blinking up at Daria and Liane stroked the tousled hair back from her daughter's forehead. 'Same cheeky face, huh?'

To Liane's astonishment, Daria reached out and put the palm of her hand on Frith's cheek, gazing hungrily at the child. Oh, no. Surely 'someone' hadn't been ill here, or worse?

Daria leaned back in her chair again. 'More her manner – the happiness in her eyes when she was sipping her drink.'

Fortunately, Frith wasn't fazed. 'It's hot chocolate. It's my favourite, after cola. We're going to McDonald's later, aren't we, Mummy?'

'It's your clinic day treat, isn't it?' No need to let Daria think she fed her child junk food as a regular thing. Liane hesitated. This wasn't the place for a complicated conversation. Whatever was going on with Daria, it wasn't good. She gestured at the crutches. 'I guess you had an accident? We must get together sometime and catch up.'

Daria smiled briefly, then pulled herself to her feet. 'I'd like that. I have to go, though. I have an appointment next door. I thought I'd come in here first to – to see the place.'

'Liane! Frith's up next for bloods!' Janine was standing at the corner, waving to them.

Liane got to her feet. 'Daria – can I help at all? Look.' She scribbled on an old shopping list in her bag. 'Here's my mobile number. And I'm on Facebook, Liane Morton.'

'I'm Daria Geddes on Facebook. I'll be fine, thanks. My husband's picking me up afterwards.'

Liane frowned, giving her old friend's shoulder a little pat. Daria didn't look well enough to be wandering around all alone. What was her husband thinking? Liane hurried back to the cardiac clinic with Frith, who was still slurping her hot choc.

Janie, one of the clinic nurses, was waiting for them at the desk.

'Your turn, Miss Frith. Let's get you through and measured.'

Liane put Daria to the back of her mind and walked after Frith and Janie. Clinic now, then she'd get her job application sent in and check out the flats-to-let advertisements. And she had a friend to find on Facebook. Superwoman was needed again.

DAY FIVE – TUESDAY 21ST APRIL

CHAPTER 10

She'd been here for days and days and she was better, except for her arm, and still Mammy wouldn't let her go home. It wasn't fair. And Mammy'd told her a lie, too – Mummy wasn't here after all.

Evie waited in her room until Mammy heaved herself out of bed in the room next door and into the bathroom with her usual cough and an 'Uff!' Now it was safe to go downstairs, and maybe she could sneak out and find Mummy. She wouldn't be too far away; she never was. Evie crept downstairs, slowly because she still couldn't fasten her trousers with one hand and they kept falling down.

The cats were prowling around the kitchen miaowing and waiting for Mammy – they wanted their breakfast. Evie counted them: Marmaduke, Topsy, Daisy, Demelza, Tallulah, Ermintrude, Tabitha and Socks. Everyone was here. She bent to stroke Marmaduke, but he was busy pacing up and down to get into position for breakfast. Evie tried the back door. It was locked, so she clambered onto a chair to wait too.

Mammy's kitchen was nothing like Mummy's. Mummy had black and grey cupboards and a shiny sink and a black table and chairs. Everything here was old and bashed. Big fat tears welled up in Evie's eyes and she bent forward, holding onto her poor sore arm with the other hand. Tallulah was watching her. She had a piece of one ear missing; that must hurt too.

'Tsk, is no one except me allowed to make breakfast?' Mammy barged into the room, coughing, and rummaged in a cupboard. 'Here, maid, you can fill up the food bowls while I make toast.' She handed over a box of cat food.

Evie shook it and immediately all the cats were swarming around her feet, miaowing up at her. She giggled. 'They're hungry!'

'Give them some food, then. These two bowls by the sink. Don't fill them all the way up.'

Evie shook cat food into the bowls. It looked yukky, just little brown blobs, but the cats couldn't wait. She was nearly knocked down in the rush for the first bowl.

Mammy laughed. She poured milk into a glass for Evie, then lifted the cats' water bowls – they had two of these as well – and filled them at the tap.

'That's the li'l rascals happy, now let's have ours.' She put a plate with toast for Evie on the table.

Evie sat up again. Mammy only ever put butter on the toast, but that was okay. Better than the yukky marmalade Mummy had sometimes. The sun shone in the kitchen window and glinted off a pile of empty glasses that were waiting to be washed. Evie moved her head back and forwards, making little sunshine rainbows dance on a glass with a broken bit.

'Can I go outside after breakfast?' She nearly said, 'Before I go home?' too, but that would have made Mammy cross. But one day Mammy would say, 'This is the day you go home, Evie.' Except Mammy called her Bridie, or maid. Evie licked her fingers. She'd seen a bride once, at the church up the road from home, a lovely bride with a long white dress and a big bunch of pink and white flowers. It would be nice to be a bride one day. But for now, she was too little.

Mammy was frowning. 'You're still flushed. Let me feel your head.'

A hand scraped over Evie's forehead.

'Much too warm. You can rest in your room this morning and have a nap before lunch. Tabitha can go with you. I'll bring you some medicine.'

Evie scowled. 'I don't feel too warm. I feel fine. Except for my arm.' She pouted at her arm, lying still as still against her tummy. It hurt whenever she tried to move it, and her fingers were all big and stiff. 'I want to go outside. I want to go home.'

Mammy thumped her hand on the table and Evie jumped.

'We're not going back to Ireland, do you hear? And don't you remember what happened when you went out to the beach with Aiden too soon after you had measles, and I was that busy nursing Maeve through it I didn't see you'd sneaked out?'

Evie shook her head. She didn't remember any of that.

'Well, I remember. Pneumonia, you got, and it was nearly the end of us both. We're not letting that happen again, are we? It's precious, you are.' Mammy coughed and banged her chest.

Evie sat, swinging her legs and pouting at the floor. It was much, much dirtier than Mummy's floor ever was. The cats had made muddy footprints everywhere and there was a splodge of brown sauce or something under the table. She didn't want to be the end of anyone. It might be best to stay inside until she was all better.

Mammy was taking little sips of tea that must be too hot because she was pulling a face at every swallow. Evie slid down and went around the table. 'Can you fix my bandage? It came loose in the night again.'

Mammy bent over to peer at her arm. 'Fingers still swollen, eh? I think that needs a splint, you know. We'll see what we can do.'

A splint? She'd never had one of those before. 'Will it hurt?'

'Bless you, child, it'll take the hurt away. Upstairs with you, and I'll come in a moment with your medicine.'

Evie went to the door, holding her trousers tight with her good hand in case she tripped over them.

Mammy laughed. 'Come here with you!' She did up Evie's trousers and gave her a little push towards the stairs. Evie went up, holding her sore arm again. It was good Mammy wasn't cross any more. Tabitha and Socks both came up with her, and Evie went over to the window to wait for Mammy.

The garden down there had lots of dandelions. Was it Mammy's garden? Behind the dandelions was a whole lot of bushes and a couple of trees, and on the other side of that was a house. The windows of the other house had no curtains so maybe nobody lived there any longer. Maybe new people would come soon.

Mammy came in with the medicine bottle and a handful of spoons. 'Let's have this arm, then.'

Evie sat down on the bed beside Mammy and they took the bandage off and looked at her arm. The bruises were getting better.

Mammy held a big spoon close to Evie's arm, then put it down again. 'Too wide. Let's try this one.' She lifted a wooden spoon.

A wooden spoon? How funny. Evie barely moved a muscle while Mammy held the wooden spoon under her arm so her hand was in the spoon bit.

'Perfect. Don't worry, this will let your arm rest while it's getting better.' She wound the bandage round Evie's arm and the wooden spoon, and when she was finished, Evie lifted her arm. It did feel a little better. She gave Mammy a smile.

Mammy smiled back. 'Let's get that medicine inside you where it'll do most good.'

Mammy used the plastic spoon that came with the bottle for that, and Evie swallowed. Mammy gave her more pink medicine than Mummy did.

'You lie down on top of your bed beside Tabitha and Socks and have a rest.'

A scratchy hand stroked Evie's cheek, then Mammy was coughing her way downstairs again. Evie stroked Tabitha's soft back. She didn't mind resting when she had cats to keep her company.

MARGIE LEANED on the table downstairs, catching her breath. This cold was settling in her chest; she was wheezing away like an old steam train today. She put the Calpol bottle into a high cupboard where the cats wouldn't get at it, and pulled out the bottle of aspirins. This bottle had lasted her for years, but there were only two left. She swallowed them both with the dregs of her tea. There.

Upstairs, all was quiet. Margie went through to the living room and dropped onto the sofa to close her eyes for a moment. Poor li'l Bridie with her bad arm. But the splint would help, and she could get some cream at the chemist's next time. She'd need to go for more aspirin anyway, it wouldn't do for her to be ill and not an aspirin in the house, would it? The chemist was expensive, but she had a stash of spare cash in the kitchen for emergencies. She'd been keeping it for Tabitha; those kitties would need kitten milk when they were a few weeks old, but time enough until then to save up again. Though somehow, her pension wasn't lasting very well this week.

Disturbed, Margie went back to the kitchen and opened the drawer where the stash was. Good, that would do for cream and aspirins. And some chocolate for the maid, too, she was being such a good girl. Memories of Bridie running wild along the beach at Bantry Bay slid through Margie's mind. What a tomboy she was. And that showed you the child wasn't quite right at the moment. Rest and medicine were exactly what Bridie needed and at least she was being cooperative, not like Aiden and – actually, where was Aiden? She hadn't seen him for a while, nor Sammy or Maeve. Margie grabbed hold of the drawer as the kitchen wavered briefly.

And Ned – but Ned was gone, wasn't he? They'd come to Glasgow and for a while everything had been fine, but then – Ned wasn't here any more. Margie's head throbbed, and she massaged her temples, stumbling through to the sofa again. Close your eyes, Margie, and dream.

Their cottage in Ireland. Her and Ned and the babies... then before they knew it the babies had grown into children, and imps they all were. Those cheeky little faces round the table, how they'd laughed. They'd never had cash to splash, but the good times had made up for that. You didn't need money to laugh and love.

Now they were in Glasgow, but it was all so hazy, it was better not to think too much. Things often came back to you when you were busy doing something else. Margie circled her shoulders to relax her breathing. There! She'd make sausage and egg for lunch, Bridie liked that and an extra sausage or two would go down well with the kits, too. Marmaduke loved sausages, and so did Sammy and Maeve and – where was Aiden?

Margie swung herself round until she was lying along the sofa, her head pillowed on Bridie's jacket. Topsy came to cuddle in by her chest, and Margie smiled.

A little sleep before lunch would do her good too.

DAY SIX – WEDNESDAY 22ND APRIL

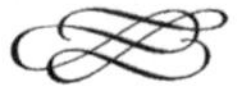

CHAPTER 11

Liane was pouring boiling water down the kitchen drain, which had blocked yet again, when a message pinged into her phone. She abandoned the kettle and grabbed her mobile. Theoretically, she wasn't going to hear anything about her job application until the end of the week at the earliest; she'd only sent the application off on Monday, but you never knew.

It was Steve. *Is this a good time to call?* Golly. What was this about?

Sure. Liane poked her head into the living room, where Frith was busy with her Lego, then sat at the kitchen table, waiting for Steve's call. It came half a minute later.

'Liane, hi. My break's almost finished so I've only got two seconds, but I've just had a phone call you might find interesting.'

Liane jerked upright. 'About Frith's test results?' Oh, my giddy aunt, were the bloods okay? They took a sample from Frith at every clinic appointment, but the results needed a day or two to come back. If everything was fine, they heard nothing – was this bad news?

'Hey, don't panic, it's nothing like that. Sorry. The call was from the chief administrator, about your application for the creche job. This is completely off the record, but you're on the interview list. I gave you a glowing reference and mentioned you'd already left your previous job and could start any time. I hope that was okay?'

'Wow! Yes. Thanks, Steve.' He was going to a lot of trouble over this.

'I reckon you're in with a really good chance.' His voice in her ear sounded warm and confident. 'It's my afternoon off – I was wondering if you and Frith would like to go for a coffee? I could give you some hospital tips and info that might help at the interview. There's a good café near Boswell Park.'

Liane's brain was still racing. He was asking her out. For a coffee. With her daughter. To talk interviews. And – why not? It wasn't as if she was inundated with coffee invitations. Almost everyone she knew had jobs to go to on Wednesday afternoons.

'Sounds good – some tips would be great. I'm what you might call out of interview practice.'

He laughed. 'You and me both, but we'll work out a strategy for you. It's the Rock Café – three o'clock okay?'

'See you there!' Liane ended the call and grinned at her phone. Was this a date?

. . .

'WHY AREN'T we going to the café at the hospital with Steve?' Frith's face was one big question mark as they walked past the park gates on the way to the Rock Café.

'He's not at work this afternoon. It'll be a nice change from the hospital, don't you think? And shall we come back to the park on our way home afterwards?'

'To feed the ducks!'

Frith skipped along, wispy blonde hair flying in the breeze, and Liane hugged herself. It was springtime, she had a decent shot at a new job, and she was out with her daughter to meet a very nice man. A good afternoon.

Heat from the café hit them the moment Liane opened the door. Frith unzipped her jacket of her own accord and ran across to Steve, who was sitting at a table near the bar. Liane followed on. The café was all imitation red leather seats, Formica tables and funky lamps, and could have come straight from the sixties. She'd never been here before, but look, there was a little stage up the back so they must have live music sometimes.

'Ladies. Good to see you.'

Steve wasn't the same person out of uniform. His dark blond hair – rather like Tony's, now she noticed it – was falling over his forehead, and the black sweatshirt he wore made his eyes look bluer. Liane hung Frith's jacket over the back of the little girl's chair and sat down. She wasn't used to meeting good-looking men in cafés. Steve's fingers were tapping his other arm – was she late? Or was he nervous? Or regretting this?

Steve handed her a menu. 'Okay. Frith and I are having a competition to see who can enjoy their ice cream most. Would you like to join in?'

Liane relaxed – sort of. 'I certainly would. Look, Frithy, they have banana splits.'

After ten minutes' chat about ice creams and other favourite desserts, Liane's fingers were tapping too. Nothing was more conversation-killing than your four-year-old making eyes at the man who'd invited you both to said conversation. The arrival of the ice creams gave Frith something more important to concentrate on, and Steve winked at Liane over the little girl's head.

'Got your list of intelligent questions to ask at the interview ready?'

She hadn't, but the following half hour gave her several ideas. This was Steve the nurse; he was just being nice. Nothing about the way he was talking was different from the professional she knew at the hospital. Not a date then, which did make things less complicated. Liane made copious mental notes, and had almost finished her Honey and Walnut Swirl when the last voice on earth she wanted to hear today spoke beside them.

'Having a good time? Spoonful for Daddy, Frithy-baby?'

Frith beamed and offered up a minute spoonful of chocolate ice cream while Liane cringed. Of all the times and places for Tony to turn up at, this was about the worst. He was going to make all kinds of innuendos, she could see them coming, but there was nothing she could do except introduce the two men, as Tony didn't appear to have twigged that this was one of the people who'd cared for his daughter in hospital – which showed how often he'd been there.

Tony's eyebrows shot up and he treated Steve to a mocking grin. 'A nurse, eh? That must be, ah, challenging.'

Liane swallowed a few pithy words. What a scumbag he was.

But Steve was more than equal to Tony. 'Not if you know what you're doing. Join us for coffee?'

'No, thanks. I have some business to attend to. See you two soon.' He patted Liane's shoulder, made a show of kissing Frith, and wove away through the tables to the bar before being ushered out the back somewhere.

'Sorry.' With Frith there too, it was all Liane could say. The little girl had finished her ice cream and those ears were waggling again.

Steve signalled to the waiter. 'No probs. Coffee? Then I should get going. I'm playing squash at five.'

'And I have to write down everything you've said. If I get this job, I'll have you to thank. I don't suppose you do a line in flats, too?'

He laughed. 'I leave that to my brother. He has an expanding portfolio. Why – do you need a new flat?'

Liane leaned back as the waiter arrived with coffees. 'Sort of. The place we're in is expensive for what we get, and the landlord does nothing in the way of upkeep.'

'I can let Jon know you're looking, if you like. How many rooms?'

'Thanks – two bedrooms, garden share if poss. I pay a hundred and thirty a week for the place we have, and I wouldn't want to go above that.'

'Got it.'

Thankfully, they managed to leave the café without encountering Tony again. Frith waved happily as Steve strode off up the road, then she gripped Liane's hand as they crossed at the lights and headed for the park.

'Can we visit the ducks now? Except we didn't bring bread.'

'They won't be ready for dinner yet anyway. Come on!'

BACK AT HOME, Liane's thoughts wandered while she sat with Frith as the daily dose of CBeebies flashed over the TV screen. It would be great if Steve's brother could find them a new flat. If he was anything like Steve, he wouldn't be a slimeball who ignored all her pleas about hot water and drains. The sound of an email pinging into her phone had Liane diving through to the kitchen and into her email account. Wow, oh wow – she had an interview at the hospital on the 3rd of May!

She abandoned her phone and danced through to the bedroom to decide on the best interview outfit. Should she go for a *Paula's* reject, or something more casual? The grey wool dress someone had returned to the shop with an unshiftable make-up stain around the neckline looked good on her, and some funky jewellery would hide the mark okay. Liane grinned at the dress, remembering how Paula's rage had simmered beneath the surface all the time she was assuring the customer that of course they'd exchange it for the black. When people were paying northwards of five hundred quid for dresses every couple of weeks, they could more or less do what they liked, and thanks be she was out of all that now. Liane thrust the dress back into the wardrobe. She would wear her black linen trousers with her black and green top and feel more comfortable.

She plumped down beside Frith again to message the

good news to Janine, Steve and Sister Annie: *I have an interview!*

Janine and Sister Annie sent their congratulations and good luck messages almost immediately, and Liane sent back flower and heart emoticons.

Her phone buzzed again, a call this time. Ah – Steve was giving her his congrats in person. Interesting...

DAY SEVEN – THURSDAY 23RD APRIL

CHAPTER 12

Every day was the same and they were all unbearable. Daria left Noah still asleep and went for a shower before Mum and Dad started to get up. Having them here was good in one way because they loved her, and being loved was what she needed, but it was hard to be with them too, seeing the grief and helplessness in their faces all day. Mum would bustle around the flat, cooking meals Daria struggled to swallow, but none of them had anything real to do and it was… it was the worst time of her life and each new day was a mountain to climb. After six days of numbness, today was day seven since Evie's death, and something was different. It was the end of the first week Evie had never seen.

Perched on the bathroom stool, Daria pulled on trousers and fastened her boot around her leg. The pain was bearable now, but everything took ten times longer than it normally did when you were on crutches, and her foot was still bruised and swollen.

Moving slowly, she swung her way down the hallway. Past the study, where deep silence told her Mum and Dad were still asleep, past her own room, and—

She stopped dead. Evie's room. The door had been firmly shut when they returned from the hospital on Sunday and it was still closed. But the longer she left this, the harder it was going to be. Daria inched close and pressed the handle down.

It was as if Evie'd been gone for months. A thin layer of dust covered everything, and the Snow White bedding on the junior bed was immaculate. Evie's toybox was frozen in time in one corner while her sheep mobile above the bed shivered in the current of air Daria had made opening the door. It was like a catalogue photo of a child's room. They'd tidied before leaving for Spain, of course. Cold fingers of fear snaked around Daria's heart – Evie would never be here again. Unshed tears smarted behind her eyes and it was pitiful; even wiping her eyes was difficult. One of her crutches banged to the floor.

Her mother was behind her. 'Daria? Are you—'

Daria took a deep breath. She had to do this. 'We'll organise a memorial for her, Mum. And I want to mark her life in some way. Not a gravestone or anything like that, something that's alive – a tree. We can plant a tree for her in a beautiful place.'

Ellen George hugged her. 'That's a lovely idea, darling.'

Daria leaned her head on her mother's broad shoulder. Nothing was lovely, but this was something she could do for Evie.

. . .

After breakfast, when her parents had departed for the supermarket, Daria sat with her leg stretched out on the sofa and opened her laptop. Where could you plant a tree for someone? And what kind of tree should it be, for a beautiful little girl who'd loved life? Evie's face flashed into her mind, and Daria suppressed a sob. It was silly to think like this, but the last child she'd touched hadn't been her girl. The memory of Frith's happy smile was stinging. What a painful moment that had been, and she hadn't even told Liane about Evie. Frowning, Daria tapped into Facebook. Liane had sent her a friend request and Daria had accepted, but they hadn't communicated otherwise yet. Liane's timeline was full of photos of Frith, and – no. Daria tapped out of social media. She wasn't ready for a friend with a child. The only friend she'd been in contact with was Kit, her best friend since primary school and Evie's godmother. Kit would want to come to the memorial too. Daria googled *plant a memorial tree*, and blinked at the number of hits that appeared.

Noah came in and peered over her shoulder. 'Looking for a place to plant the tree? Any ideas?'

'I've just started. What kind of tree shall we get? If we can choose?'

He shrugged. 'I guess it'll depend on where you want to plant it.'

Where *she* wanted...? 'Don't you want to as well?'

'I wanted her to live. Not this.'

His voice tailed away, and Daria slumped. 'I so wish she'd been flung from the taxi too.'

'I guess the car seat stopped that happening. How ironic is that?'

'She wasn't in—'

He jerked away from her. 'She wasn't in a car seat? How come?'

Had he never been in a cab with Evie? 'They don't carry child seats, Noah. It's perfectly legal as long as the child's belted up in the back seat.'

'Legal or not, it wasn't bloody safe, was it? You should have taken ours with you.'

'And done what with it at the airport?'

'I'm sure they have left luggage lockers somewhere.'

Daria buried her face in her hands, then realised. 'But she wasn't thrown out anyway. It made no difference.'

He turned his back on her, shoulders hunched. 'She wasn't thrown out, no, but she'd have been thrown around the taxi. A little thing like Evie, can you imagine what that would have done to her? A car seat would have spared her that.'

Daria's world collapsed. Was he right? If she'd taken the car seat, would their daughter still be alive today?

'I'm sorry! Do you think—?'

Noah jumped back, stumbling into the coffee table, his eyes huge in a sheet-white face. 'I think she's dead, Daria. "Sorry" doesn't cut it.' Clutching his head, he strode into their bedroom and slammed the door.

The worst pain in the world stabbed through Daria as she cowered on the sofa while images of Evie lying crumpled in a wrecked taxi seared through her head. Or Evie, flying through the windscreen, her beautiful face bloody and torn. *No.*

Her daughter's death was all her fault.

CHAPTER 13

Grey daylight was flooding through the window when Margie woke up. No sun today, then, and up you get, Margie. She sat on the edge of her bed, rubbing her bony chest to get rid of the wheeze. Nice deep breaths, lovey, you'll be right as rain in no time. But the sick, dizzy feeling was slow to move on this morning.

The sound of a metal bowl scudding across the kitchen floor spurred her downstairs. The girls and boys wanted breakfast. Bridie was sitting in the corner playing with Socks and Tallulah and an old tea towel. She jumped up to have her trousers fastened, and Margie's back twinged as she bent to push the reluctant button through the buttonhole. Her back couldn't be doing with rainy days.

'Let's get some toast on the table. Look at that rain, and us needing shopping.' Margie opened the bread bin. Only one slice left, and they'd run out of milk, too. A trip to the shops was a dire necessity, but… she fumbled in her purse, fingers trembling. Not much left here. And the kits were running short of food too.

Misery clutched at Margie's throat. She didn't have enough money to get everything, so she was going to have to go to the post office and get some from her account and that was always so complicated. They'd given her one of those cards for the machine, but it was easier to go inside and talk to a person. Hopefully, it wouldn't be the woman who turned her nose up, dopey madam that she was. Still, the maid was getting better, that was the main thing.

She gave Bridie the toast and sat for a while with a cup of milkless tea to see if the rain would go off. If anything, though, the clouds were getting darker and eventually Margie gave up. The sooner she went, the sooner she'd be back. She put her head into the living room, where Tallulah, Bridie and Socks were curled up on the sofa. Now there was an unlikely sight for you; Socks wasn't normally one for snuggling with the girls. Margie went to say goodbye, stroking each furry head as she passed and dropping a kiss on Bridie's.

''Bye, lovey girls. Socks, young man, mind you're a gentleman.' The other kits were all outside and a nice mess they'd make when they came in later with muddy paws. But never mind. That was cats for you.

Margie battled her way along the road and around the corner. This was miserable – her umbrella was useless in a wind like this. And for pity's sake, if it wasn't one thing, it was another – water was seeping into her left shoe, making every second step a cold, uncomfortable squelch. She'd already lost one shoe this month, so she was down to her last pair. Come on, Margie, grit your teeth and carry on. Here were the shops, so while she might not have a dry inch of skin on her body, at least her trip was halfway over. Margie grappled in her purse for her post office card and glared at it. Cards and machines you couldn't work were no use when you had a family to feed.

She trailed into the post office, waited in a long queue of steaming jackets and sour sniffy faces, then shouted her way through a conversation, a pane of glass separating her from Mrs Toffee-nose. Money tucked into her inside pocket – they might snatch her bag, but they wouldn't snatch her cash – she left the post office and stood in the rain to plan.

The food bank was half an hour away, much too far when she was feeling rough. Margie coughed, then shuffled into the little convenience store on the corner. It was run by a lovely Indian family and it was certainly convenient, but the prices were enough to make your eyes water. Still, a tin of beans and some soup wouldn't break the bank, and sometimes they had bread from yesterday on half-price. She had to save where she could.

Margie wrestled a basket from the pile by the door and started off down the left-hand side where the cat food was. A large-sized box landed in her basket. The kits loved this one so it was worth the extra money. She'd get it in the food bank next time, and some more of that tinned tuna Bridie liked. It was lovely with some rice. The kits enjoyed it too. Round to the next aisle and here was the tuna and the beans – pity she wasn't more full of beans today, hah! – and she'd get some tomato soup, too. Bridie's favourite. A glance at the bread shelves told her there were no old loaves today, so she splashed out on a packet of morning rolls. And milk. There, that wouldn't ruin her, and she'd be home in ten minutes. Coughing, Margie rounded the corner to the solitary cash desk and took her place in the queue.

A voice came from behind her. 'You okay, love? You're looking a bit peaky.'

Margie jerked round and oh, gracious, it was a big policeman cradling two packets of sandwiches and two cans of Irn Bru. Margie's mouth went dry. Why did you always think you'd done something wrong when you saw a policeman? He was waiting for an answer, too.

'I'm just fine. Looking forward to the warmer weather coming in.'

He chortled. 'Aren't we all?'

He was staring at her basket, and Margie changed it to her other arm where he couldn't see it so easily.

'You want to feed yourself as well as you feed your cat, love. That's the expensive stuff you've got there.'

'And worth every penny. Don't you go worrying about me. I did the big shop yesterday.' She ignored the glance the policeman exchanged with young Abhi on the till – it was none of their business. Margie kept her head down. Good, it was her turn now. She stuffed her shopping safely into her bag as soon as it was scanned, then a smile to Abhi, a nod to the policeman, and she was outside. Home, Margie, quick as you can.

This rain… you'd think it was December. Her foot had gone numb with the cold and the wet. Margie limped along, fighting with the umbrella until it blew inside out and flew out of her hand. It skittered across the road and ended up under a hedge, and it could stay there, too, useless thing that it was.

A car drew up beside her and the tall policeman wound down his window.

'You're getting wet, love. Want a lift home?'

He was kind. Her grandma had always said, if you get lost in the city, find a policeman. But she wasn't lost and she certainly didn't want a nosy-parker do-gooding copper in her house upsetting Tabitha.

She forced a smile. 'Home's half a minute around the corner. No worries. Thank you.' Quick march, Margie, look fit and business-like, and he'll leave you alone.

He did. His gaze bored into her neck as she strode to the corner, wheezing, but when she looked back, the police car had disappeared. Good. Ten miserable minutes later she was in her own hallway, hanging wet things on the stair post. Topsy and Marmaduke came running and as she'd expected, there were muddy paw marks all over and someone had coughed up a hairball in the kitchen. But she was home. A cup of tea and she'd be right as rain. Now where was Bridie? Margie heaved herself upstairs to find the child standing in the smallest bedroom, where the window overlooked the street.

'Come and have some milk, lovey, and I'll do your bandage for you.'

'I think it feels better today.' A hopeful face staring into Margie's.

'That's good. Give it a couple more days and you'll be right as rain.'

Bridie's face brightened. Downstairs, Margie tended to the child then made tea. She sat in the armchair with Tabitha to drink it, but her shivers were making it hard for her to hold the cup. She'd forgotten to go to the chemist's, too. But her cuppa would help, and some of Bridie's pink medicine would be just as good as an aspirin. A rest, that was what she needed, to get rid of these shivers. Margie coughed. Ouch.

Bridie, on the sofa with Tabitha and Demelza, was staring at her with wide eyes.

Margie put her cup on the coffee table, hot tea slopping over onto her hand. Was she to have no peace today? 'I'm all right! Leave me alone!'

The three of them fled the room, and misery almost choked Margie. She wasn't all right, was she? But she had to be. She had her family to look after. Come on, Margie, drink that tea and pull yourself together.

Bridie was alone in the kitchen when Margie went through for a second cup. Poor maid, she was missing her brothers and sister. Where were they again? Margie shut her eyes to think, but here was Bridie, pulling at her sleeve, wanting something.

'The kits have all gone out the window. I want to go outside too.'

Margie opened the back door. The rain had gone off, but the paving slabs by the door were wet and slimy with moss. 'Look, everything's soaking out there. You don't want to be falling over and making that arm worse again, do you?'

Bridie drooped. 'When am I going back to the other house?'

How many times? 'Will you stop that nonsense! And you're not going out, do you hear? Skedaddle upstairs and play in your room for a while. I have things to do.'

Bridie about-turned and thumped upstairs, and Margie closed the back door, hot misery flushing through her. Poor maid, she'd been too harsh there. She reached for the bottle of Calpol. Bridie's dose was one spoonful, so two should be right for a grown-up. There. That would help. Now, where were the toys? Poor Bridie needed something to distract her while her arm was bad. Didn't they have a toybox somewhere?

She stared around the kitchen, then went through to the living room. The whole place was strangely toy-free; someone must have had a tidy. It was usually bears and dollies all over the place, and those jigsaws Aiden liked. He never managed to finish them, though, did he? Margie chuckled and opened the cupboard under the stairs. Hah – here was the toybox!

It was empty, though, apart from a couple of books and Maeve's bear. Margie lifted it – one bear was better than no bears, but where on earth had those rascals put everything?

She forced her tired legs up to Bridie's room, where she nearly died of fright when the maid popped up from under the bed.

Margie held out the bear. 'Look what I found.'

Bridie scrambled up and took it. 'He can play too. We're making a den, me and Socks!'

Margie coughed. Look at the child's face. Grubby didn't come into it. 'That's good. Tell you what, I'll have a lie down, then afterwards we'll give you a lovely bath. And I'll make some bean butties for tea, would you like that?'

Bridie nodded, and Margie gave the child's head a pat. 'Don't worry, Bridie, love. Your arm will be good as new before you know it.'

. . .

BATHTIME AT MAMMY'S was peculiar. There was no shower for one thing, and the bath was all dusty. Mammy wiped it before she put the water in, but bits of grey fluff were still floating about in the water and the plughole was still green. Mammy put a kettleful of hot water in first, because the tap water wasn't always warm enough, she said. She took Evie's clothes away and put a blue towel on the basin ready for coming out. Evie touched it with one finger before climbing into the bath. It wasn't a nice fluffy towel like she had at home.

Mammy didn't have bubble bath, either, and the soap smelled different to Mummy's. Mammy puffed and coughed because she had to kneel down beside the bath. Evie sat still, holding her arm so it didn't hurt while Mammy washed her hair with the soap first, and then the rest of her. It was scary having her arm washed, but Mammy was gentle as could be and it only hurt a tiny bit.

'You can play in the bath while I fetch your clothes.' Mammy held onto the side of the bath and got up with her usual 'Uff'.

Two tears welled up and ran down Evie's face as soon as Mammy wobbled out of the bathroom. There was nothing to play with here, and she had to hold her arm anyway. When was she going home to Mummy and Daddy and the big tub with lovely bubble bath and her toys to skoosh around the water?

Bang-bang-bang! came from downstairs. Evie jerked in fright. Someone was at the front door – that had never happened before.

Mammy bustled back into the bathroom with an armful of clothes that weren't Evie's. 'Keep quiet! It's that woman next door again. Always complaining, she is. The cats this, the cats that. Nosy besom. She'll go away.'

Evie made herself teensy-weensy and quiet. After a minute Mammy picked up the towel.

'Out you come. Clean as a whistle, you are now.' She helped Evie out of the bath and dried her off while Evie held her arm.

They only had the one green bandage, but Mammy rolled it up the other way, so the clean bit was on the outside, and wound it around the wooden spoon again. Evie was glad when that part was finished, but the bandage was making her arm feel much better. The clean clothes were old blue trousers and a red T-shirt. They were more like boys' clothes, but Evie said nothing. They would be finished quicker if she was quiet. She waited while Mammy brushed her hair.

'There! Shall we make those bean butties now?'

Evie sat in the kitchen while Mammy heated the beans. She'd never had beans in a butty before, but it was good and Mammy put a tea towel over her front so she didn't have to worry about dripping on her clean clothes. Evie dropped three beans on the floor, but Demelza came and ate them, so that was all right. Afterwards, Mammy gave her a spoonful of medicine, then took two big spoonfuls herself.

'Right as rain, we'll be, Bride, with this inside us.'

She smiled at Evie, lifted up Demelza and went to sit in the living room with Tabitha. Two seconds later, Demelza was back in the kitchen and Mammy was snoring. Evie went upstairs to the window where you could see the street. Maybe Mummy would come today.

DAY EIGHT – FRIDAY 24TH APRIL

CHAPTER 14

Frith skipped along beside Liane on the way home from the supermarket. 'I like not going to Mrs P's every day.'

'Don't you miss the other children?' Liane opened their gate. Hopefully it hadn't been a mistake, allowing Frith to stay at home with her now she didn't have a job to go to. School was looming for her daughter after the summer hols, and come to think of it, if they were going to move, this would be the time to do it. Starting school then changing to a different one would be really tough on poor Frith.

Frith followed her inside. 'Sort of. Can Lucy come to play tomorrow?'

'I'll text her mum, but don't hope too hard. Families often have things to do at the weekends.'

Liane put the shopping away, then pulled out her phone to message Lucy's mum while she remembered. Oh – she'd missed a call from Steve. Was this a good time to call back? She tapped to connect.

'Hi, Liane. Jon has a place that might suit you – a two-bed semi with a garden in Mansewood. Do you want to call him about it?'

She certainly did. But – a semi? 'Is it in our price range?'

'Yes. It's an old place, apparently.'

Liane saved the number and called as soon as Steve hung up.

His brother had the same deep voice on the phone. 'It's two-up, two-down, bathroom upstairs and downstairs loo under the stairs. An elderly couple lived there for years, but they went into sheltered housing a couple of weeks ago. The garden is what you might call a challenge. Would you like to see it?'

Would she just. Liane organised a time that afternoon and tossed her phone back into her bag. Please, please let this house be suitable. Tony lived in Mansewood, which was a dubious kind of recommendation, but it was a nice enough area and a garden of their own would be brilliant. They could grow veggies. Wow – Frithy could have a trampoline. They'd need to win the lottery for that first, but you never knew. If the job worked out too – but that reminded her, she should be looking for more jobs. It wouldn't do to bank too hard on this one, no matter what Steve said.

THE HOUSE WAS in a quiet street with a park at one end. Liane and Frith arrived first, and Liane took stock of the place while Frith walked along the garden wall at the front. Big windows, shabby paintwork, a patch of scrubby grass in the tiny front garden. She wandered along the pavement to see up the side of the house. An elongated patch of grass at the back led to a jungle of trees and bushes at the far end – you couldn't see the far end.

Liane stepped back onto the road to see the roof properly. All those home improvement programmes she'd watched over the years were going to come in useful today. No obviously missing tiles, good.

A black van pulled up and an older version of Steve got out, grinning. 'Roof's fine!' he called across. Liane went to shake hands.

Jon jabbed a key into the front door. 'Okay. This place has what estate agents call "potential". I bought it for my portfolio last year with the tenants in place already, and they didn't want the disruption of having it done up while they were in situ. In other words, it needs a makeover, but I'll get that done soon.'

He led the way inside. The hallway and stairs had a worn green carpet and faded flowery wallpaper while the wooden banisters and doors were painted white. Everything was shabby and old, but the house had a homey feel about it. You could sense that people had been happy here. Liane took Frith's hand before the little girl ran upstairs. A house with an upstairs was an exciting prospect for her daughter – for Liane too, actually.

Jon handed her a floor plan and opened the first of two doors on their left. 'Living room. Nice bay window. Central heating.'

Liane walked across the room. It was smaller than the living room they had now, but considering she'd decided they didn't need a living room at all if the kitchen was large enough, she couldn't complain.

'And kitchen.'

Jon opened the second door, and Liane and Frith followed him in. The kitchen was the same size as the living room, which was fine, but oh, dear, talk about dated. Those fittings might have been from the 1950s. Liane squinted at Jon. He'd gone a bit pink.

'Okay, it's straight out of a museum, but you can ignore that because the entire place will be renovated before anyone moves in. I'm going to knock through to the living room and make it open-plan, too.'

'Sounds good.' The window overlooked the back garden, which consisted of a small patio, a patch of grass and the jungle at the back. He'd been right, it was a challenge. A vegetable plot was conspicuous by its absence, and the grass was patchy and dandelion-infested.

Upstairs, the front bedroom was large and the back one small, and the bathroom was a similar vintage to the kitchen. Frith went straight to the window of the back room. 'Can this be my room? You can see for miles over the garden, can't you, Mummy!'

'It's a room with a view,' agreed Liane. She inched closer to Jon and lowered her voice. 'It would make a lovely home and the size is right for us, but I'd need more details about price and when it would be available.'

He glanced at Frith. 'The price is the one you gave Steve as your maximum and it'll be ready by the end of October.'

Damn. Liane heaved a sigh. 'I'd prefer somewhere I can move in a lot sooner than that. Frith starts school after summer.' Why was a new kitchen and bathroom, a wall coming down and a lick of paint going to take so long? On those home improvement programmes, they practically rebuilt places in four weeks or less.

'Ah. The problem is, I'm renovating another place I own on this street, but the tenants there don't move out until the end of August. I want to do them both at the same time.'

'Wouldn't it be possible to do this place up with us already living in it?'

Jon hesitated, scratching his chin.

'Mummy! There's a little girl at the window of that house and she's waving to me!' Frith jumped up and down at the window, waving madly. 'We could be friends if we lived here!' She twisted round to beam at Liane, then spun back to face the window. 'Oh! She's gone! Can I go outside?'

Jon rustled the papers he was holding. 'Why don't we go downstairs, and Frith can explore the garden while we talk business?'

'Ooh, yes!' Frith was off like a shot, and Liane hurried after her.

She and Jon stood at the back door, watching as Frithy galloped around the garden, disappearing into the bushes at the far end. Liane shoved her hands into her jacket pockets and crossed her fingers hard. Frith would love living here – it was a real paradise for children. An almost impenetrable jungle at the bottom of the garden was every child's dream, surely.

Jon sat down on an old iron bench below the kitchen window. 'Living in the place while it's being renovated wouldn't work, I'm sorry. There would be days of having no water, no electricity, no kitchen, bathroom, no windows – and that's before you get the painters in stinking the place out.'

Liane was silent as dismay welled up. Oh, for a local

grandparent for Frithy. This house would be perfect, but it wasn't looking hopeful, was it?

Jon was scratching his chin again. 'You like the place, don't you?'

'I'd take it straightaway if we could move in for Frith starting school. Problem is, we have no handy relatives to put us up for the time it's being fixed up.'

'Okay. How about you take it, move in whenever you like, and I'll find you another place locally to lodge in while the renovation's ongoing? But remember, you'd have a lot more hassle than if you waited to move in when it was finished.'

Frith ran down from the far end of the garden, joy written all over her face. 'I looked over the fence to see if the other little girl was there, and she wasn't, but I saw three cats in her bushes. They have a lovely jungle too. Mummy, are we going to come and live here?'

Liane held out a hand to Jon. 'I'll take the hassle. Done.'

'When are we moving to the new house?' Frith attacked her raspberry ripple ice cream with gusto.

Liane was savouring her forkful of coffee and walnut cake. They were in a South Side café, celebrating their new home. Jon was going to drop by with the contract tomorrow. The agreement was a nominal rent for the months when the property was unrenovated, the same amount in their lodgings during the renovation, and full rent afterwards. All fair enough, though they had four weeks' notice to pay on their old place, so she'd have double rent for a while. On the upside, there was nothing to stop them moving in as soon as the contract was signed.

'We'll need to organise lots of things first. People to help move furniture, and things like new curtains, and of course there's the garden. We can't cut the grass with the kitchen scissors, can we?'

'I'll push the lawnmower!'

Liane smiled. They had lots of work in front of them and lots of additional expense, too, though that would go back to normal after the removal. Fingers tightly crossed that finding a new job would be as uncomplicated.

DAY TEN – SUNDAY 26TH APRIL

CHAPTER 15

Mammy must really like beans on toast, because they had them nearly every day. Evie quite liked them too, but it would be nice to have something different now and again. She liked things like puddings and carrot sticks and chocolate fingers, and Mammy never had anything like that.

She stabbed her last bean and ate it up, then sat back to drink her milk. She didn't like this milk much. Strawberry milk was much nicer. Mummy didn't have it all the time, but some days she'd say, 'How about some pink milk?' and Evie would run into the kitchen and climb up on her special stool so she was high enough at the breakfast bar. When was she going home?

The kitchen window swung open as Topsy came in along with the sound of a plane. Evie stared up, but she couldn't see it from her seat at the table. Had Mummy gone to Spain to see Grandma and left her here? She must have, it was such a long time since they'd packed to go there. It was nice in

Spain. They'd gone at Christmas too and Mummy was so sad to leave Grandma and Grandad again when they came home. Daddy sometimes went to Spain, too. He was never at home much, but it was fun when he was. Evie stuck out her bottom lip. Every time she asked, Mammy got cross, so it was better not to. Two tears tracked down her face. When she rubbed them away there was a smear of dirt and bean sauce on her hand.

'Glory be, maid, what are you pulling faces for? And what a mucky pup you are – upstairs with you, and we'll get that face washed.'

Mammy was banging her chest again. She did that a lot. Evie slid off her chair and ran up to the bathroom quick as quick while Mammy panted along behind her.

'Wheezing like an old steam train, I am.'

Mammy sat down on the edge of the bath and made a flannel wet and soapy at the basin. Evie stood still until the dirt was washed off, then Mammy gave her hair a pat with a brush. She frowned.

'We should you get some more clothes, too. What have you done with them all? I can hardly find anything.'

Evie blinked. Mammy didn't seem to expect an answer, though. She was looking at the hairbrush and her face had gone all pink and funny. A moment later she stamped from the room, and drawers banged in Evie's room. Evie went through.

'Have you scamps been hiding things again?' Mammy was panting away, opening all the drawers and rummaging around.

Evie went over to Tabitha, who had come in to look for a

place to snooze in the sunshine. She liked the window ledge in Evie's room.

'No. Do cats hide things?'

Mammy laughed, then coughed. 'Cats are experts at hiding. We'll find you more clothes, don't worry. You've grown again, haven't you?'

Evie swallowed hard. 'Daddy said I grow like a runner bean.'

'Did he? I don't remember that.' Mammy was rummaging in the bottom drawer. 'Ah, look. Let's see what we have here.'

She sat down on the bed with an armful of old clothes and shook them out one by one.

'This should fit you now. And try these. And why didn't I think of it—'

She bustled out while Evie sat looking at the blue jumper and trousers. These were for boys, weren't they? But that didn't seem to matter here. Mammy came back with a big bag of clothes and started to sort them out on Evie's bed.

'Can you do my bandage?'

'Tsk. Give me a moment, will you?'

Mammy was shaking out jumpers and socks and things, so Evie went over to the window and stroked Tabitha, who was stretched out in the sunshine. It would be lovely if she saw the little girl at the window of the house across the garden again. But nothing was moving over there today.

Mammy was taking a long time with the clothes, so Evie went downstairs again. The kitchen was lovely and sunny – it would be so nice to go out somewhere. Mammy never went to the park – or if she did, she didn't take Evie with her. The cats were lucky, they could get out of the window. Evie yanked at the door handle – oh! It wasn't locked today. She sat down on the sunny doorstep and straightaway Socks and Topsy ran up to play. This was better.

It was a lovely garden here. Hundreds and hundreds of dandelions were waving their yellow heads in the grass. She could pick some for Mammy later. But then, dandelions made your hands all brown. Mummy said daisies were better, but Mammy's grass didn't seem to have many. Evie stretched her legs out, and Socks came to nose at her feet. Better stay on the step for now. She might not be allowed out here all alone.

'Where's this bandage, then?'

To Evie's surprise, Mammy sat down on the doorstep beside her to unwind the bandage. Evie sat waggling her fingers while Mammy got the bandage ready to put back on. They weren't sausagey any more. 'Will it take much longer to get better?'

'It'll take as long as it takes, maid. Be patient.'

Mammy sat for a moment when the bandage and the wooden spoon were back on, then she gave Evie a little cuddle. Evie wrinkled her nose. Cuddles were lovely, but she wanted Mummy to cuddle her too.

'When can—' She stopped. It wasn't nice when Mammy was cross.

Mammy hauled herself up and went back inside. A moment later the stairs creaked. Evie waited before tiptoeing upstairs. Mammy was lying on her bed with her eyes closed. Good, she could go back down and play in the garden for a little while.

The grass at the back stretched up to all the bushes and trees. Behind them was the house where the little girl had been at the window. Evie pushed her way through to the back fence – it was made of wood and was almost as big as she was, though there were plenty of holes in it to peek through. She still couldn't see the other house very well because there were so many bushes and trees on the other side too. She was about to turn back when a bang and a child's voice made her stop.

'Mummy? I want to see if the cats are in the jungle today!'

Evie grabbed the fence and stood on tiptoe – was this the little girl?

A woman answered. 'All right, but don't go out of the garden. Steve and I will be inside measuring for curtains.'

Evie waited. Marmaduke pushed past her and went all the way into the garden next door, and vanished. A moment later the little girl spoke to him.

'Hello! What's your name?'

Evie called through the bushes. 'It's Marmaduke.'

'Ooh!'

Branches rustled, and Evie stood still as a little girl with wavy blonde hair and wearing jeans and a yellow sweatshirt pushed her way through the bushes and came right up to the fence. She was bigger than Evie but not much.

The little girl spoke first. 'I saw you at the window last time we were here. Do you live there? We're moving in soon. Why have you got a bandage?'

Evie licked her lips. 'I bashed my arm, so Mammy put a bandage on – it hurts when I don't have one.'

'Do you live with your Mammy? I call mine Mummy but her name's Liane. Steve is her friend and he has a brother called Jon and this is his house but we're going to stay in it. Is that your cat? I've never known a cat called Marmaduke before.'

'I—' Evie stopped. It was hard to know where to start. 'Mammy has lots of cats. One's called Tabitha and she's got kitties in her tummy. Mammy says they'll be here soon.'

The little girl gave a gasp. 'Ooh, you lucky thing! Can we…'

'Bridie! Where are you, child?'

Oh, no, Mammy was coming. Was she cross?

The little girl waved behind Evie. 'We're here!'

Evie wheeled round to see Mammy pushing her way through the bushes.

'What are you doing? And – who's this?'

The little girl gave Mammy a big smile. 'I'm Frith. I think Bridie's a lovely name!'

Mammy smiled back, but it was only a little one. 'Bridie's a lovely girl.'

Frith was hanging over the fence. 'My mummy's called Liane. That's a lovely name too, isn't it? What's your name?'

Mammy's smile twitched again. 'Margie. Come on, maid. We have clothes to try on.'

She held out her hand and Evie took it, giving Frith a little wave with her green-bandaged arm.

'I'll come and look for you when we've moved in!' Frith waved back, then dashed off.

Mammy held onto Evie's hand all the way back to the kitchen, where she shut the door firmly behind them.

Evie squinted up. 'I wanted to play in the garden.' Mammy didn't look cross, but she didn't answer either. They went upstairs where there was a big pile of clothes on Evie's bed, and Mammy made her try on a lot of trousers until they found two pairs that were about right. And some T-shirts and jumpers and knickers and socks. They were all old, and Evie didn't like them, but her own clothes weren't here.

'I want my other clothes.' It was out before she'd thought.

Mammy threw the too-large pair of trousers she was folding up into a drawer. 'I want, I want! I want gets nothing, that's what my mammy used to tell me. You need more than one set of clothes and these are your spare ones. You stay up here and play with the cats – it's not good for you, running around the garden with that arm, and I'm not up to chasing after you.'

She coughed so hard she had to sit down. Evie brought her a glass of water from the bathroom. When she'd drunk it, Mammy reached for the pink medicine.

'I need to go to the chemist's, maid. Here's me poorly and not an aspirin in the house.' She took two big spoonfuls then raised her eyebrows at Evie.

Evie shook her head. The medicine made her sleepy, and her arm was nearly better.

'All the more for me.' Mammy gave Evie's head a little rub and went back to her own room. The bed creaked loudly.

Evie sat down on the floor with Socks. Frith was a lovely name too. Maybe they could play together when Mammy was asleep, or at the shops. It would be nice to have a friend who could talk.

DAY TWELVE – TUESDAY 28TH APRIL

CHAPTER 16

Daria settled into the back of the car with her mother, one hand reaching over the seatback to steady the little lilac tree that they'd positioned diagonally across the boot space. Thankfully, having a hatchback allowed you to transport things like this. Noah drove silently towards the north of the city. He was still sunk in despair and, while that was understandable, he was freezing her out. The lack of a child's car seat in the taxi Daria had taken with Evie sat between them like a smouldering volcano. Daria stared at the back of his neck as he drove. Would he have decided any differently if he'd been in her place that day?

Her father was bowed in the front passenger seat, as silent as Noah, but at least his grief wasn't accusing her of causing her child's death. Daria pressed her lips together. Her parents had wanted a religious ceremony, but… no. A funeral with all the ceremony of a church service, with friends who were gutted for them, of course, but the lingering, unspoken and unspeakable thought at the back of every mind would be: *thank God it didn't happen to us*. It was out of the question. And in a way, the absence of a coffin pushed the cold fact of death farther away. Evie wouldn't be at her own memorial, so it wasn't real, was it? And Mum – Daria winced as yet another hopefully upbeat remark about the tree ceremony came from her mother's side of the back seat. Poor Mum, she was trying so hard to hold Daria up, but it was driving a huge wedge between them. Daria shifted in her seat. It would have been better if she'd been able to confide her fears about the lack of a car seat to her mother, but Mum was barely coping with her own grief. Impossible to burden her with Daria's guilt, too. It would actually be a relief when her parents went home to Spain on Sunday; they all needed time and space to grieve in their own way.

Daria twisted in her seat to look out behind them, where Millie and Roger were following in their own car while Evie's godmother, Kit, drove behind them with her partner Adrian. Thank God Kit was here and on Daria's side, because Noah's parents weren't happy about today either. Rog had suggested getting someone outside the immediate family to officiate at the tree ceremony, suggesting a humanist friend of his, but Daria hadn't wanted that. She'd wanted to scatter the ashes under the tree as they planted it, but according to Noah, the ashes were still being held while the investigation was ongoing, though Daria couldn't see why this should be. Unlike the drivers of the taxi and the other vehicles, Evie had played no part in causing the crash. If they'd been allowed to have her cremated, why weren't they allowed to have her ashes? It was another example of soulless officialdom, but ashes weren't Evie and they could scatter them around the tree another day. So here they were, eight people going to plant a tree for a happy little girl they'd all loved, and not many of them were agreeing with any of the others about it. Evie deserved better, but this was what grief did.

Once outside the city, the scenery became hilly and wild, with sunshine and shadows chasing across the green rolling hills silhouetted against a perfect blue sky. The estate they were going to was famous for its beautiful gardens, open to the public all year. Daria had been coming here for years; it was a part of her childhood. About half of the estate was woodland, and it was here they were planning to plant the tree. The father of one of Noah's friends was head gardener and he had arranged it for them. He'd offered to provide the tree, too, but Daria had wanted to choose that herself.

The three cars swung through black wrought-iron gates, crawled up the main driveway and skirted the house before driving on towards the river.

Jim was waiting with a wheelbarrow in the car park. He came over as Noah parked, and there was a round of awkward introductions and commiserations. Daria fixed her eyes on the trees, most of them deciduous, now greening up and coming to life after winter. The woodland area was at the back of the estate, and all the buildings were out of sight. Yes, this was a good place to remember Evie. She gripped her crutches.

Noah loaded the tree into the wheelbarrow, and Jim pushed it along a pathway.

'I've prepared the place – it's not far from the river, so you get the sound of that in the background, but there's plenty of drainage and sunshine. We have other lilac trees along both banks, so this one will do well there.'

Noah answered him, walking beside Jim and supporting the tree while Daria swung along between her mother and Kit, with the others bringing up the rear. Mum was stifling tears and Dad behind her was stony-faced and silent. Oh, it was all so – hard. The warmth of Kit's hand on her arm was the only thing that kept Daria going. They passed a massive lilac tree that was sending perfume over the entire area, and she breathed in deeply. Yes. This was what she wanted for Evie's tree.

She called ahead to Jim. 'How old is that one?'

He turned. 'Twenty-five years, give or take a few. It's a beauty.'

Daria pulled out her phone and handed it to Kit to take a few photos. In another twenty-five years, she'd compare these with Evie's tree.

'It's here.' Jim was standing beside a hole that was waiting several metres away from the path, a pile of earth beside it. Like a grave. Daria moved over to join him, gripping her crutches hard. Her mother accepted a tissue from Millie, but Daria's eyes were dry. She was beyond tears now.

Jim unpacked Evie's tree and teased out the root ball, then straightened up. 'This is a good 'un. Put it in and hold it while you fill the hole, then press the earth down firmly. I'll leave you alone now, but I'll come and water it in when you've gone. Take all the time you need.'

He shook hands all round again, clapped Noah's shoulder, and left.

Daria inched forward and held the tree with one hand as

Noah shovelled in the earth and stamped it down. Kit had brought white roses, and they all laid one at the base of the little tree, then stood silently. The babbling of the river in the background combined with the rustle of treetops in the breeze, and the perfume from the older tree downstream wafted through the air. A beautiful spot, but not half lovely enough to be Evie's memorial. Noah came to stand beside Daria, and she leaned in as he put his arm around her. They had to heal, as a couple, they had to get through this.

ON THE WAY HOME, all the parents went in Rog and Millie's car. Probably they'd organised that beforehand, to give her and Noah some time together after planting the tree. Kit, who lived north of the city, hugged Daria hard before they drove off.

'We'll leave you to be alone with your families, love. I'll be in touch in a day or two.'

Daria gazed out as they started back to the city. All too soon they were in the middle of the usual urban scenery, with cars and houses and people as far as the eye could see. Kit and Adrian swung away to the left, and Noah drove on without speaking. Daria was silent too; the air in the car was thick with silent accusations. *Your fault your fault...* She didn't even know if they were her accusations or Noah's. Dry-eyed, she sat motionless as they drove through the affluent north side suburbs, into the Clyde Tunnel and out again, on towards home.

Noah pulled up at traffic lights by a row of shops, and a blonde child skipping out of a newsagent's caught Daria's eye. Frith! Liane emerged too and took her daughter's hand, and the pair of them beamed at each other. Envy and grief speared Daria's heart. Lucky, lucky Liane, having a daughter to smile at and love.

The lights changed and Noah drove on. Daria closed her eyes, pushing away the memory of touching Frith's face that day.

And now that she'd seen Frith, children were popping up everywhere, skipping along beside a parent, running into a park or a shop to spend their pocket money. She was increasingly conscious of them, those children milling around the city streets, some of them little girls with Evie's zest for life. Daria pressed cold fingers against her eyelids. All her life, she would come across little girls who had something of Evie about them, whether it was appearance or clothes, or, like Frith, that indefinable air, the same mannerisms, and… oh, *God*, this was tough. And here they were, almost back, and she and Noah hadn't uttered a word to each other.

After a brittle conversation over coffee and fruit cake at Rog and Millie's, the rest of them went home. Daria's parents promptly went into their bedroom and closed the door, and she limped on through to the living room. Either Mum and Dad were trying to be super-tactful and sensitive or they wanted to talk about something she wasn't supposed to hear.

Noah was slumped in the sofa. Daria propped her crutches against the wide sofa arm and sat down beside him. He didn't move.

She touched his knee. 'I think it's a good place for Evie's tree. Hopefully, it'll flower next year. We can scatter the ashes there as soon as we get them.'

He jerked upright. 'I don't care what you do with the – ashes. It's not Evie, is it? That bloody taxi! It makes me so angry. Evie's gone and nothing in the world is going to bring her back, so please just shut up about the tree. I want to keep her in my head as my happy little girl, not a never-ending series of conversations about a bloody lilac tree!'

He strode into their bedroom, leaving Daria sunk in the corner of the sofa. He couldn't have hurt her more if he'd taken a whip and beaten her. Oh, he'd stopped short of blaming her for Evie's death this time, but the accusation was still there, unspoken. It wasn't as if he'd been the perfect father all Evie's life – he'd rarely done things alone with his daughter. Daria leaned her head back, blinking violently to keep the tears in.

Listlessly, she reached for her phone to put the lilac tree photos into a folder where they wouldn't get lost. An email had come in, from a name she didn't recognise and headed 'Class Reunion'. Daria opened it. Ruby Clark, who used to be Ruby James, had organised a reunion of their old secondary school class in a couple of weeks. Oh, no. Definitely not. Some things were impossible in the months after your child was killed, and this was one of them. There was a group for the class on Facebook, and Daria tapped through. Someone had added her name without asking. Her thumb hovered over 'leave group', then she scrolled down the list of group members – Liane was there.

Daria scrolled further down the page. A few photos of their school days were up too. Here was one of her and her Kit, all smiles and holding the area trophy while the rest of their netball team beamed in the background. She'd been happy back then, and oh, if only she could go back. Relive her life in exactly the same way, right up until that taxi journey.

All-consuming emptiness swirled around in her head, and Daria closed her eyes. Help me, someone. This is so hard.

DAY THIRTEEN – WEDNESDAY 29TH APRIL

CHAPTER 17

Her cough was worse this morning, and her legs weren't doing too well either. Margie leaned heavily on the banister on the way downstairs. She hadn't felt this rough for many a long day – for two pins she'd have stayed in bed, but the family was waiting. They needed her, and she needed them to keep her going.

Most of the cats were milling around yowling for food. Bridie ran out of the living room when Margie arrived at the bottom of the stairs – seeing the maid so bright and ready for breakfast was the first good thing about today. Bridie shook cat food into bowls while Margie made toast and provided fresh water, then collapsed onto a hard chair at the table and leaned her head on one hand. It was hard when you were ill and had little ones – especially now, when she was alone with such a big family to take care of. Oh, they should have stayed in Ireland.

Bantry Bay... Life had been more sociable there, especially when she was a little one. In those days, neighbours had helped you. Food was scarcer but people had shared, they'd come by with a few extra spuds or a cabbage. And if a mother was ill, well, everyone in the street would rally round. Margie wiped her eyes on her sleeve. Bad days didn't usually get to her like this.

'Can you get me a glass of water, Bride, darlin'?'

Bridie left her toast and went to the sink. Margie gulped the whole glass down, wincing. She should get something from the chemist's, but that meant going there, and medicine was expensive. Still, she needed something to get her back on her feet again.

Most of the cats vanished outside when the food was gone. Tabitha was on the kitchen table but that was all right, she was allowed to do what she liked, li'l mama she was. Marmaduke was still sniffing around the empty bowls, and Ermintrude and Bridie were playing with a piece of string in the hallway. Margie lifted her purse.

'Out with you, Marmaduke. Bridie, Ermie, darlin's, you keep Tabitha company in the warm while I'm out.'

She shooed Marmaduke outside then ushered the other three into the living room. The kitchen window was always open in case someone needed to get in or out. Her bag… here it was. She was ready. Where was she going, again? She coughed – oh, that hurt. The chemist, yes.

Margie croaked a goodbye, closed the back door behind her but didn't lock it – she'd lost the key somewhere this week. But no matter. The front door was locked, and nobody ever came around the back except Mrs Fancy Curtains at the side, and she'd only done that once. All the old friendly neighbours they'd had when they moved here were long gone, more was the pity.

The road to the chemist's was as long as it had ever been. Margie's feet dragged along the pavement as her head grew hotter and her breath shorter. She would have a sit-down on that strip of scratched grey plastic in the bus shelter outside the chemist. You couldn't call it a seat; it wasn't wide enough to sit on properly. You were supposed to lean on it and poke at your mobile phone. She came to the bus shelter and leaned thankfully on the grubby rest. They were nosy parkers and busybodies in the chemist's too; if she went in all breathless, they might not let her out again.

Watching the traffic filled a few minutes, and thanks be, no one paid any attention to her. Margie swung herself forward and stood straight – yes, that was better. She'd be fine in no time with some medicine.

'Bottle of aspirin, please.'

The lass behind the counter didn't look old enough to be at secondary school, never mind out working. 'I'll give you a packet, shall I?'

Snooty li'l madam. Margie slid a note over the counter, scrabbled up the change that was slid back to her and retreated. Twenty piddling little aspirins wouldn't last her long, would they? What was wrong with a bottle of a hundred pills like you used to get? All they wanted nowadays was to make you spend more money and she didn't have it. She had Bridie and the others to buy things for, and the kits. The walk home had Margie's head throbbing with every step, and she was almost in tears by the time she arrived at her street. Two more minutes – she would manage.

Inside, she went straight to the living room. Empty. What rascals those three were, but surely Bridie hadn't gone out after she'd been told not to. Tabitha should take better care too; those kitties could come any day.

'Bridie!'

A thud came from upstairs, and Margie relaxed. 'It's all right – stay in your room!'

She coughed, then collapsed onto the sofa to recover her breath. It was a moment before she was able to go for some water to wash the aspirins down. She glanced out, but the other girls and boys were all out of sight. So precious, they were, especially Tabitha and Bridie. Her little family. She had to get better for them.

DAY FOURTEEN – THURSDAY 30TH APRIL

CHAPTER 18

Liane scrabbled around in the bottom of the removal box for the garlic press and a stray bottle-opener that had escaped the bag of miscellaneous bits and pieces they'd started out in, and dropped them into the cutlery drawer. Another box unpacked. Whoever had said that moving house was one of the five most stressful things you did in life had got it dead right – and it was especially true when you went from sitting still to full speed ahead in three seconds flat, like they had. Her legs were aching; you'd think she'd run a marathon every day since last Wednesday.

Steve came in with the ironing board 'This for the cupboard in here?'

'If there's space.' Liane added the empty box to the pile by the back door. 'I think we're winning, you know.'

He closed the cupboard door on the ironing board and grinned at her. Liane grinned back. It was amazing, spending time with Steve. They'd had a trip down the Clyde Coast on

Monday afternoon when he was off work, and even with Frith monopolising the conversation, being with him had felt right. Now he was helping them with the speediest removal of the century. Life was looking up.

'Mummy! I knocked down six skittles!'

Frith was out on the patio, playing with the skittles set Steve had bought her on Monday, the picture of a happy child. Liane sent a thumbs up through the kitchen window. Just think, they had a garden all of their own; that was heading towards a dream come true. Not to mention two parks within walking distance, one a mere hundred yards away, and the primary school Frith would go to after summer was in the next street. It was perfect. They were also quite a lot closer to Tony's flat, which was questionably less perfect. One thing she'd need to do today was inform him of their new address.

Frith appeared at the back door, accompanied by an enormous orange cat. 'Can I have a biscuit? Look, Mummy, Marmaduke's here – he's so friendly! Do you think he'd like a biscuit too?'

Liane bent to stroke the cat, who purred obligingly and stepped into the kitchen. Help – she didn't want every cat in the neighbourhood coming by for afternoon tea every day. Liane handed over a chocolate digestive and ushered Frith outside again, relieved when Marmaduke followed on.

'We shouldn't feed him, Frithy – look, he's not exactly skinny. He obviously gets plenty of grub at home. You can be garden friends, huh?'

Frith was charmed. 'We can make a little house – or a den – in the bushes! Come on, Marmaduke!' She skipped off down the garden, and Liane turned back to the house to see Steve leaning in the back doorway.

He lurched upright, producing a bottle of Prosecco from behind his back. 'Well fielded, Mummy. How about we toast your new home?'

'Good plan. I think I know where the glasses are.'

His eyes were warm, and Liane's insides tugged in a delicious, shivery way. Golly, this really could be the start of something big in her life. New house, new bloke (potentially) – all she needed was the new job to complete the trio. She shook nuts into a bowl while Steve poured drinks, and they adjourned to the elderly iron bench beneath the kitchen window.

Liane called down the garden. 'Frith! Want some nuts?'

Frith's voice was audible, talking presumably to the orange cat, but the little girl was lost to sight in the bushes. Liane called again. Imagine losing your child in your own back garden – this couldn't be more different to the patch of crazed, crumbling concrete they'd shared with three other flats at their old place.

Frith bounced across the grass and plumped down at Liane's feet. 'Bridie's not here, but I met one of her other cats. He's black and he's much smaller than Marmaduke. He came through a hole in the fence.'

'Marmaduke and Mr Black.' Steve ruffled Frith's hair. 'Wonder who the next one'll be? Mr White? Or Mr Black Patch over one eye?'

Frith giggled 'Or Mr Stripy! Bridie said they had lots of cats! And one's having kittens soon!'

'You can ask their real names when we meet Bridie and her mum properly,' said Liane, a vague idea entering her mind at the mention of kittens. Frith would love a little cat of their own and, with a cat-owning neighbour, they'd be able to exchange holiday feeding duties.

Frith gulped down her apple juice and grabbed a generous handful of nuts before vanishing into the undergrowth again.

Steve put an arm across Liane's shoulders and gave her a quick hug. 'She's a lovely kid, you know.'

'She's my world. It's going to be so much better for her here. Hey, I think I'll have a house-warming party in a week or two. There are loads of people I'd like to thank for babysitting and helping me when Frithy was poorly – a celebration would be fun.' Especially if she was celebrating a new job, too. The chances were good – as well as the creche job, she'd applied for an admin one in a logistics company and another in a medical supplies depot. Neither of the others came with childcare attached, though, so the hospital one would be best.

Steve went for the Prosecco bottle, and Liane tapped into her phone contacts, planning her invitations. There were dozens of people here. Steve, and Jon and his family, Sister Annie, plus the old neighbours and the new ones here they didn't know yet, not to mention people like old school friends – and that reminded her, she should reply to that email about the reunion. It would be fun to see what everyone had been up to in the twelve years or so since they'd left school. She'd need to find a babysitter, preferably one where Frithy could spend the night. Sister Annie might help there… Liane stood up. The chatter in the bushes had stopped. Where was Frith?

'Frith!'

Silence. Did Frithy realise you shouldn't start exploring other people's gardens? They would have to work out some rules here.

'She'll be concentrating on her game,' said Steve, reaching for Liane's glass to refill it.

A sudden giggle was accompanied by a flash of red T-shirt between the bushes, and Liane sat down again. A neurotic mother was the last thing any child needed.

She accepted a full glass from Steve. He'd already offered to lick the garden into shape for her. 'Do you think you could thin those bushes out a touch?'

He shot her a look then cast his eyes heavenwards. 'How (not) to endear yourself to your new girlfriend's child.'

Ooh. Liane flapped her hand in front of her face to cool the flush. 'Am I your new girlfriend, then? Do I have any say in this?'

'Aren't you? I know it's early days, but... I'd like you to be.'

He'd gone all pink too. Liane raised her glass. 'Here's to us, then.'

They clinked, and Steve took her hand as they sat sipping and chatting about things they could do that summer, though part of her was on constant alert for sights and sounds of her daughter. What was it going to be like when Frithy went on her first sleepover, her first night out, not to mention her first date? And to think that a year or two ago she'd have given everything she owned to see her girl playing so happily. Parenting wasn't for wimps.

At coffee time she yelled for Frith, and a moment or two later the little girl came running up the garden.

'Mummy, I've met lots of Bridie's cats in their garden! She came out to play for a little while. The little black one's called

Ermintrude and I met Daisy and Socks and Demelza too. The others don't come outside so much, Margie said. The one who's having kitties soon is Tabitha, Mummy, can we...?'

Unbearably hopeful eyes bored into hers, and Liane didn't try to hide her grin. 'We'll think about it. Is Margie Bridie's mum? You should come and check with me before you go into people's gardens, Frithy.'

'Bridie said it was okay. We were playing houses. I was Dad and Bridie was Mum and Marmaduke and—'

She chattered on, and Liane gloried in those pink cheeks, and the sheer love of life streaming from her child. She would have to go by and say hello to Margie, but immediately after consuming three glasses of Prosecco wasn't the best time to introduce yourself to the neighbours.

STEVE HAD coffee with them before leaving Liane to sort Frith's possessions into the little girl's new bedroom. At six o'clock Frith announced she was hungry, so Liane went downstairs to make dinner. Spaghetti and sauce from a jar would do; this had been a tiring day.

Her mobile vibrated on the work surface and Liane lifted it, sighing. Life did keep on getting in the way. It was an email from Ruby, the woman who was organising the reunion. A list of people so far attending was attached, and a reminder to anyone else interested that they'd need to accept by May 5th to get tickets. This was going to be great – she would ask Steve to be her plus one. It would be fun, meeting people she hadn't seen for yonks. Liane scanned the list of ex-schoolmates – Daria wasn't there, but most of her other old friends were. Spontaneously, she tapped to make a voice call to Daria.

'Hi, Liane.'

Daria's voice was dull. She said nothing more, and Liane sat down at the kitchen table, which was still piled high with stuff she had yet to find a home for. Had she been too spontaneous, calling like this?

'Hello – I've just seen the message from Ruby about the reunion. I guess you got one too?'

'Ah, yes. I won't be able to go, though.'

'Oh, what a pity. I think it'll be brilliant to see everyone again. I've more or less kept up with Gill and Karen, but that's all. They're both still in Glasgow.'

'I haven't kept up with anyone except Kit. She's working in insurance in the city centre.'

'Are you able to work at the moment, with your leg? Is it healing well?'

'No. I don't know when I'll start again. It's improving every day, though.'

Daria sounded terribly down, and Liane frowned in sympathy. It couldn't be much fun, getting about on crutches and not being able to do everything you usually did.

The spaghetti water boiled, and Frith ran in from the garden.

'Mummy, I'm hungry!'

'Coming, love bug.' Liane made an impulsive decision. 'Daria – how about a coffee sometime? It would be nice to catch up, especially if you can't come to the reunion. When would suit?'

'Um – that would be nice. Any time suits.'

'Great. Tomorrow at two?'

Daria agreed, and Liane gave her new address before hanging up and looking through her kitchen cupboards for the spaghetti. This had been the best day ever – moved in, Steve being lovely, and an old friend coming tomorrow. Now to concentrate on feeding her ravenous daughter. Having a garden made you extra-hungry, according to Frith.

DAY FIFTEEN – FRIDAY 1ST MAY

CHAPTER 19

Mammy wasn't well. Evie ate her toast quietly, blinking across the table as Mammy coughed her way through a cup of tea. She'd been coughing a lot in the night, too. It sounded sore. Evie had woken up twice when Mammy went to bang around downstairs – looking for medicine? The packet of pills was sitting beside the kettle.

Mammy sneezed, then she wiped her nose with her sleeve and leaned her head on one hand. Evie peered around the kitchen, but there weren't any tissues. It was all a big mess here, even more than usual, and Mammy had forgotten to fill one of the cats' water bowls. Evie jumped up and filled it, spilling quite a lot of water on the floor, but Mammy didn't say anything.

'Can I play outside?' Maybe Frith would be out too.

'It's raining. Leave me in peace to get better, maid. Play in the house for now.'

Mammy coughed again, and Evie changed her mind

about asking to have her bandage done. Her arm was much better anyway. She went through to the living room, but there wasn't anything to play with here and the TV was nothing like the one they'd had at Mummy's. This one was old and tiny, and it was in a dusty fat wooden box and not on the wall. The remote was nowhere to be seen. Evie stood in front of the TV – it had knobs on the side. She turned one, but nothing happened. Ah – it wasn't plugged in. The plug was a bit old, too. Evie lifted it, then looked at the door. She wasn't allowed to plug things in at home, but Mammy was still coughing in the kitchen. Evie shoved the plug into the socket on the wall and tried the knobs again. The TV made a crackly noise a few times, but nothing happened. Evie gave up. The cats were better fun, anyway.

A lorry splashed up the street, and Evie went over to the window. Mammy's front garden was untidy too, and it was much smaller than the back. And it was still raining. And—

Something smelled horrible. Evie swivelled round – oh no! It was the TV. Was that smoke coming out of the back?

She whimpered and scooted back to the kitchen, where Mammy was bent over her tea at the table.

'I wanted to watch TV and now it smells all burny!'

Mammy gaped at her, then sniffed the air. 'I don't smell anything.'

Evie pulled Mammy's arm, and she swayed through to the living room. It *was* smoke coming out of the TV, and Evie began to cry.

'Tsk. It's been broken for years. Leave it alone, maid.' Mammy yanked the plug from the wall, then flopped down on the sofa.

Evie crept back to the kitchen. Mammy's cup was empty,

but Evie was too little to make her a cup of tea. She filled a glass with water and took it through to the living room.

'I brought you a drink.'

Mammy took the glass and gave her a cracked little smile. 'Fetch me the pills too, and then we'll remember Ireland.'

Mammy's Ireland stories were nice, though Evie didn't remember the things they'd done there. It must be the same as Spain, though, because there was a beach and rocks to climb over. She hurried back to the kitchen for the pills. Mammy swallowed two, then Evie clambered up and Mammy pulled her onto her lap.

She gave Evie a little squeeze. 'What was the best thing about Bantry Bay?'

'The sea?'

'That's right. Your daddy had a boat when you were little and we all used to go fishing. Swimming sometimes, too, but you liked it best when we were on the beach and you all went paddling.'

'Did we have ice cream?'

'For a treat. You liked having raspberry sauce on yours and Maeve liked the chocolate.'

Raspberry on your ice cream was yummy. Mammy coughed, and her chest heaved against Evie's back. She jumped down and handed Mammy the glass of water.

'Good girl. Let me have a little sleep while you play for a bit, darlin'.' Mammy sipped her water. Very soon she was snoring.

Evie went back to the kitchen. Poor Mammy. But it would help if she washed some of the cups and glasses, wouldn't it? Mammy didn't have a dishwasher. The water was cold but there was plenty of it, and Evie soon had a row of clean glasses and cups on the draining board, though she got her bandage all wet. The tea towel was dirty, so she searched through drawers until she found a clean one. It had a big hole and the picture was all washed away, but she dried the things anyway.

She was almost finished when Mammy came through to the kitchen and opened a tin of tomato soup for lunch. Evie cleared a space on the table and found bowls and spoons for the soup. She was helping, and it was nice.

The sun came out while they were having lunch, and Evie went to the kitchen window as soon as they'd finished their soup. 'Can I go out to play?'

Mammy was drinking pink medicine straight from the bottle. 'Don't go on the grass until it's dry or you'll catch your death too.'

Evie ran out before Mammy changed her mind. Everything was quiet in Frith's garden, so Evie played a game with some twigs she found to waggle about while Socks pounced on them. She would listen all the time, though, and – yes! That was Frith talking in her garden. Evie wriggled through the jungle to the back fence.

'Frith! Are you there?'

Frith came squashing through the bushes. 'Ouch – my jungle's thicker than yours!' She poked at a scratch on her arm.

'Can you come and play with the cats?'

'I'll ask.' She pushed her way back, and Evie jumped up and down to see more of the other garden. It was true, Frith's jungle was more jungly.

After a minute Frith was back. 'I can't stay for long. We're having ice cream and cake with a friend of Mummy's and when she's gone home we're going to the shops and then the park. I'll be back afterwards, though.'

She crawled through the biggest hole in the fence and joined Evie, and they started a game of Catch the Twig with Socks at the back of Mammy's house. They'd only been playing for five minutes when Frith's mummy called, and Evie was alone all over again.

Mummy used to take her to the park too, but that was before. Evie kicked a stone around for a while, then sat on the step with half a packet of biscuits she'd found in a cupboard in the kitchen. They'd gone all soft, though, so she spat the first bite out then went back inside and put the rest in the bin. The packet of pills was in there, all squashed up. They hadn't made Mammy better, had they? Evie put her head into the living room, but Mammy was asleep on the sofa, her breath rattling in her chest. Evie closed the door and headed for the stairs. She'd better play in the house in case Mammy needed her to fetch something.

Upstairs, she went into the smallest room where nobody slept. She would build a house for her and the cats, yes, there was a big box with a lot of little boxes inside it in the corner here. By the time Mammy called, Evie and Socks were having a lovely game in their own houses, though Socks only sat in his box and miaowed at Evie when she tried to make him visit hers.

Back in the kitchen, Mammy had started to make tea. Her face was pink and shiny, but she smiled at Evie and held out one hand.

'Come on, Bridie, maid. Let's get that bandage fixed.'

Evie sat still while Mammy took the bandage off. It was dry now. 'Why am I called Bridie?'

'It was your grandma's sister's name. She went away to Dublin when she was a young woman, then she married a man from the north and went there to live. Maeve is after my little sister – she died of tuberculosis when she was just two.'

Oh no – a little girl died? 'Didn't she go to hospital? And what's tuber— what you said?'

'It's when your lungs are sick and you can't breathe properly. They took her away for a while, but my mammy brought her home again. There was nothing you could do in those days.' She coughed and reached for the medicine bottle.

'Are you sick too?' It would be awful if Mammy was as sick as little Maeve who died.

'Nothing but a silly cough. I'll get something else at the chemist soon, that'll fix it.'

Mammy fastened the bandage again and Evie tried out her arm. It was almost as good as new. She smiled at Mammy, but then Mammy started coughing again, harder than before.

She waved Evie to the sink. 'Water!'

Evie fetched a glassful and Mammy sipped, but the cough kept coming back. Mammy stood up and leaned on a space beside the kettle, making a funny noise as she breathed. Evie was breathing fast too – what if they took Mammy away to hospital? Would she go back to Mummy then? Was Mummy home yet? And what about the cats?

A shivery-scared lump was heavy in Evie's tummy now. She ran to fetch the pink medicine – oh, no, the bottle was nearly empty. Mammy grabbed it and fumbled the top off, but then it slipped from her hand and crashed to the floor.

Pink medicine oozed out, and Evie's throat went all thick and choky. Oh, poor Mammy.

Mammy leaned her head on her hands, pushing the toaster to one side. Her shoulders were shaking.

Evie stood still. What should she do? It was dreadful when grown-ups cried.

CHAPTER 20

Daria tucked tissues into her handbag, and lifted her jacket from the coatstand. Was she ready for this coffee invitation? She and Liane had been friendly for a few years, but that was a long time ago. She had no idea what Liane had done in the meantime. Except, have a baby. Was Frith an only child? Imagine being confronted today with Liane, several children and a happy family life. How could she even start to tell them about Evie? Maybe this wasn't a good idea.

Her mother's voice came from the bedroom. 'Do you need help, darling?'

Too late to change anything now. Daria slung her handbag over her head, and reached for her crutches, propped against the coatstand.

Noah was driving, and Daria settled into the back seat beside her mother. They were dropping her off at Liane's, then Noah and her parents were going on to Silverburn Shopping Centre. Mum and Dad were flying back to Spain on Sunday, so they wanted some home-stuff to take with them. No doubt too the three of them would seize the opportunity to talk about her and how she was coping. Daria swallowed rising apprehension. In five minutes, it would be Liane and her family she'd be coping with…

Noah pulled up on a wide street near a park and came to help Daria out. 'We'll be back for you between three and four. I'll text you when we're leaving Silverburn.'

'That's fine. If I need to leave before that for any reason, I'll let you know.'

'Why would you?'

Daria struggled to reply pleasantly to his petulant tone. Mum hated it when she and Noah snapped at each other. It was easier to keep the peace.

'I don't know if she has anything else planned.' Daria ducked her head to speak to her parents. 'Have a good shop.' She swung her way up Liane's front path.

Liane opened the door and stood back to let her in. 'Lovely to see you, Daria. Now, do you want to sit on an armchair, or would we be better at the kitchen table?'

Daria handed over her crutches while she shrugged out of her jacket. How nice of Liane to ask. 'The kitchen table would be easier, thanks.'

Liane led the way into a bright but ancient kitchen. 'I was on crutches for a while when I was a teenager. It's amazing how much we take for granted about moving around the place, isn't it? Grab a chair.'

Daria sat, and leaned her crutches on the wall to her left. 'How long have you been here?'

Liane looked at her watch. 'Almost twenty-eight hours.' She jerked her head at the pile of boxes in one corner. 'That's why cardboard is such a major part of the ambience at the moment.'

Daria gasped. 'Gosh – you've settled in quickly! It was weeks before I even considered inviting people for coffee when we moved into our place.'

Liane laughed. 'What're a few boxes between friends? We'll be living in chaos for a few months, anyway. The house is being renovated soon and we'll move out for the duration.'

She chatted on while she was setting out coffee mugs, and Daria circled tight shoulders. Frith wasn't here. Would this be a good time to tell Liane about Evie? The thought had barely formed in her mind when the back door burst open and Frith charged in.

'Are we having cake now? Hello, Daria!'

And there it was, Evie's love of life. Most happy little girls would have it, but it was still heart-wrenching for Daria to see.

Liane winked at her. 'Frith, sweetie-pie, that was very nearly the perfect way to come into the room when we have a visitor. Next time, say hello before you ask about the menu, and you'll have cracked it.' She dropped a kiss on Frith's blonde head, and Daria's heart broke.

The next hour was spent at the table, with Frith eating a huge portion of chocolate ice cream as well as a chunk of apple cake while she interrogated Daria and Liane about their school days. It was hard not to laugh at the little face opposite, so serious while she asked her questions. Daria's cake vanished before she realised she'd eaten it – for seconds at a time, this was like being back in the universe she'd been catapulted out of on the day of the accident. But in between, again and again, reality hit her like a kick in the stomach. Evie should have been here too.

Eventually, Frith ran out of questions and dessert. 'Can I go and play with Bridie again until we go to the park?' Bright eyes met Daria's. 'Bridie's my new friend – she's got lots and lots of cats.'

Liane was shaking her head. 'The rain's back on, look. Why don't you unpack more of your toys?'

Frith's face fell as she stared outside, but she thundered upstairs obediently. Silence fell in the kitchen, and Daria drained her mug. This would be the ideal time to—

'More coffee?' Liane went over to the machine.

Daria watched idly as she pressed buttons, and the clock on the microwave swam into focus – gosh, it was well after three. Noah could turn up any second. 'Half a cup would be lovely, thanks.'

Should she...? No. She wasn't going to start a difficult conversation today. They'd had a nice afternoon and anyway, Frith could reappear at any second too. A conversation about Evie was best had when there were no children present and they had plenty of time. And to prove the point, here was Frith again, a picture book clutched to her chest.

'Daria, would you like to see my fairy book? And can I show Daria my game on your phone, Mummy?'

'We're in a phone-free zone this afternoon, love bug. Show Daria the book, though – the illustrations are gorgeous.'

Frith slid her chair round the table, and a whiff of lemon shampoo reached Daria's nose. Oh, how many times had she sat leafing through a book with Evie? Her girl would have loved these pictures too. Daria forced out a few questions about the story, loving Frith's answers and hating the fact that her heart was torn between the joy of the moment and the twin holes of loss and grief.

Her mobile buzzed in her bag, and Daria was glad to see Noah's text. *With you in five.*

'That's my husband. I'll wait by the door, if you don't mind. He has Mum and Dad in the car too. Liane, Frith, thank you so much for a lovely afternoon.'

Liane walked with her to the door and helped her into her jacket. 'We'll do it again sometime. And see if you can make it to the reunion, Daria – I think it'll be a lot of fun.'

It would have to be fun without her. Daria swung her way to the car when Noah drew up outside. She waved to Liane and Frith in the doorway, and dropped into the back seat beside her mother. Who'd have thought that spending an hour or two with a little girl who wasn't Evie would be so tough – and so wonderful?

DAY EIGHTEEN – MONDAY 4TH MAY

CHAPTER 21

Liane awoke on the day of the interview to rain battering against the windows, almost drowning out her mobile ringing on the bedside table. Shit, had she overslept? Panic surged until she saw it was only half past six. She scrabbled to connect; bummer, this was Karen, who was supposed to be looking after Frith while Liane was at the interview – please, please, don't let her say she was backing out.

'I'm so sorry, Liane, but Susie's been up sick all night. Can you find someone else to take Frithy?'

Liane dredged up her Superwoman skills. 'Oh, poor little thing. Don't worry, I'll manage something.'

She dropped the phone as soon as Karen disconnected, and flopped back on the pillow. Who on earth could she ask at three seconds' notice? All her other friends had work to go to and Steve was on duty this morning too. Tony? Gawd. It was going to come to that, wasn't it? The only other person she could think of was Daria, who Frithy barely knew and who was on crutches. She tapped to connect to Tony's number, grinning wryly. A 6.33 call; how to make yourself popular with your ex who'd most likely been partying all weekend. Her call went to voicemail. Liane tried three times with the same result, then thumped the pillow. Tony was most likely still in bed with a massive weekend hangover. There was no reason to suppose he'd answer a text in a useful time frame. She'd have one more go in half an hour.

Liane showered, then put on her bathrobe – it wouldn't do to spill half her breakfast down her interview outfit, and the way her hands shook every time she thought about half past nine, that was almost inevitable. Okay, should she have coffee for the energy boost, or a nice herbal tea to calm her nerves? No question really, was there? She pressed buttons for cappuccino and chewed her way through a bowlful of healthy muesli.

Okay. Now to try Tony again. Pick up, pick up... Voicemail. They were onto plan B. It was half seven, late enough to try Daria. Liane swiped down her contacts list. Daria and Frithy'd got on like a house on fire on Friday and Daria didn't have a job to go to while her leg was healing, so fingers crossed. A text might be a good way to start.

Babysitter fail – any chance you could take F for 1–2 hours this a.m. while I'm at my interview? Liane sent it off and went for more coffee.

Her phone rang before she'd pressed a single button. Daria – wow, this was hopeful.

'Hi, Liane – I have a hair appointment at half eleven, would that suit your times?'

A wave of relief flashed through Liane. 'Yes! The interview's at half nine. I'd be in your debt forever. I know it's a big ask when you're on crutches. Perhaps your mum can help?'

'Mum and Dad went home yesterday, but if you bring Frith here, I can manage. It's not as if I'd have to run around after her all the time.'

Sorted, if not a hundred per cent ideal. Liane made a note of the address and went back to planning. It might be best to damn the expense and get a taxi to Daria's and then on to the hospital. She couldn't sit down in front of the interview panel all rushed and sweaty, not to mention rain-splashed. So much was riding on this interview.

Frith was charmed when she learned about the new plan for the morning. 'Shall I take my fairy book? Daria liked that.'

Ten to nine saw their taxi pull up in front of Daria's building. Liane leaned forward to speak to the driver. 'I'll see my daughter inside and be straight back.'

She raced in with Frith, who was carrying a huge bag of books and toys, and bundled her up the stairs to Daria's flat door.

'Be good!' She kissed Frith and rang the bell, grinning at Daria when the door opened. 'I'll be back ASAP – I'll text you when I'm on my way. You're a star; I owe you.'

Back in the taxi, she sat organising her head into a more interview-like mindset. This simply had to go well.

THE CHILDREN'S HOSPITAL WAS BUSY, and Liane crossed the entrance hallway with her heart beating in her throat. Quarter past nine; she was in good time. A quick trip to the loo, then she'd be ready for anything they asked her. She hoped. The next hour could change her life.

The interview passed in a blur, with Liane on one side of a large and shiny wooden conference table and the panel of three on the other. The head of the admin staff was there, plus the leader of the playgroup and some high-up person in the nursing hierarchy, though Liane wasn't clear what his role on the panel was. They were all older than she'd been expecting – the administrator must have been past retirement age – and while they were pleasant, they weren't friendly. Liane sat with her hands clasped tightly on her lap, struggling at first to keep her breathing under control. Once she settled down it was okay, though; the one question that threw her slightly was why she hadn't asked her previous employer for a reference.

'Ah – I wasn't there for long and I left because I was never able to finish in time to collect my daughter punctually from the childminder's. The shop owner wasn't pleased when I – handed in my notice.'

'I see. If you get the job, would your daughter need a place in the playgroup?'

At least she had anticipated this one. 'She had a place with an excellent childminder who I'm sure would take her again, but I'd be able to be more flexible if she were here with me, until she starts school. If I get the job.' Was that a good answer? Mrs P would take Frith back, surely, if push came to shove.

'I see. And I understand you'd be able to start soon?'

'Yes. I've been busy moving house, but we're settling in nicely.' Liane smiled across the table.

A few more 'What would you do if…' questions ended

the interview, and Liane landed on the other side of the door at last. Golly, she'd been put through the wringer there.

She started back to the lifts, her heart skipping a beat at the sight of Steve waiting at the end of the corridor. He came to meet her, his face expectant.

'How did it go?'

'All right, I think, but they were pretty neutral. I'll hear by the middle of next week, one way or the other.'

He walked downstairs beside her. 'I'm sure you've smashed it. Hey, how about going to an art exhibition this week? A guy I was at school with has one on – Dave Struthers. It's nothing Frith would enjoy, unfortunately, but we could go when she was on a play date? It's on until the tenth.'

'Sounds good.' This would be their first date exploring something cultural. Liane made a mental note to Google Dave Struthers before they went.

Steve opened the door to the entrance hallway for her. 'I'm on evenings all week but if we went at half one-ish, we'd have time for a coffee afterwards.'

'That would be great. Where is it?'

'The Gallery of Modern Art in town. How about Wednesday?'

Liane agreed, anticipation fizzing inside her. She and Steve hadn't had a lot of us-time yet, and much as she loved Frithy, it would be nice to be a twosome for a while. He walked to the main doors with her before kissing her cheek chastely and leaving her to run for the approaching bus. Wow, oh, wow. Liane plumped herself down on the first empty seat, her heart singing. He cared, and so did she. And they were going on a date. Whatever the interview result was, she was walking on air right now.

Ten dreamy minutes later, she jumped off the bus and started towards Daria's flat. The rain had eased off, but everything was soaking. And heck, she'd forgotten to text her ETA. Better do that. *On my way, with you in 5.* Liane marched along the street and up Daria's driveway. This was a much more upmarket area than theirs; lucky Daria to live in such a gracious old house.

To Liane's surprise, Frith and Daria were waiting on the landing outside the flat. Daria was pale, but she smiled kindly at Frith and gave her a little hug goodbye before turning to Liane.

'How was the interview? It's been lovely having her. I hope you'll let me do this again sometime?'

Liane glanced at Frith, who was grinning up at Daria and nodding. Daria did seem to have the magic touch, so…

'It went okay, I think. As you've asked, and only if it's not too cheeky, could you manage Wednesday afternoon? I'm supposed to be going to an art exhibition and heaven knows if our usual babysitter's little one will be well enough by then to stand a visit from Frithy.'

'I'd love to.'

Daria hugged Frith again, and Liane hesitated. Were those tears in her old friend's eyes? Daria was smiling, though, and Liane relaxed.

'Brilliant – I'll call you later. Put your feet up at the hairdresser's, you deserve it.'

An awkward clap on the shoulder later – you couldn't exactly hug someone who was balancing on one leg and crutches, could you? – Liane and Frith were running downstairs.

'Daria has a lovely big TV and I played tennis on it. Can we get some TV games, Mummy?'

'One day. We'll have to save up first – they're expensive.'

'I'll ask Santa.'

Oops. But there was plenty of time to channel Frith's Christmas wish list in the direction of more affordable toys. And hallelujah, she could chill for the rest of the day. It was a longish walk home from Daria's, but Frithy'd been inside all morning and some pre-lunch exercise would do them both good. And she'd pop by the neighbours this afternoon, the ones with the little girl Frithy'd met, and say hello. A friend next door was just what Frithy needed.

Frith skipped along, chatting about this and that, and Liane revelled anew in the sight of her pink cheeks and energy. Maybe if she saved every possible penny, they could get a Wii at Christmas after all. Frithy had missed a lot during her illness, it would be lovely to make it up to her a little. She could—

Liane rounded the corner into their street and stopped dead. Tony was hanging around outside their gate, hands in pockets and a frown on his face she could see from twenty yards away.

'Daddy!'

Frith dropped her bag of toys and ran to be scooped up in Tony's arms. Liane trailed along the pavement to join them. Something was bugging Tony big-time, if those knitted brows were anything to go by. His hair was greasy and uncombed and his clothes looked as if he'd slept in them –

which, knowing him, was perfectly possible. He was a 'crash on the sofa after a night out' kind of guy.

Liane forced a neutral expression onto her face. 'Frith, love bug, I'm going to ask you to be very good and play in the garden for a few minutes while I have a chat with Daddy. You can see him again afterwards. Okay?'

Frith's shoulders drooped, but she nodded dumbly and trotted up the path to the back garden. Liane put the bag of toys down beside the gate. Was he here to scrounge some lunch?

'I wasn't expecting you, Tony.'

He sniffed. 'That's blatantly obvious. What was that with the midnight phone calls? And when were you going to tell me you'd moved? I had to ask the neighbour at your old place.'

'Tony, I sent you a message with the full address days ago. It's not my fault if you don't check your texts.'

'I noticed you had your phone switched off all morning.' He scrolled down his message list, then sniffed again.

No need to tell him where she'd been. If he thought she was in with a chance of a better job, he'd be round for cash every five minutes instead of every two weeks. Liane sighed. What had happened to the good-looking, fun guy who'd give you his last penny? The one she'd fallen in love with? But then, Tony's main problem was he didn't have any pennies to give now she'd left him and taken her income – or lack of it – with her.

Tony was still frowning. 'I want to see Frith a lot more regularly, Liane, do things with her, show her things. She's my daughter too.' He strode over to the front door, forcing Liane to follow on.

She opened the door and led the way to the kitchen, where she could keep an eye on Frith, who was playing skittles on the patio. Marmaduke had come to visit, good.

Okay, there were two things to consider here. Tony was right; as Frith's dad, he did have rights. But he hadn't exactly been a hands-on father when Frith was ill, so why was he starting now?

'We can arrange something, yes, of course. But I'd like you to visit her at home more regularly before you take her out anywhere, Tony. You barely know each other.'

'I think I'm capable of entertaining a four-year-old in an appropriate manner. And don't forget you owe me – you've had her to yourself all this time.'

What the hell was he talking about? Liane choked out a reply, tears of rage burning in her eyes.

'Tony. I owe you nothing. You're the one not supporting your own daughter.'

'I'm an artist, aren't I? All my career needs is one little push, and you block me every time.'

His voice was loud and petulant – had he been drinking?

'What planet are you on? I'm fed up with this, Tony. Grow up.'

Liane moved over to the window. Looking at him for two seconds longer would have her exploding. Outside, Frith was running to meet a dark-haired little girl emerging from the jungle at the far end of the garden – this must be Bridie. A slight child with a solemn little face that brightened when Frith took hold of her hand and pulled her towards the house. The pair set up the skittles and began a new game.

'Liane! Did you hear me? I said, I have the same rights as you do.' Tony folded his arms and stood glaring at her.

Liane kept her tone neutral. 'When you want to spend more time with Frith, you can phone and we'll arrange something.'

He strode to the back door. 'We'll make that tomorrow afternoon then, shall we?'

Brilliant. A visit from Tony two days running. Ah, well – Frithy would be happy.

DAY NINETEEN – TUESDAY 5TH MAY

CHAPTER 22

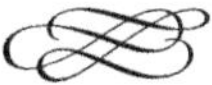

Tabitha was having a wash. Margie stroked the cat's soft fur beside her on the sofa, then abandoned her after-lunch cuppa and swayed to her feet. Her legs weren't quite as shaky today, and after three rainy days on the trot, the sun was struggling through again. That trip to the chemist might even be possible this afternoon. She had to go, didn't she? Her throat hurt and this cough was still dreadful – once she started, she couldn't stop. Her chest was playing a tune as if all the bells and whistles in Ireland were in there.

Bridie was in the kitchen, sorting through the cupboard by the door. Exploring the cupboards and making houses with cardboard boxes had kept the child occupied during the bad weather, but she'd want to go out today. Margie gazed out to the sunny garden. Leaving Bridie out there while she went to the chemist wasn't safe, but taking her wasn't a good idea either. That traffic was dangerous.

A car backfired outside, and Margie shivered. Bridie. Her Bridie had an accident, didn't she? The world faded into grey and Margie leaned both hands on the table, shaking her head to get rid of the buzzing. She was fine.

Demelza jumped inside through the open window and streaked past to the hallway. Bridie stood up, and Margie grabbed her before she ran off too. 'Let's do up that bandage before it falls right off. Then you can look after Tabitha while I'm at the chemist. We need to take care of her until the kitties come, you know.'

Bridie perched on a chair while Margie unwound and reapplied the bandage.

'How many kitties will there be?'

'They sometimes have three or four. We'll have to wait and see, won't we?'

Bridie waved her arm around when Margie was finished. 'It's almost better.'

'Good. Off you go and keep an eye on Tabitha – she's on the sofa.'

'I'm going to the loo first.'

Bridie sped off, and Margie rummaged around in the kitchen drawers for her purse. It must be here somewhere... yes, here it was at the back, and thanks be, she had enough money for a visit to the chemist's. A spasm of coughing shook her ribs, and Margie held onto the edges of the drawer. Her chest was on fire, full of everything but air. She needed more than aspirin to beat this bug. Margie wiped her eyes, turning and tripping over Topsy.

'Scram, you!'

Topsy slunk through the window while Margie leaned over the sink, panting. Poor darlin' Topsy.

She poured herself a glass of water and shuffled out to the hallway, where Daisy was tapping at an envelope lying on the floor behind the door. Margie tutted and went to pick it up, leaning against the front door while she peered at the plain white envelope. Her eyes were worth nothing now, and her specs were long gone. The address was handwritten, so it probably wasn't a bill, and – she turned it over – there was a name scrawled on the back too, though she couldn't for the life of her make out what it said. Another spasm of coughing left her breathless and Margie tossed the letter onto the hall table and went for a sit down. It wouldn't be important; nobody ever wrote to her.

She sank down beside Tabitha, water slopping over her glass and seeping through her trousers, making them cling to her leg. Two minutes, then she'd go. She took a few mouthfuls, but swallowing was an effort.

Ach, Tabitha puss – such soft, warm fur, such a contented purr when Margie rubbed behind the torn ears. Oh, for the days they were all safe at home in Ireland... but they weren't gone, not really. She only had to close her eyes and she was back there, with Ned and all her babies. Oh, it was wonderful then. Tabitha dug her claws in, and Ireland was gone. Come on, Margie. Another few sips of water and she'd be ready to go. Ready as she'd ever be, anyway. Where was that girl?

'Bridie! Come to Mammy!'

Thumps on the stairs, and Margie staggered to her feet, swaying as Bridie skipped over to the sofa to join Tabitha. Margie's heart swelled with love – Ireland was gone, but Bridie was right here.

'Good girls. And you stay inside this time, hear? I'll be

back before you know it.' A glance told her the windows were closed – not that she often opened these ones – and Margie wheezed her way to the door, closing it behind her. There.

The pavements were wet, but at least the rain had gone off. Margie lifted her chin and set off for the row of shops. This uphill part was murder, but it would be downhill on the way back and she had to do this; she had to be well for her family. Ireland loomed in her head again.

Remember what fun it was when the babies were small? Aiden and Sammy, then Maeve, and then – oh, and then her darlin' baby girl.

Tears blinded Margie as she stumbled along, grabbing the odd handful of hedge to help her balance. The holes in this pavement were a disgrace.

'All right, hen?'

Another do-gooder. Margie swiped a hand over her eyes, then stuck her chin out at the postman staring at her from a thin, spotty face. Upstart. Who was he, call her 'hen'?

'I'm fine.'

'Off to the shops, are you?'

'None of your business.' She inched past him, nose in the air.

'Give you a lift if you like. I'm heading back to the depot in Thurston Street.'

Margie stopped. A lift. What a luxury. She shouldn't take it, but a lift would make such a difference today.

'Thank you. You're – very kind.' And many a long day since she'd said anything like that. Margie followed him across the road to his van and dropped into the seat when he opened the door for her. Whistling, he started the engine. Two minutes, that was all it took, and here they were at the shops already.

'Which one?'

'Chemist. Thank you.'

He pulled up beside a motorbike parked on the pavement and came round to help her out. 'Looks like the chemist's the right place for you, love. Or the doc's. You take care.'

Lucky, she was, all that energy saved. Margie walked into the shop with her head high. 'Something for my chest, please.'

It was a different woman on today, an older one. She narrowed her eyes at Margie, a frown gathering behind thick glasses with red frames. 'What's the problem?'

'Bit of a wheeze. Sore throat.'

The woman raised her eyebrows. 'Is this something new?'

'Aye. Two or three days.' Not true, but it was no one's business but hers. Margie fixed her eyes on the assistant and held her ground.

The woman went through to the back and returned with a box of something and a packet of sweeties.

'These are powders, take one sachet in hot water four times a day. And you can suck one of the throat pastilles every two hours. If you're not better by Friday, see your doctor.'

Margie sniffed. 'Chance would be a fine thing.' She wasn't going to walk nearly an hour to the new medical centre to queue for an appointment she wouldn't get for three weeks.

The woman grimaced. 'They're overworked. Drop in again if you need more advice. Anything else?'

Margie took another bottle of Calpol and paid – the price was shocking, she wouldn't come here again, anyway – before shuffling out. The woman was staring after her, nosy besom that she was. So what if she didn't have posh clothes? She'd paid for her medicine, hadn't she? And while she was here, she'd best stock up on soup and beans. Heavy to carry but cheap and nourishing. And she'd get some jam, too, Bridie would like that. Margie stepped into the minimarket. At least there were no nosy busybodies in here, and no policemen either today. And look, they had aspirins too. She added a packet to her basket, peering at the chocolate on the stand by the cash desk; a bar of milk always went down well at home. Aiden and the rest had always enjoyed a treat, in the old days. But she'd already spent too much.

A throat sweetie to suck helped her on the way home. Blackcurrant, they were. Nice. Took her back to the days when her granny made cordial with the berries they gathered down by the beach. And here she was, home in no time just like she'd said. Margie stepped through the back door and dumped her bag on the kitchen table, then rummaged for the packet of medicine. Lemon, good, her granny had sworn by lemons when she had a cold. Margie put the kettle on and looked around for a clean mug. Tallulah was sniffing at the empty cat bowls.

'Bridie, lovey! Mammy's home!'

Silence. Had the maid fallen asleep? The kettle boiled with its usual shriek, and Margie poured water into a mug for her lemon drink, then stirred. The mug was hot to lift, so she wrapped a tea towel round it to take it to the living room to drink in comfort. Wheezing again, she swayed through to the hallway, knocking the letter off the hall table as she passed. The living room door was open…

And no, no, no – Margie's legs gave way and she lurched over to the armchair, hot lemon scalding through the tea towel while a howl of anguish tore at her throat. Marmaduke was alone on the sofa, and Bridie and Tabitha were nowhere to be seen.

CHAPTER 23

Evie sat on the sofa beside Tabitha, listening while Mammy left the house. It was always less homey here when Mammy went to the shops. Evie poked at Tabitha's stripy fat tummy, but Tabitha spat at her and scratched before going to sit on the armchair. It would be nice if the kitties came out soon. Evie sucked her finger where the scratch was. Ouch.

The house was ghostly quiet without Mammy coughing and banging around, or snoring when she was asleep. Evie wriggled, still sucking her finger. It wasn't fun, waiting in here, especially when Tabitha only wanted to sleep. Maybe Frith would come out to play until Mammy was back home again?

Evie jumped up and ran to the door, Tabitha following on. Evie stopped. 'You have to stay in here or Mammy'll be cross.'

Tabitha didn't understand, though. Evie went back to the sofa, and Tabitha went with her. They settled down again, and Evie held her breath. Yes, shh, Tabitha was asleep. She inched up as slowly as she could and tiptoed back to the door – made it!

The house was still too quiet. All the kits except Tabitha were outside, that was the problem. Evie skipped through the kitchen and opened the back door.

The grass at the back was wet, and Evie stood on a pile of cat poo before she noticed it. Yuk. She scraped her trainer on the grass until it was clean again. Through the jungle to the fence at the end of the garden – but there was no sound from Frith's side and nothing was moving there either. Evie scuffed her feet across the grass, but when she was almost back at Mammy's house, someone's back door slammed.

Evie tore back through the bushes to the fence. 'Frith! Are you there?'

The bushes on Frith's side rustled. 'Yes! Are you out to play? My daddy's coming to visit today. Does your daddy live with you?'

Evie's tummy wobbled inside. 'He used to. But he has a lot of – of confer-things that he has to go to.'

Was Mummy back from Spain yet?

'My daddy doesn't visit often but sometimes he comes for tea and then he gives me my bath, too. He plays the guitar – what does your daddy do?'

'He goes to work. Can you come and play with the cats?'

'Mummy said not to go away. You can come here. I have a lovely yellow bush. We can make a den underneath it.'

Evie squeezed through the fence and followed Frith through the jungle to the back corner. Frith stopped in front of a big bush with tiny yellow flowers all over. Mammy had one in her jungle too. They crawled underneath as far as they could go and sat looking out through a curtain of yellow. Evie grabbed a branch and sniffed. They didn't smell of much.

'We can bring a blanket to sit on and something to eat and drink.' Frith got up again. 'I'll go and see if—'

'Frith! Daddy's here!'

Frith leaped up. 'I'll bring him to see our den! Wait here!'

Evie sat still. It would be lovely if her daddy came to play too, but he didn't often do things like that. Sometimes they went to the park, but he was usually too busy to play. Ermintrude arrived with Socks, and they settled down beside Evie. This was better – waiting all alone in Frith's garden wasn't nice.

More rustling and Frith was back in the den. 'Mummy's cross. Daddy wanted to take me to the park and get ice creams, but Mummy won't let him so he's gone alone to get them. I told him you were here too. He'll be back in two ticks, he said.'

Ooh. Ice cream! Mammy never bought ice cream – she didn't have a freezer to keep it cold.

Frith crawled off again. 'I'm going to get us a blanket to sit on!'

Evie's tummy gave a big wobble. She and Mummy had chocolate ice cream at the park once, and once Daddy took them for a hamburger and they had ice cream then, too, but Mummy hadn't liked that much.

'Mummy says to ask if you're allowed sweeties 'n' stuff?' Frith was back with a big towel.

'Uh-huh.' Evie helped spread the towel on the ground, and Frith reached into her pocket and brought out two tiny packets of Smarties. She gave one to Evie.

'Ooh!' Evie fished in her packet. 'I like the red ones best!'

'Me too!'

They sat there munching until a deep brown voice called down the garden. 'Frithy-baby?'

Bushes rustled, and Frith giggled. 'We're in here!'

Evie pressed her back against the yellow bush as Frith kneeled up to hold the branches open for her daddy. He crept in, all bent over, then plumped down beside Frith. He was holding three ice-cream cones with chocolate flakes in them.

Frith whooped. 'Yay! You got 99s!'

He passed one over. 'I did. Hello, Bridie! I hope you like 99s too?'

He handed Bridie a cone, and she took it carefully, remembering to say thank you. She hadn't had a 99 for such a long time.

Evie watched Frith's daddy while she was licking her ice cream. He was nothing like her daddy. Frith's daddy was wearing jeans that were almost as dirty as hers were, and his hair was longer than hers, too. But he liked 99s, so that was good.

Frith and her daddy were talking all the time, so Evie didn't have to say anything. She sat there eating her ice cream and getting sticky while they were talking about going on a bus trip to the Tall Ship, though Evie wasn't sure what that was. She wiped her fingers on her jeans when she was finished – she'd got a little drip on her bandage, too. She smudged it almost away.

Frith's daddy waggled his eyebrows at her. 'What happened to your arm, then? Cool bandage, by the way.'

Evie frowned. That was the bit she didn't remember very well.

'It got bashed in a car.' She held up her bandage for them to look at. 'Mammy put the bandage on. It's nearly better.'

'Good-oh.'

He licked his fingers and grinned at her – he was nice.

'Bridie, darlin'!'

Mammy's shaky voice came drifting over the garden, and Evie scrambled up. 'I have to go.'

'Nice to see you, Bridie.' Frith's daddy gave her a pat on the head as she crawled past, then Evie ran to the fence and squashed through. Was Mammy cross?

Mammy was standing at the back door, and oh, no – was she crying?

'Bad girl, giving me a fright like that! You could have fallen and hurt yourself again, playing outside while I'm not here to keep an eye on you. Come inside and stay where I can see you.'

Mammy grabbed hold of Evie and gave her a little shake and then a big hug. Evie went with her into the living room and sat beside Tabitha on the sofa while Mammy drank her new medicine. It smelled lemony, and it made Mammy go to sleep. Evie crept upstairs to the room where she could watch the street outside.

After tea Mammy made another lemon drink and they went into the living room. The medicine was working, Mammy said, but she still wasn't happy because she wasn't talking much. Stories about when they'd been in Ireland would make her cough, she said. Evie picked at a hole on her sleeve. This was boring.

'Can I go and tidy the cupboard in the hall? I haven't done that one yet.'

Mammy gave her a tiny nod, but she didn't smile. Evie crept out and opened the cupboard door. It was full of old boxes and a vacuum cleaner that was covered in dust – was it broken? She held onto the door frame and stood right up on tiptoe to see the shelf above her head – ooh, a chocolate box. Evie reached up and pulled it down, and a cloud of dust flew off the top. All Mammy's things were old.

She dropped down on the hall floor and opened the box – there were no chocolates left. A pile of old papers was sitting at the top, envelopes and things held together with an elastic band. Boring. And some old black and white photos underneath. In most of them, two little boys and two girls were playing at the seaside.

Bang! Bang! Evie's heart thumped, and she pulled her knees up to her chin. Someone was thumping on the front door again. She held her breath – but Mammy was coming to answer it.

Instead of opening the door, though, Mammy stood there with her finger on her lips, staring hard at Evie, who kept still as a mouse. What was happening?

'Margie Donohue! I know you're in there. Those cats of yours have been digging up my vegetable patch again – it's disgusting. If you can't keep them under control, I'll report them – and you!'

Footsteps stamped off, and after a moment, Mammy winked at Evie. 'That was Mrs Posh next door again. She has fancy curtains and a vegetable patch.'

Good, Mammy was smiling. Evie stood up. 'And she doesn't like cats.' She gave the box to Mammy. 'I found this.'

Mammy took the box to the sofa. 'Dearie me, look at this. Bills – but I paid them, I think. Ah!' She lifted the photos out. 'How on earth did they land in here?'

'Who are they?' Evie leaned against Mammy to see better.

Mammy sat forward and spread the photos out on the coffee table. 'These are of when we were in Ireland, maid, don't you remember? Home. Ah, my Ned – this was the day we went to Cork. You weren't born yet. We took some pigs in a trailer and had a picnic on the beach after they were unloaded. Then we drove home the long way, by the sea. That was a grand day, that was.'

She lifted another photo, one of the ones with children on it.

'And here's my babies. Maeve, my big girl. And my boys.'

She stroked the photo with one finger, then gave Evie a cuddle. 'And my Bridie.'

Evie stared at the picture. Was that her? But someone was knocking on the door again – not an angry bang this time, and no shouting, but Mammy whispered to stay quiet. Nothing more happened, and after a moment Evie tiptoed to the window. A man in a suit was walking away – oh! Daddy? But no, this man had different hair.

Evie skipped back to the sofa and lifted the photo of the bigger girl with curly hair. 'Where's Maeve now?'

Mammy gave a little jump – she'd been away in a daydream again.

'Eh? Maeve? Dublin, she went to. And Aiden and Sam, they went further. Over the sea and far away. But my Bridie's not going to do that, are you, darlin'?'

Mammy closed her eyes, and half a second later she was snoring. Evie put the photos back into the box and put it on top of the TV where the cats wouldn't get it. She didn't want to go over the sea and far away. It was good she was here with Mammy.

DAY TWENTY - WEDNESDAY 6TH MAY

CHAPTER 24

Wednesday started with the worst headache she'd had since her student days. Daria grabbed her crutches and tottered from her bed to the bathroom, where she crashed around in the cabinet for some paracetamol. She'd drunk her share of the bottle of Chablis Noah had opened last night, mainly to stop him drinking the lot – and it hadn't worked, had it? He'd gone on to whisky when the bottle was empty, and the silence between them was telling its own story. She'd read that relationships often didn't survive the loss of a child – but she'd never have thought it could happen to them.

She swung her way through to the kitchen, dotting her foot on the floor like the nurse had told her when the stitches came out. Noah was busy with the toaster, and resentment burned through Daria when he barely glanced up. How dare he ignore her?

Deliberately, she banged one of her crutches against the

leg of the table. At least that made him look up. 'Noah. We have *got* to talk. About us, about the accident, about Evie.'

'What is there to say? She's gone, because you had her in a bloody taxi with no child seat when it was hit by a fucking tanker.'

Daria remained motionless, her hands turning damp on the plastic grips on her crutches. He was looking for someone to blame, and that someone was her. It was horrible for her too – she hadn't been there to hold her child in the last few seconds of Evie's life. A new, jagged sensation was jabbing about in her head. It took her a few moments to work out what it was.

She was angry. No, she was raging – at Noah. He was back to ignoring her – it was pitiful – and she couldn't even march off with her head in the air. Daria about-turned as briskly as she could and limped back to her bedroom.

The flat door slammed behind Noah and his briefcase before she was dressed. Daria slumped on the bed. This was appalling – they would have to go for bereavement counselling, or marriage guidance. They needed help with this.

She went back to the kitchen and sat sipping her coffee, the silence in the flat chilling through her. The ceiling was falling in on her today – she had to get out of here for a while. This afternoon's babysitting session might allow her to spend a few hours in someone else's four walls. If Liane agreed to it. Daria reached for her mobile.

'Liane – would it be better if I came to you this afternoon instead of Frith coming here? I was thinking, that way you'd know she had plenty of toys and you wouldn't need to feel obliged to hurry back.'

What a hypocrite she was. Daria rubbed her hand over

her face. Liane was the one person in her life at the moment who treated her normally, but that would stop the moment the other woman knew about Evie. If Liane set foot in here, she'd see all the photos and things like Evie's jacket still on the coatstand. They'd need to change that sometime, but oh, not yet.

Liane was cheerful as ever. 'Sure – but wouldn't it be easier for you at your place?'

'My leg's much better, I'm allowed to put weight on it now. And to be honest, being at home all day, every day is doing my head in.'

'Okay. How about I ask Steve to pick you up on his way here and take you home again afterwards? Frithy'd love to show you her things. If you're lucky, you might see some of the cat family next door, too.'

Daria laughed, then ended the call and burst into tears. Spending time with Frith was torture, but now she'd started, she couldn't stop. Those moments of being a mother again, looking after a child – they were like a drug. The fact that it wasn't her child was the worst agony in the world.

Her mobile pinged as Liane's text came in. *Steve will pick you up at half one. See you soon!*

Daria pushed her mug away and propped her elbow on the table, resting her chin in her palm. That was one thing sorted. The situation with Noah was going to take a little longer.

CHAPTER 25

Liane strolled round the first group of paintings, Steve a few steps behind her. The Gallery of Modern Art was bang in the middle of Glasgow city centre, not an ideal place to park, so they'd left the car on the other side of the river and walked across the footbridge into town. The gallery was busy without being crowded, and Liane breathed in deeply as she went from one image to the next. Such colours – they reminded her of a Monet exhibition she'd been to once.

She stepped back to better admire a canvas of green and purple swipes and smudges that brought the rural scene to life. She'd expected to enjoy Steve's company; enjoying the paintings too was an added bonus.

'I can't believe how fabulous these are. I wouldn't mind a couple of prints for the walls at home.'

Steve joined her. 'We can have a look in the shop on the way out. Tall trees seem to be a theme of his, don't they? Which would you choose?'

Liane gazed around. Here, with Steve – it was right. Easy. They were on the same wavelength about enjoying the paintings for the colours and landscapes without looking for deep hidden meanings.

'This one of the river, I think. Look at the light in it – you can almost feel the sunshine.' Liane's phone vibrated in her pocket and she pulled it out. Yikes.

'It's Daria. I'd better take it.' She stepped into an empty corner and tapped to connect, apprehension crowding in. Frith and Daria had been busy with a jigsaw when they left an hour ago – surely nothing had gone wrong?

Daria's voice was low and echoing. 'Liane, Frith and I are at the park along from your house, in the loos. A man – Frith said he's her dad – appeared when we were at the swings and I can't get rid of him. He says he wants to take over from me and spend the afternoon with Frith. What shall I do?'

Liane pressed the phone against her ear as panic rose in her throat. Tony in the park? That wasn't a coincidence; he must have been watching them. Waiting for his chance to – what? *Take Frith?* And what the shit was Daria doing, going to the park when she was on crutches?

'Stay in the loos and keep Frith with you. I'll come as fast as I can.'

Steve was beside her, his eyebrows raised. Liane strode to the exit, explaining as they went. 'I don't know what he'll do. He talked about wanting to take her out somewhere the other day, but you know how little contact he had with her when she wasn't well, and he's so unreliable – I don't want to see her hurt and I don't trust him to look after her properly.'

This was when she needed the car twenty yards away and not over half a mile. They jogged down Queen Street and around back roads to the footbridge, Liane's breath catching in her throat. She collapsed into Steve's Ford and hyperventilated in the passenger seat as they sped back to Mansewood.

Steve pulled up at a red light. 'Maybe all he wants is some normal father–daughter time, now Frith's able to do stuff?'

'Then he should have organised it properly with me. And he was never interested in doing things while she was in hospital, or at home sick. You can't be a father on good days only. He's never been alone with her, not even for a few hours. And I have an awful feeling that what he's actually trying to do is scare me into—' She broke off. This was so sordid, and she didn't want to sound bitchy.

'Scare you into what? Liane, has he ever hurt you?'

Steve's voice was at least an octave higher than usual as the car moved off again, and Liane rushed to reassure him.

'No, no. He shows up regularly begging for cash, that's all. He thinks I should support him while he's trying to get his big break.'

'Oh, for God's sake. What is he, thirteen? Don't worry, we'll be there in two minutes.'

Liane's mobile rang again, and she put it on speaker. Daria.

'He's got her! He called out for her and she ran out of the loos before I could stop her. I can't see them anywhere!'

Steve spoke while Liane was smothering a shriek of horror. 'Where are you exactly, Daria?'

Liane clutched her head. Her baby – Frith must, she absolutely *must,* stay safe.

'I'm on the long path coming down to the main gate. It's

the quickest way out, but I can't run with my leg – should I call the police?'

Liane fought for self-control while Steve spoke.

'Wait until we're there – we're at the far end of the park now. Meet you at the gate.'

Liane disconnected and jabbed anew at her phone. Pick up, Tony, you scumbag. But of course, he didn't, and she shoved the phone into her pocket. Steve parked on a double yellow line. Liane fumbled to open the door, gazing wildly up and down the street. Daria was standing at the park gate. She swung across the road on her crutches while Liane and Steve got out of the car.

'Still no sign. Liane, I'm so sorry—'

Liane brushed that aside. The first thing was to find Frith. 'You can wait here in case they appear. Steve – how about we run through the park? If we go right and left round the boundary path, we can meet at the other side and come back along the main path. That way, we'd see pretty much all of it. It's not a big place.'

'Okay. But if we don't find them, you should call the police.' He handed the car key to Daria and grabbed Liane's hand.

She held on for dear life as they dived through traffic, horns blaring from both directions. Inside the park gate they parted company. Liane jogged steadily, her feet light on the path and her eyes darting right and left. There were so many bushes here – but Tony had no reason to take Frith in among them, unless they were playing hide and seek, and Frith was more likely to want to play on the swings. A stitch jabbed in Liane's side, and she held one hand to her ribs, her breath hot and painful in her throat. She could murder Tony right now.

Steve was waiting at the other side of the park. 'No sign. Come on – we'll check the swings on the way.'

He was holding her hand again, pulling her along the main path, and thank goodness he was because she wouldn't have been able to move so quickly without him. They stopped at the swings and Liane gawped around the clusters of kids making the most of the mild spring sunshine, but no small girl with a pink jacket and blonde hair was in sight.

Steve's face was grim. 'I think you should call the police.'

Liane leaned both hands on her knees. 'Tony wouldn't hurt Frith. I'd like to try his place first.'

Back in the car, she sat massaging her side and giving directions to the flat Tony shared with two other would-be musicians. Without much hope, she tried his phone again. Nothing. Daria was apologising non-stop in the back seat, but Liane didn't answer. This was all Daria's fault; she should shut up. Oh, that wasn't fair. Liane wiped her eyes – she'd left her precious child with a woman who couldn't run after her. If it was anyone's fault, it was hers.

Tony's street was deserted. The houses here were terraced, and a long row of grey roofs stretched down either side of the road. The small garden in front of Tony's building was overgrown, the solitary rose bush unpruned.

Steve parked about ten yards from the entrance. 'I'm coming in with you.'

It wasn't a question, and Liane didn't try to stop him. Face it, she could use the moral support.

Daria undid her seat belt. 'Shall I come too?'

Liane shook her head. 'You'd better stay here. Steve and I

will deal with him.' For the life of her, she couldn't keep the anger from her voice, and Daria flinched.

Liane led the way up a short flight of steps to the front door. She'd been here before, when she and Tony were still together. What would she do if he and Frith weren't inside?

Like the other buildings up and down the street, the stairwell door was open to anyone who wanted to go in. Liane took the stairs two at a time to the dimness of the first floor. She leaned on the doorbell and it rang frantically inside the flat, and – voices. Someone was there.

Liane banged a fist on the door. 'Frith!' Never had she yelled her daughter's name in such a tone. There was the sound of heavy footsteps, and the door creaked open.

'Here already? She's having some ice cream.'

Liane stormed past Tony's smirk without another word. Frith was cross-legged on the living room floor, still in her jacket, tucking into a generous bowl of chocolate ice cream. Liane crouched beside the little girl. Oh, to be able to yell at Tony that he was a word she couldn't use in front of Frith, grab her child and hold her tight all the way home – but that would only frighten the poor kid.

'Are you okay, sweetheart? I was worried, I didn't know where you were.'

'Uh-huh.' Frith gripped her bowl and inched away from Liane. 'I'm allowed to be with Daddy. He said so.'

Swallow the rage, Liane. 'Yes, but we should always organise it properly first. Finish your ice cream, and we'll get going. You can have a ride home in Steve's car.'

Frith spoke through a mouthful of chocolate ice cream. 'I don't want to go home. I haven't played with Daddy's guitar yet and I want more ice cream, too.'

Liane stroked Frith's head. Knowing Tony, he'd have promised her all the ice cream she could eat. 'You can play with the guitar another day, sweetie.' She stood up and glared at Tony. 'What did you think you were doing?'

He was grinning away as if this was the funniest thing he'd seen all week. Liane pulled herself together; she shouldn't give him the satisfaction of seeing her upset. Steve was in the doorway with an expression like a bulldog chewing a wasp, which would be hugely entertaining to someone like Tony.

Liane forced herself to sound calm. 'You can't take her without asking, Tony. If you want access, we'll get it properly organised. I'll contact Social Services and find out how to go about it.'

His face fell all the way to Australia. Nice one, Liane. That had hit the spot.

'No need for that, is there? We can come to an informal agreement. I should have joint custody, she's my kid too.'

In his dreams. 'I'm not into informal agreements, Tony, and as Frith's primary carer, I get to organise any help we need to make this arrangement.' Liane had no idea if this was correct, but Tony didn't know any better either. He stood glowering at her as Frith finished her ice cream. Liane ignored him.

Frith gaped into the bowl for a moment then stood up. 'I've had enough.'

Thank goodness for small mercies. Liane took the little girl's hand. 'Say 'bye-bye to Daddy.'

Half a minute later they were at the car again. Liane opened the back door. 'Can you sit in the front, please, Daria? I want to come in here with Frith.'

Daria moved without speaking, and Liane got in beside Frith.

Steve reached back from the driver's seat and touched her knee. 'Liane, you were really good in there, well done. I don't know if I'd have been so calm with him.'

Liane barely managed a smile. If Frith and Daria hadn't been in the car too, she'd have been in floods. 'I wasn't calm. But letting him think that was the right way to go. He's a big kid. Stand up to him and he'll crumble.'

Frith lifted her arms as Liane clicked the seat belt on for her. 'There you go, love bug.'

Daria jerked round in the front seat and gave them a wide-eyed stare. 'She shouldn't travel without a child seat!' Her face was sheet-white.

Liane nearly burst into tears. 'I don't have a car seat, Daria, because I don't have a car.'

In any other situation, the expression of horror on Daria's face would have been comical. Her eyes flitted from Liane to Steve and back. 'She's not safe without one.'

It took a Herculean effort, but for Frith's sake, Liane kept hold of her temper.

'We'll be home in a few minutes, Daria.'

Daria shrank back in her seat, and Liane hugged Frith, who was mercifully unaware of the fright she'd given them. 'Daddy and me came two stops in the bus. We went upstairs.'

Liane slid one arm around Frith. Oh, how good it was to cuddle her girl. 'You like going upstairs, don't you?'

Frith leaned against her, inhaling loudly. 'The bathroom's smelly at Daddy's.'

Liane swallowed a smile. Good. Frith wasn't stupid. She'd noticed Daddy didn't represent an ideal way of life, even if he was trying as hard as he could to be the fun parent. Relax, Liane.

Home again, she settled Frith with her Lego in the living room and turned to Daria, who was hovering in the doorway. 'We'll go through to the kitchen.'

'I'm sorry. It was all my fault.' Daria sagged onto a chair and rummaged in her bag for a tissue.

Liane pulled up a chair too. You couldn't yell at someone who wasn't on your level. 'It was Tony's fault. He took advantage – but what did you think you were doing, going to the park when you're still on crutches?'

Daria's fingers were working on the hem of her woollen jacket. 'I know. I'm sorry. My leg's improving and she wanted to go, but – it's no excuse.'

Liane dabbed her eyes with a tissue. 'Suppose she'd run off after another kid, or a duck or something? Or had an accident or—' She stopped abruptly. The thought of what could have happened to her precious daughter was too much. 'I think you should go now, Daria. Frith – I – need to be alone.'

Daria was white. 'I'm so sorry. Steve, can you take me home, please?'

Liane sat motionless as they left, then she reached for the kettle. All's well, etcetera, but she'd had the worst fright of her life today. By a mile.

DAY TWENTY-ONE – THURSDAY 7TH MAY

CHAPTER 26

Daria woke at six and hobbled through to the kitchen on her crutches, leaving Noah snoring. She had lost Evie, and she'd nearly lost Frith, too. What a mess. What if Liane never forgave her? She might never see Frith again, and she could add Liane to the list of people currently blaming her for making a mistake. And Liane was right; she shouldn't have taken Frith to the park. So Noah might be right too. Oh, God. Evie...

Daria switched on the coffee machine, then made herself a large mug of black coffee. This was a new low point. She'd thought the memorial would be the worst thing, but worst things just kept on coming, and maybe they always would.

Noah was up now, crashing around in the shower. Daria sipped her coffee. She couldn't let her life disintegrate any further and home was the best place to start rebuilding it. She'd suggest bereavement counselling, but surely they could make a start together, first.

She waited until he was sipping coffee too, waiting for his toast to pop up.

'Noah, I was thinking. Let's go back to the park after work tonight, visit Evie's tree. We should talk, and that would be a good place. The forecast's okay. What do you think?'

His face darkened. 'I told you: I want to remember her alive. It's beginning to feel as if the more we talk about her, Daria, the more dead she is. I'm not going to start making pilgrimages to Evie's tree every few weeks.'

Daria grabbed her self-esteem before it melted irrevocably. 'What do you suggest, then? We can't go on like this.'

'No, we can't. But twenty minutes before I go for the train is no time to start a conversation about anything.'

He grabbed his toast and mug and strode back to the bedroom. Daria slumped in her chair. The sun was tipping over the roof across the road, sending a tiny shaft of yellow into the corner of the kitchen, but nothing, nothing was bright any more. Why was Noah taking out his anger and hurt on her? She was supposed to be his partner, the love of his life, but although she was aching for closeness, love, mutual support, he was freezing her out. The end of their marriage… was this it? Noah left the flat, shouting goodbye without coming into the kitchen, and dammit, she wasn't going to be treated like that. Daria got up and hopped across to her mobile on the work surface. It wasn't too early to call Kit, in fact this was a good time; Kit would be on the train on her way to work. She tapped into her contacts.

'Kit – I was wondering if you'd have time to do me a favour tonight?'

'I've nothing planned. What do you need?'

'I want to go back to Evie's tree, and Noah won't come with me. Could you drive us there?'

'Oh, Daria, love. Of course I will. I'll pick you up at seven, okay?'

Seven was perfect. Daria ended the call and dropped her phone into her handbag. What on earth was she going to do all day?

BY HALF PAST FOUR, she was in danger of going stir-crazy and her eyes were aching from staring at the laptop, but she'd made an album of the best photos of Evie. Four years and one month of life, from the first ultrasound photo to the last outing to feed the ducks, each photo with a sentence to describe it and the date it was taken. Daria sent the file off to be printed and went for a walk around the flat. Noah would be back soon. If he made a scene about her proposed outing with Kit, well, she would do what he'd done and walk out on him.

He arrived home early, and Daria shoved a frozen quiche into the oven.

'Kit and I are going to visit Evie's tree. She's picking me up at seven.'

He shrugged. 'It's up to you. We have different ways of dealing with grief, Daria.'

That was obvious. It didn't seem to occur to him that dealing with grief could mean helping each other to work through it. Daria made a salad to go with the quiche and they ate a strange, silent meal at the kitchen table. Noah's eyes were luminous and his voice unsteady, but all they talked about was salt and salad dressing, and every sentence that ignored the problem between them was a stab in the back. Daria left him to see to the table and went down to wait for Kit outside. There was only so much silence you could take.

Kit arrived punctually, and reached across to hug Daria when she took her place in the passenger seat. 'You and Noah are having a ghastly time – I'm so sorry. Let me know if you ever need help again, Daria, I'm here for you.'

Daria breathed out in relief as they drove across the city and out to the north. Evening sunshine was making the hills golden-green tonight. She'd been right to come; this was a healing kind of place.

They parked in the visitors' car park and walked by the river, approaching Evie's tree from the other side this time. There was only a handful of other visitors, and Daria was glad. She'd never thought about other people looking at Evie's tree, wondering why it had been newly planted in the middle of all the established ones. Should they have a plaque of some kind made, one that could stand beside the tree? 'In memory of Evie' for everyone to read and wonder who she was. It was something to think about.

They didn't talk much, but that was all right. Kit was here for her, and wordless love and support were doing more than a stream of words ever would. Daria took both crutches in one hand and put an arm around Kit as they stood in front of the tree.

'Thanks, Kitty.'

Five minutes was enough. They wandered back to the car park, where the sight of Noah standing beside their car sent shock fizzing through Daria. She limped across, Kit by her side.

He stared at her awkwardly. 'I've come to pick you up. It'll save Kit another trip across the city and back again.'

Kit rubbed Daria's back. 'It's up to you, love.'

Noah's face flushed red, and for a micro-second hurt blazed from his eyes. Daria gripped her crutches hard. If she went home with Kit now, it would be the end for her and Noah. And he wouldn't be here if he wanted things to end.

She nodded at Kit. 'I'll go with Noah. Thank you, Kitty, for everything.'

Kit kissed her cheek. 'I'll call you tomorrow, huh?'

They drove in convoy to where Kit branched off to go home. Daria waved, then sat back. Noah hadn't spoken since they'd left the park. This was like the drive back from the memorial all over again, and the same desolation was creeping into her gut.

'What is it you want us to do, Noah?'

He crashed into second gear to take a corner. 'I want you to accept what you did.'

Daria bowed her head. It didn't get much more condemnatory than that, did it? This had been a mistake. They were back with everything being her fault, and nothing she said would get through to him.

'I loved my daughter, Noah.'

He didn't reply.

DAY TWENTY-TWO – FRIDAY 8TH MAY

CHAPTER 27

Goody – it was sunny today. Evie bounded out of bed and ran to the window. Maybe Frith would be out to play later. She pulled on the trousers and pullover Mammy had put ready for her after her bath last night, and made a face at the frayed cuffs. She didn't have nice clothes here, but it didn't matter, because she played in the garden so much and she always got dirty anyway. She reached for her trainers under the bed – Mummy had bought these for her in Spain, at Christmas. Would she bring presents when she came home again this time?

The green bandage had come loose; it always did in the night. Evie unwound it and put the wooden spoon on the chest of drawers. She didn't need a splint any more. Her arm was better and the bruises were almost gone, though you could see the marks where the spoon had been pressing.

Mammy was snoring even louder than usual today. Evie peeked into her room when she went past, but she didn't go in. Mammy'd been up in the night, because the new bottle of pink medicine was beside the bed and it had been in the kitchen last night when Evie went up for her bath.

The cats were all miaowing around downstairs, and Evie filled their food bowls and gave them some fresh water. Mammy came in before she was finished.

'You lot would waken the dead, you would.'

She put the kettle on and started making toast, so she wasn't cross.

Evie sat up to eat her toast. 'Can I play in the garden after breakfast?'

'I should think so. But you're not to go out of our garden, hear? No trailing over next door. I'll be watching.'

Mammy stirred her lemon medicine and brought it to the table. She hadn't made any toast for herself.

'Aren't you having breakfast?'

'I'm going for a lie-down first. But I'll be listening for you, all right? I'll hear if you do anything you shouldn't.'

She wheezed her way back upstairs. Evie finished her milk and toast and wiped her hands. It was easier without the bandage. She opened the back door, and cold air hit her face – brrr! The grass was still wet, but the dandelions were all standing with their faces turned up to the sun. She'd pick some for Mammy later. It didn't matter here if she got brown on her hands. Was Frith out already too?

Evie stood on the doorstep where you could see most of the house at the bottom of the garden. Oh – Frith was at her window upstairs! Evie waved, jumping up and down, and Frith waved back before vanishing. They both arrived at the fence at the same time, and giggled.

Frith leaned over a broken bit of fence. 'Has Tabitha had her kitties yet? Shall we play in my den?'

Evie shook her head. 'I'm not allowed to go out of the garden. You can come here – we can make another den. I've got some big boxes, they can be our beds – or boats!'

'Ooh, yes – or caravans! The cats can be horses!'

Frith squashed through the fence and joined Evie. They found a good bush for the new den; it didn't have yellow flowers, but there were some tiny bluey-purply ones growing beside the leaves. Evie rushed inside for some big boxes, and Socks and Topsy joined them in the den.

'Is this Tabitha?' Frith sat down in a box, cuddling Topsy.

'No, she's inside. She's the little stripy one with the fat tummy.'

'Can we go in and look at her? Pleea–se?'

Evie put her head on one side. It would be nice to do something Frith wanted. But what would Mammy say? She stood up. 'Mammy's gone for a lie-down. I'll see if she's asleep, then we can go in.'

Tallulah was lying on the sunny step at the back door. Evie took a big high step over her. Tabitha wasn't the only puss who'd scratch you quick as quick if she got cross.

She didn't need to go upstairs to know that Mammy was asleep, because loud snores were coming all the way down to the kitchen. Evie jumped over Tallulah again and raced back to Frith in the den.

'Mammy's asleep upstairs. We can go and see if Tabitha's in the living room.'

They ran back to the house, Frith giggling behind her, and Evie pushed the back door open. Tallulah had shifted from the step so it was easier to get inside.

Evie put a finger to her lips. 'If Mammy wakes up, she'll be cross.'

Frith stood in the back doorway, frowning into the kitchen. 'It's messy here.'

'Mammy's not well, that's why. Shh!'

Evie led the way to the living room, Frith close behind her. And oh, lucky – Tabitha was lying on the sofa, fast asleep.

Evie knelt on the floor beside her. 'This is Tabitha. Be careful, she scratches.'

Frith stepped back. 'Oh. She does look fat, doesn't she? Can I have one of the kitties?'

Evie gave Tabitha's head a little pat. For once, she was more in charge than Frith. 'I'll ask Mammy. Let's go back outside.' If Mammy heard them, they would get into trouble.

Frith walked over to the TV. 'Is that a television? Does it work?'

'It's broken. I plugged it in once and it nearly went on fire.'

Frith jerked back the hand that was about to touch the TV, and went over to the coffee table. She picked up the photos Evie and Mammy had been looking at yesterday. 'Who are these people – is that the beach at Largs?'

'No, that's Ireland. Mammy tells me stories about when we used to live there. That's Aiden and Sammy, and that's Maeve. It's at Bantry Bay.'

'Where are they now?'

'Mammy says the boys are over the sea and far away, and I don't remember about Maeve. Come *on*!'

Back outside, Evie relaxed. It was better when Mammy wasn't cross.

Frith skipped back to the den. 'You do have a funny old house. We're getting a new kitchen and bathroom soon. Hey,

Mummy's taking me to the story club at the library next week. Why don't you and your mammy come too?

Evie pondered. Story club – Mummy had taken her there too. It was nice. But Mammy never took her anywhere. 'Can I come with you?'

'I'll ask Mummy to ask your mammy. She went to say hello already but you weren't at home.'

Dismay thudded into Evie's middle. Mammy didn't answer the door, did she? When would Mummy be home from Spain? But then, she didn't want to go home before Tabitha had her kitties.

They played at going to the beach until Frith's mummy shouted her to come for lunch. Evie wandered back inside too – she was hungry.

Mammy wasn't snoring any more. Evie tiptoed upstairs and put her head into the bedroom. It was empty, but then the toilet flushed and Mammy came out and got back into bed.

'Give me another hour, maid.'

'I'm hungry.'

'Have a piece of bread. I'll make you some soup in a while.' She rolled onto her side, and a minute later she was snoring all over again.

Evie went back to the kitchen. She didn't want bread, but soup would be nice – she could make some for Mammy, couldn't she? She rootled around in the cupboard for a tin – tomato, good! She and Mammy both liked it best.

The pan was still all beans juice, so she gave it a wash, then tried to get the ring-pull off the can of soup. It was too tight, but she'd try what Mummy did once when she had a cut finger. Evie tiptoed upstairs for the wooden spoon, then she levered the ring pull up with a teaspoon, slid the handle of the wooden spoon through it and pulled the top up. She couldn't get it right off, but it opened enough for her to pour the soup into the pan. There! Now to light the gas.

The gas lighter was a bit scary. Evie hefted it, then made up her mind. She'd seen Mammy do it hundreds of times. A quick try without the gas – good, the sparky thing was working. She turned on the gas until it was hissing like it did when Mammy lit it, and pressed the lighter twice. Plop! It came on so fast she got a fright, but it was lit. Now she had to turn it down to a baby flame – there! Evie kneeled up on a kitchen chair, stirring slowly with the wooden spoon until little bubbles showed in the soup.

'What on earth are you doing, child?'

Evie jumped. 'I'm making you some soup. I think it's ready.'

Mammy took the wooden spoon from her. 'Yes, it is. But don't you do this again, you hear? You're not big enough to light the gas.'

She gave Evie's head a little rub, so she wasn't really cross. Evie got the bread out while Mammy poured the soup into two bowls, then they sat up at the table and had lunch. Mammy didn't eat much of hers, though.

Evie watched miserably as Mammy went to make more lemon medicine. It might be better not to ask about the story club yet.

DAY TWENTY-FIVE – MONDAY 11TH MAY

CHAPTER 28

Nothing had changed; it was the same slap in the face every morning. The alarm would go off, Noah would crawl out of bed and into the bathroom, and Daria would lie there, weak with relief that he was gone from her bed, taking with him the silent accusation that came in a never-ceasing stream from every pore of his body. *Your fault, your fault.* Would it have made so much difference if she'd taken the car seat with her? They'd never know.

She lay still until the flat door banged shut behind him, then sat up and reached for her crutches. Her three-week check-up at the hospital was at eleven-thirty.

Daria ordered a taxi, then made coffee and sat on the sofa with her laptop and a gaping hole in the morning to fill before she had to leave. Clinic visits always brought the accident back to centre stage in her life, and Daria's fingers hovered over the keyboard. She'd never searched online for newspaper reports or articles about the accident. Imagine what they'd have said about it in the gutter press: *Four-year-old perishes in horror crash*. Or: *Evie, 4, dead at scene*. No, no. It was bad enough without reading sensationalist junk about it. Daria banged the laptop shut again.

There was still so much she didn't know – it was frustrating. Noah had taken over all the paperwork, and he always managed to duck out of giving precise details. The procurator fiscal report, for instance. It would be good to know how long that would take. Presumably, they'd have to wait until it came before they could collect and scatter Evie's ashes. How very much easier this would be if she and Noah were working as a team and helping each other. Daria wilted into the sofa, her arms limp by her sides. Every day this situation lasted between her and Noah brought them one day closer to what might be the end of their marriage. It wasn't what she wanted.

THE FRACTURE CLINIC WAS QUIET. After a ten-minute wait, Daria was ushered in to see the doctor – not the one who'd operated, nor any of those she'd met as an inpatient. Two to three more weeks using the crutches while gradually increasing weightbearing was his advice, and Daria was glad to hear it. This was the only part of the disaster that was going according to plan.

She strapped on her boot and stood up to leave, an idea hovering in her mind. 'I don't suppose you know which doctor saw my daughter at the Children's Hospital, do you?' Impossible to ask who had certified her girl dead, but if anyone could give details of Evie's injuries and death, that person could.

The doctor swiped around on his tablet, a shifty expression on his face. He hadn't mentioned Evie, so possibly he didn't even know about her.

'Sorry, no. Do you want me to...?'

'It's all right. I'll go over and ask in Children's A&E while I'm here.'

Daria swung her way to the main door and across to the adjacent Children's Hospital. Passing through the entrance hallway here reminded her of Frith and Liane – another disaster in her life. She'd messed up there and no mistake; it was understandable that Liane had been so upset.

A long queue of people was waiting in front of an information stand at the back of the entrance hall, and Daria grabbed a seat round the corner to wait for a quieter moment. Come to think of it, something to drink would be an idea. She hadn't eaten since last night.

The nearby machine gave her a packet of cheese and pickle sandwiches and a bottle of water. Daria stuffed both into her bag and swung back to her chair. Oh, for the day when she didn't need both hands as well as her feet to walk around with.

Sandwich finished, she got up to check the queue again, but it was longer than ever, and anyway, she couldn't possibly ask about Evie's doctor with a queue of people – some of them children – listening in behind her. Daria stood still. This possibly wasn't the best idea.

'Are you all right? Can I help with anything?'

An elderly priest was standing behind her, complete with clerical collar and black robe. Help, you'd think they'd wear more cheerful, child-friendly clothes here. But it was kind of him to ask.

'I wanted to speak to someone about, um, when my daughter came in a few weeks ago. We were in an accident, but I was taken next door so I don't know who saw her.'

It sounded odd as she said it; he must be wondering why on earth she didn't know. His expression didn't change, though.

'Has she been discharged?'

'She died before she ever arrived here. I don't know exactly where they took her.' Damn Noah. Tears spilled over, and she didn't have a hand free to wipe them away.

His face creased in sympathy, and he gripped her elbow. 'How terrible for you. Come and sit down in my office. I'll find someone to help you.'

It was easiest to do as he said; she couldn't stand in the middle of the hall with tears running down her face. Daria followed him into a small room halfway along a short corridor. The priest introduced himself as Father Morgan, asked for Evie's name and the date of the accident, and gave Daria a glass of water before leaving her alone.

Daria mopped her eyes. This was a mistake – another mistake – but at least she had a moment to pull herself together.

It was quarter of an hour before Father Morgan returned with a thirty-something woman in green scrubs, and introduced her as Mrs Anderson, consultant in the Paediatric Trauma unit. To Daria's relief, he left her alone with the woman, who pulled up a chair and put her tablet on the desk.

Daria explained again, and if this woman thought it was peculiar, she said nothing, merely nodding and lifting the tablet.

A few moments of swiping and tapping later, she frowned up at Daria. Oh, no – what was coming now? Daria pressed one hand to her chest.

'Mrs, um, Daria – is Evie's father here too – are you together?'

'We're – no. I mean yes. We're having problems.' What did this have to do with Evie's injuries?

Mrs Anderson put the tablet down and took her hand. 'I'm so sorry – Evie wasn't brought here after the accident. One of the vehicles involved was a petrol tanker, and there was an explosion shortly after the crash. No bodies were ever recovered.'

Daria clapped her hands over her mouth as the headlights from the lorry that afternoon swept in front of her eyes again. Someone had said it was a tanker, and tankers held petrol. Oil. But – an explosion? *No.* Why had nobody told her? She'd been thrown onto the ground and then removed from the place where flames and heat had enveloped a living, breathing, beautiful child, her child, incinerating Evie's small body and sending particles and ash swirling into the skies. Particles of Evie. This was why no one had known what to say to her when she'd come round in the hospital. Her child was already cremated.

Heat was coursing through Daria; her cheeks were burning. Why hadn't Noah told her this? He must know. And Millie and Roger – and her parents – they must all have known, yet they'd let her believe Evie'd come here to hospital, been cremated. Oh, they'd been trying to spare her the anguish, she saw that, but she should have been told.

The doctor reached out a hand and took one of Daria's. 'I

imagine they had to evacuate the area very quickly. Believe me, if they could have saved Evie, they would have.'

'Did they see her? The paramedics, the police?'

'I don't know. This is dreadful for you.'

Daria bit her lip and tasted blood. She'd never know what happened, would she? Evie could have been hurled through the windscreen to hit God knows what, and lie hurting and broken before she was pulverised and blown away on the wind. Bile rose in Daria's throat. No wonder Noah wouldn't talk to her.

BACK HOME, she lifted the pile of mail behind the door and flung it on the kitchen table. First thing was to get hold of Noah; they were going to talk this through no matter what he thought. She tapped his number and sat drumming her fingers on the table. Now she was the one with cold anger, but in her case, it was justified. Noah would think his anger was justified too, mind you, and possibly it was.

His voice was clipped. 'Daria?'

'I'd like you to come home straightaway, please. We need to discuss something I found out at the hospital this morning.'

'What? Are you all right?'

At least he'd asked. 'Yes. Just come home now, please. I'm not talking about this on the phone.' She ended the call. What would she do if he didn't come?

His key jabbed into the lock less than half an hour later, though, and Daria wiped clammy palms on her trousers.

Noah strode into the kitchen and flung himself into a

chair. 'Surely this could have waited until tonight, Daria, if there's nothing wrong with you.'

Everything was wrong with her. 'I went into the Children's Hospital after my clinic appointment today. Why didn't you tell me about the explosion?'

His face flushed fiery red, and he slammed both hands on the tabletop. 'The explosion that killed our daughter, you mean? Because no way would she have stayed put on the back seat, Daria. She'd have gone straight through the windscreen. It was the last few minutes of her life and they were ten times more painful for her than they need have been.'

He thumped the table again, tear-filled eyes looking everywhere but at her.

They were back to the lack of a car seat. Daria struggled for words. 'You should have told me. I—'

'Oh, believe me, I didn't keep quiet for your sake. Your parents decided there was no need for you to know about sordid details like their granddaughter being ripped apart in a bloody inferno. Mine agreed with them. "We'll keep it to ourselves as long as possible," that was the idea. And if you have any mercy in you, you won't tell them you know about it. Leave them what little peace of mind they still have.'

Daria flinched. Of all the things he'd said and not said since the accident, that hurt the most.

'Noah – what's happened to us? This is so unfair. You'd have made the same decision about the taxi.' Daria clenched her fists under the table.

'I wouldn't. Not once have I taken her in the car and not put her in a child seat appropriate for her age. I can't do this, Daria. I can't cope with losing Evie and what you did.' He pushed his chair back and left the room.

Daria remained motionless, thoughts racing. She might be the only person involved in the accident left alive for him to blame, but she wasn't going to put up with this. What they needed was time alone to – to get used to what had happened to them. Mum and Dad were too far away to flee to, but… Daria reached for her phone. Kit had a spare room, didn't she?

CHAPTER 29

The library story club was a big hit from the moment Liane and Frith went in and Frith was given a library ticket all of her own. Janet the librarian had arranged a circle of child-sized chairs in a corner of the junior library, and Frith joined a boy and two little girls already sitting there. Liane went off to explore the crime fiction shelves. She was planning to stay in the building, as it was Frithy's first visit and the poor kid didn't know another soul, but knowing her, there wouldn't be any problems. Her daughter was no shrinking violet.

After a pleasant hour in a comfy chair with a book and a coffee from the machine, a buzz of high-pitched chatter filtered through the library and Liane glanced up. Story time was finished, apparently. And wow, Frithy had found a little boyfriend. Liane grabbed her things and went to investigate.

'We had three stories and we made one up ourselves too!' Frith's face was flushed with excitement. 'Oliver and me were best!' She beamed at a dark-haired little boy with a snub nose, and he gazed at her adoringly.

Liane hid a smile. This was what Frithy needed – more friends in the area. Apart from Bridie, there were no kids Frith's age in the houses around home.

Janet came over to say goodbye. 'Coming back next week, then, Frith?'

'Yes!'

Liane helped Frith with her book selection and her jacket. Oh, there was Oliver's mum come to collect him; she would go and say hello. Barbara, Oliver's mum, was as keen as Liane was to organise a playdate, and they settled on lunch at Barbara and Oliver's on Thursday. Frith's face was a picture.

The little girl skipped all the way home, and Liane smiled. This was a good day for her and her girl – story club for Frith this morning, and dinner out with Steve for Liane tonight. Frithy was looking forward to spending the evening with Steve's brother and his family. They had a trampoline in the garden, and Frith had already spent several happy hours there with Jon and Ella's kids.

In their street, Frith bounded ahead to open the gate, then wheeled round again. 'I want to— Look, Mummy, there's Margie!'

Liane turned to see where Frith was pointing. She'd tried three times, but she'd never managed to catch Bridie's mum at home. The only person in sight was an old woman at the crossing further along the road. She disappeared, heading in the direction of the shops.

What the—? 'That can't be Margie?'

Frith had never sounded so indignant. 'Yes, it is. I've met her.'

Oops. A few wires had got crossed here, somehow. Liane walked up the path. 'Is Margie Bridie's grandma, then?'

Frith scowled. 'No! I told you – she's Bridie's mummy, except she calls her Mammy. They're from Ireland.'

Liane opened the door. 'Okay, okay. I'll pop over soon and say hello.' And when she'd done that, she'd be able to disillusion Frith properly. A quick chat about the biology of having babies would be a good idea, too.

Frith spent the next hour playing with her skittles and two of the cats, as Bridie didn't put in an appearance. Liane fetched her outfit down to iron for that evening's outing – it was a real butterflies-in-the-tummy thought, a lovely meal out with Steve, just the two of them. She was hanging up her blouse when Frith whooped out that Bridie had arrived.

Liane switched off the iron. Margie must be home again now, and this was as good a time as any. She grabbed a couple of mini boxes of Smarties for the girls and went out.

'Look, Frithy – why don't you have a skittles competition? A Smartie for every skittle downed, and see who gets through their packet first. Is, um, your mammy at home, Bridie?'

Bridie nodded, her eyes widening. Liane left the girls setting up skittles and squeezed through the back fence. She fought her way through Margie's garden – almost as jungly as theirs – to cross a square of grass that was ninety per cent weeds, most of them dandelions, and ten per cent cat poo in various stages of decomposition where the cats had scratched the weeds away. Liane pulled a face – might be a good idea to start a 'leave shoes at the back door' rule at home. Three cats were lying around in the sun behind the house. Liane knocked briskly on the back door. She'd say a quick hello, issue a coffee invite, then scoot home again.

The door opened and Liane stepped back. An old woman in black trousers and a baggy grey pullover stood glaring at her; it was hard to judge her age but she must have been at least eighty. Sparse grey hair straggled across a deeply furrowed brow, and two bright red spots flamed in pale cheeks. Ill health was written across the woman's face, and the hand holding the door was trembling. Liane had to make an effort to sound normal. This poor soul didn't look as if she was strong enough to take care of a little girl.

'Hi – we've moved in across the back, and I came to say hello. I'm Liane, Frith's mum. It's Margie, isn't it?'

A smile flickered and vanished. 'I saw you cross the grass. Pleased to meet you.'

Margie's accent was a pleasant but hoarse Irish brogue. Her eyes met Liane's briefly before sliding away, and Liane searched for something to say.

'Frith loves your cats. She's always talking about Marmaduke and, um, Socks and Topsy. She loves playing with Bridie, too. Um, does Bridie always live with you?' Was that too cheeky?

Margie's face stiffened, and Liane hurried to explain.

'It was just – Frith mentioned Ireland. I guess you have family there?' Heck, this was getting awkward.

'My daughter's in Dublin. She'll be back soon, though.'

That must be Bridie's mum. Liane seized the chance to leave. 'I have to get home, but why don't you pop over for a coffee sometime? I'll be around most mornings this week. Nice to meet you, Margie.'

The old woman bowed her head, coughed, and closed the

door. Liane returned home the way she'd come, mentally planning her birds and bees chat with Frith.

Her mobile shrilled out while she was admiring Frith and Bridie's skittle-playing. An unknown number. Hmm. Liane stepped inside where it was quiet.

'Liane Morton? I'm Alexis Mack, head of hospital administration – we met at your interview on the fourth.'

Oh, my. Liane's butterflies returned and crashed around inside her. 'Ah – hello. I remember, yes.' What an idiotic thing to say. The phone slid in her hand.

'We'd be very pleased to offer you the job, starting the first of June. There's a place in the creche for your little girl, too.'

'Wow – I mean, thank you so much! That's wonderful news.' Liane spun around the kitchen, her phone pressed to her ear.

Alexis laughed. 'Excellent. We'll send you the contract and all the usual info, and we can take it from there. Welcome to the team!'

She ended the call, and Liane was about to yell her news to Frith when Steve appeared at the back door. He was way too early, but how was this for good timing – or did he have inside knowledge?

'I've got the creche job!' She burst into tears.

He put a bottle of Prosecco and a bowl of strawberries down on the table and pulled her into his arms.

'Mummy? Are you crying?'

Frith was yanking at her sleeve, and Liane pulled the little girl into a group hug. 'Happy tears! I have a fab new job at the hospital! And there's a playgroup for you, too. Won't that be fun?'

'Uh-huh. Ooh – strawberries! Can Bridie and me have some?'

Liane dabbed her face with a tissue as Steve shook the strawberries into four bowls and opened the Prosecco. He handed over a glass.

'Cheers, Mrs. Well done.'

Liane kissed his cheek and clinked glasses. 'I'm glad you came early.'

He tapped his nose. 'I may have heard you were being offered the job.'

SHE TOLD Steve about the conversation with Margie over crab starters in the restaurant – the best fish restaurant in Glasgow, according to Steve, and it was right on the river bank, so they had a fabulous view from their window table. You didn't get much more romantic than this.

'I do wonder why Bridie's staying with her. She seems to be one of those terribly independent old people who're struggling but won't ask for help, even when they're not well.'

'You could go back and check she's better in a day or two. Frith hasn't mentioned anything negative about her, has she?'

'No. But I'm worried. Margie was coughing badly, could that hurt Frithy?'

Steve laid his fork on his empty plate. 'Frith's as tough as the next kid these days, don't worry. And she's well occupied with Jon and the family tonight.'

Liane tried to push the worries away and concentrate on the good stuff. At least Tony'd been conspicuous by his absence this week. Hopefully he'd got the message that he couldn't march in and do what he liked with Frith.

She reached for the carafe of water and refilled both their glasses. 'I'm looking forward to the reunion on Friday – I'm glad you can come. I wonder if Daria's going. She said it was unlikely.'

Steve sipped. 'Have you heard anything more from her?'

'No. I may have overreacted, kicking her out like that, but I was really scared, Steve.'

The waiter removed the starter plates and Liane sat back, shoving the uneasiness about Daria to the back of her mind.

DAY TWENTY-SEVEN – WEDNESDAY 13TH MAY

CHAPTER 30

Margie struggled into a sitting position on the edge of the bed. Bridie's little voice chatting to the cats in the kitchen floated upstairs, and Margie gritted her teeth. She wasn't going to let this bug overwhelm her – she had to go down and make breakfast for the family. One, two, three, up, Margie. Her legs had gone all weak and shaky again and everything hurt – she couldn't do this. Margie clutched her chest, groaning as she collapsed back onto the bed. Oh, to be back in Ireland, where neighbours came to help, not hand out coffee invitations like that other little maid's mother had the other day.

Sick at heart, she pulled the blanket back over her, allowing memories to flood into her head. Why was it all so different now?

Come and watch me swim, Mammy! I can do it, I did ten strokes! Mammy! Sam's got my rubber ring! Where are the biscuits, Mammy? Margie stretched out a hand to the happy little face, but it wavered into nothing before her fingers touched it.

'Are you sick, Mammy?'

The beach and Ireland were gone. This was her bedroom, and Bridie was standing beside the bed.

'I'm tired, maid, that's all. Be right as rain after a rest.'

'I fed the cats.'

'Good girl. Have some bread and jam, and I'll be down in a minute or two.'

Bridie thundered downstairs, and Margie closed her eyes again. Maeve would help her sister; they were good little souls.

A crash from the kitchen had her rolling on her side and sitting up again.

'Bridie? What was that?'

Silence. She'd have to go and see, but she wasn't strong enough. Margie staggered two steps before losing her balance and tipping backwards. The bed broke her fall, and she slid down to sit on the floor, leaning against the bed. She moaned. Proper medicine, that was what she needed, but Bridie was too small to make the lemon drink for her.

'Bridie! Come and help!'

The child's eyes were round as saucers when she came into the room. 'Why are you sitting on the floor?'

'Bring me the pills and the pink medicine, there's a good girl.'

Bridie ran off. Margie closed her eyes.

Three loud thumps came from downstairs. As if she didn't have enough to worry about. Bridie came back with the new packet of aspirin and the Calpol.

'There's somebody at the door.'

'Just stay quiet, maid. They'll go away.'

Three more bangs came, though, and Margie cursed her weak legs. Bridie went over to the window and peeked from behind the curtain.

'It's a man again. He's going away now.'

A man? From the pensions office, no doubt, come to do her out of her money. Margie took a painful swig of Calpol. 'Good riddance. Bring me a glass of water too, darlin'.'

She cracked two aspirin from their plastic bubbles and washed them down with water.

'There! Help me back into bed, maid.'

Bridie wasn't much help, poor lamb, but she was doing her best. Margie crawled to the top end of the bed, and after a moment she was able to haul her backside up and onto the mattress. It was sleep she needed now.

'You be a good girl for Mammy.'

'Shall I get Frith's mummy to help?'

Margie bit back a shriek of protest. 'No, no. I'll be fine after a sleep, you'll see. Come and give me a cuddle.'

Her Bridie in her arms, and the world was perfect. Some things never changed. 'Tell me about Ireland, maid.'

'We like going to the beach there. And the water's cold. We run up and down to get warm and we catch prawns for tea. Do I like prawns?'

Laughter caught in Margie's throat, and she coughed. A sip of water helped, then she gave the glass back to Bridie, forcing a reassuring tone into her voice.

'You do. Off you go and play in the garden until I'm down. Be a good girl for your mammy.'

Bridie's worried little face cleared. 'I'll go and play with Frith in my den.'

It was thump, thump down the stairs as usual, then the back door banged shut. Margie grabbed the bottle of Calpol from beside the bed and had another few swallows. At last, she could rest. The world swam, and Ireland was back.

CHAPTER 31

Frith brought her cereal bowl to the dishwasher, where Liane was loading in her breakfast plate and mug.

'What are we doing today, Mummy? I want to go and play with Bridie and the cats.'

Liane emerged from a lovely daydream about Steve and how he was making her feel. If she hadn't been going to collect her noisy, over-excited daughter yesterday, the evening would have ended with them in bed. After years of being a single mum, she had landed at the 'My place or yours?' stage of a relationship, except of course neither was possible without organising something complicated for Frithy. What they needed was a useful grandma in the background – or even a useful daddy.

'I've got things to do around the house this morning, but we could go to Rouken Glen in the afternoon, if you like?' Rouken Glen park was a short bus ride away. It had a brilliant play area for kids and a pond with ducks, not to mention a waterfall.

'Ooh, yes!' Frith shot upstairs to clean her teeth before vanishing into the depths of the jungle.

'Don't go out of the garden!' Liane yelled after her, then ran upstairs to change the beds. She wrestled with duvet covers, then dumped the dirty linen at the top of the stairs. She'd whizz through the bathroom with a cloth before going downstairs again.

A text from Steve interrupted her when she was stuffing sheets into the washing machine, and Liane sat down to enjoy the moment. *Jon says Frith can stay the night on Friday while we're at your reunion. Think she'd like that?*

Frith would be all for it. *I'll talk to her. Cross your fingers.* She sent the message, then glanced outside. Nothing was moving in the garden so presumably Frith was in her den with Bridie or a cat or two. Liane started the washing machine, then called out of the back door.

'Frith! Want some elevenses?'

It was more like tenses, but no one was counting and an offer of food always brought Frith running. Liane's phone rang on the table, and her heart rate soared. Steve? She grabbed the phone – no, it was Barbara, Oliver's mum.

'Hi, Liane, glad I caught you. Have you heard about those kids that are terrorising the little ones in the park here?'

Liane grabbed a chair and sank into it. 'No! What's happened?'

'Another mum just called me about it. Young lads going up to smaller kids and making them hand over their sweeties or skateboards or whatever. Little hooligans – they're no more than twelve or thirteen, but of course that looks like a big boy to a younger kid. Alice's daughter lost her skateboard to them. Alice was at the swings with Colin and Poppy was on the path, not twenty yards away.'

Barbara ranted on and Liane listened, depression settling over her. What was the world coming to when you couldn't let your kid skateboard twenty yards away?

Stranger danger, that was another conversation she should have with Frithy. And where was the child, anyway? Liane called from the back door again, but no giggling daughter came into sight. She glared down the garden, searching for a glimpse of yellow T-shirt. Surely the girls would hear a yell, even if they were immersed in their game. Time to investigate.

A cool breeze was stirring the bushes in the jungle but apart from that, nothing was moving. And no one was giggling, either. Liane arrived at the ramshackle fence and pushed through into Margie's jungle. No Frith. She went up to the back door and thumped. Marmaduke and two of the more nondescript cats were by the step, but no one answered her knock.

'Margie! It's Liane – is Frith there? Frithy!'

Yet again, silence.

Liane picked her way across Margie's poo-ridden grass, fear dragging at her gut. Hopefully Miss Frith would be waiting in the kitchen along with a semi-reasonable explanation for all this. A giggle came from behind a large lilac bush at the far end of the jungle. Those monkeys! Liane ducked behind a tree and came face-to-face with Frith and Bridie, sitting on a blanket under the bush with three cats and a packet of Rich Tea biscuits.

'Frith, didn't you hear me call you?'

Look at those faces – they'd heard her, all right, and chosen to ignore it. 'You should always tell me when you're coming to Bridie's. I was worried. If I can't trust you not to leave our garden, you'll have to play where I can see you. You can stay inside for the rest of the morning. Say goodbye to Bridie.'

Bridie sat frozen to the spot, and Liane marched a pouting Frith back through their own jungle and into the kitchen. The little girl fled upstairs, and Liane leaned against the sink, relief mingling with guilt. Had she done the right thing? And come to think of it, she should tell Margie about those kids at the park. They could look in at the house before they went to Rouken Glen that afternoon.

THE WASHING KEPT Liane busy for the rest of the morning and, judging by the commentary coming from upstairs, Frith was playing with her doll's house. Footsteps thundered down the stairs a microsecond after Liane called that lunch was ready.

'Are you still cross?' Frith took her place at the table.

Liane passed over a slice of quiche. 'No, I'm not cross. Do you understand about telling me where you're going?'

Violent nods from the other side of the table. 'Are we still going to the park?'

'Sure. I want to pop by Bridie's house on the way. And Frithy, I had a little chat with Margie the other day. She's not Bridie's mum, she's her grandmother. I guess Mammy's what Bridie calls her, like some kids say Nana or Granny.'

Frith tilted her head to one side. 'Or Grandma.'

'Yes, exactly. I knew a girl once who called her grandparents Mumsmum and Mumsdad, but that's a bit unusual.'

Frith giggled. 'Can we ask if Bridie's allowed to come to Rouken Glen with us?'

'Why not? We'll see what Margie says.'

Liane watched as Frith demolished her quiche and salad, her heart full. In a way, this morning's disobedience and punishment were a milestone in Frith's journey through life as a normal child. An everyday situation for most families, a first for Frith and her mum.

When the meal was over, she sent the little girl upstairs to get ready, and at two o'clock they were walking up to Margie's front door – not across her garden, or it might look as if they were using the place as a short cut to the bus stop.

Liane pressed the bell. Silence – was it working? She tried again with the same result, then knocked, Frith bobbing up and down beside her. More silence.

A voice came unexpectedly from the other side of the low fence dividing Margie's property from the one next door. 'She won't answer. She never does.'

An elderly woman was standing by the door of the neighbouring house, obviously on her way back from somewhere. Liane stepped over to the fence. 'Oh? I mean, hello – I'm Liane Morton and this is my daughter Frith. We moved into Grace Street a week or so ago.'

The woman gave them a grim smile. 'Jan McGarry. Margie Donohoe's the bane of my life – or her cats are, anyway. Messing the place up and digging in my vegetables. She really lowers the tone around here, I'm afraid.'

Frith's eyes and mouth were round with astonishment, and Liane hid a wry smile. Oh, dear, hopefully Mrs McGarry wouldn't notice a new cat, once they had one of their own. She ended the conversation as quickly as she could.

'Nice to meet you, Mrs McGarry. We have to go for the bus now – we're off to Rouken Glen for ice cream, aren't we, toots?'

Frith brightened. 'I'm having a 99.'

Liane grabbed the child's hand and ran down the path with her before the other woman started on about sugar or spoiling children. Thank goodness Mrs McGarry wasn't living next door to them.

DAY TWENTY-NINE – FRIDAY 15TH MAY

CHAPTER 32

Kit's flat was on the far side of the Botanic Gardens, near the busy West End. Daria waited in front of the building, gripping her crutches, her bag looped over her head and left shoulder. Staying with Kit for a while had been a good idea. Without the accusatory vibes streaming out of Noah all the time he was at home, she had the peace and quiet to come to terms – how impossible that sounded – with what was happening in her life. She'd moved into her friend's spare room on Monday evening. For the first two days Noah had sent frequent whiny texts, but after the first one, Daria hadn't replied. They both needed space. And as no new text had come since Wednesday, Noah must have realised that too.

The taxi pulled up by the pavement, and the usual pain speared into Daria. It was a gut-wrenching reminder, being forced to go everywhere in a cab. Today's destination wasn't even somewhere she wanted to go – but she had to. She should have done it long ago.

'Broome Street Cemetery, please.' She got into the back of the minicab. And, oh, God – not only was she in a cab again, with the memory of that fatal journey uppermost in her mind, today she would be retracing some of that journey.

In a macabre way, it was fortunate that the site of the accident was so close to the cemetery – the taxi driver was unlikely to start an unbearably jolly conversation if he thought she was going to a funeral or to visit a grave.

They drove to the South Side in blessed silence. Daria rubbed her face as they joined the road *that* taxi had taken on the afternoon of the accident. Along the main road… and this was where she'd cuddled Evie and Evie had smiled that last gorgeous smile at her. Now they were turning the corner into the side road, driving towards the motorway and—

Sweat broke out on Daria's brow. The site of the accident. Her old life had stopped here.

'This okay for you, love?' The driver pulled up outside the cemetery.

'Thank you.' Daria leaned forward to pay. 'Can you pick me up here in half an hour, please?'

The driver shook his head. 'Sorry, love, you'll need to call central.' He handed over a card. 'Here's the number. Don't worry, this time of day someone'll be with you in minutes.'

Daria stuffed the card into her pocket, then gripped her crutches. As soon as the taxi drove off, she turned her back on the cemetery and swung to the edge of the pavement. Over there.

It was easy to see where the crash had been. Skid tracks criss-crossed the road, and a large patch of tarmac was scorched black. A tall fir tree at the college gate diagonally opposite was badly burned; a wonder they hadn't removed it.

Maybe they were going to, of course. It hadn't been a month yet. And this was it. She was standing within feet of the place where, four weeks ago today, the path of her life had changed and Evie's had ended.

Daria crossed over and stood beside the tree, staring around as cars drove past. There weren't many pedestrians – it wasn't the kind of road you walked along to go anywhere, unless you were a college student or going to the cemetery. She thrust her hands into her pockets. Somewhere nearby she'd lain on the ground, Evie's cries in her ears. Then they'd come and moved her away, so her poor girl's cries must have been silenced by then. Before the explosion. Why, why couldn't she remember more? Daria's throat closed in despair. This was unbearable; she should never have come here.

'Are you all right, hen?' An elderly woman clutching a bunch of flowers stopped beside her, peering into Daria's face with a concerned expression. 'Can I help you?'

Get a grip, Daria.

'I'm fine. I was in an accident here a few weeks ago, and it struck me...'

The woman finished for her: '...how lucky you were. I saw it on the TV. It was dreadful.' She stared curiously at Daria. 'Were you in a car, then?'

There was morbid fascination in the woman's eyes, and Daria pulled her jacket shut around her neck.

'Yes. Thanks, I have to go.'

She smiled briefly, moving away while the woman crossed over to the cemetery. Daria pulled out her phone. Thank heavens she didn't have to wait half an hour for the taxi.

. . .

BACK AT KIT'S, Daria pushed the front door open and manoeuvred herself inside. Home, except it wasn't. She didn't have a home any longer.

Kit's flat wasn't unlike hers and Noah's, in a once-elegant but now aged and converted detached house. This one was smaller and on the ground floor, though, which did make things easier when you were on crutches. Daria flopped onto the sofa. The visit to the accident site had brought her nothing, not even the relief of tears. How relentless time was, passing and passing, taking Evie ever further away from her. Here she was, alone in an achingly empty flat, and it would be another two hours before Kit was back.

Tonight would be hard; the two of them were going to the class reunion. Daria had refused point-blank at first, but Kit had talked her round. Her theory was that Daria had to face people someday and getting it over with for all her old school friends on the same evening would make things easier. Daria had given in. What Kit said was true, and she could make her leg an excuse for leaving early. The event was being held in a hotel a little further along Great Western Road, so five minutes in a taxi would have her back here again. No one was likely to stop her leaving – a bereavement like hers wasn't what you wanted to think about at your class reunion, was it? Oh, dear – she should never have said she would go.

Daria made coffee and slumped into a chair at Kit's kitchen table. In a perfect world, she and Noah would have been going together to the reunion, with Evie excited to be having a sleepover at Millie and Roger's. The memory of her daughter's joy on similar occasions flooded into Daria's head before frustration seared in after it. What the *fuck* had she ever done to deserve this, and what had Evie done? Nothing, nothing at all, and it was all so hopeless and so—

She rose, shoving her chair back. It clattered to the floor behind her. In one swift movement Daria swept her coffee mug, the wooden fruit bowl and a little pile of coasters to the floor, an almost-silent high-pitched scream escaping from her throat. She couldn't even scream properly. Her heart was going to burst with the horror of it all because everything, everything she'd ever loved was gone, and she didn't know how, or why. What good were memories? They were driving her insane. The memory of her own child was destroying her.

'Daria? Are you okay?'

Kit was standing in the kitchen doorway, her eyes round. She took two steps forward and pulled Daria into a bear hug. Daria held on for dear life, the shriek she'd been unable to form before ringing in the air.

'You're okay, I've got you. Let it out, Daria.'

Her legs – they were barely holding her up. Daria leaned on Kit, her head pillowed on the other woman's shoulder while howls shook her body. Kit edged her down on a chair and pulled up another beside it, holding Daria tightly but saying nothing as she fought for control.

Slowly, slowly, the horror abated. Daria pulled away. 'I'm sorry.'

'Don't be. I guess you've needed to do that for a long time. How about I make us something hot to drink?'

Daria sat there, waves of anguish flooding through her

while Kit cleared up the mess of fruit and coasters from the floor, then made tea when the kettle boiled.

Daria gaped at her blearily. 'It's hit me – I'll never have clarity about what happened.'

'I guess realising that is enough, for the moment.' Kit's expression was agonised, but she didn't say more.

Daria was silent too. It wasn't enough, but it would have to be. She straightened her back and let air flow into her lungs. 'Thank you. You're the best friend I have. Why are you back so early, anyway?'

Kit grimaced across the table. 'To give us time to get ready for the reunion. I guess that's a bad idea now.'

Daria screwed up her face. This was where she could prove to the world that she was strong enough to get through this. 'No, I'll come. I won't stay late, though.'

'You're a trouper. But don't decide yet, huh?'

Daria sipped her disgusting sweet tea. She would go for an hour at the start, say hello to a few people, see Liane, if she was there, and then come back here and leave them all to discuss what had happened to her. Was that the right thing to do? Who knew? But the class reunion had turned into a kind of personal challenge. If she could get through this, she could get through the rest of her life.

THE BIRCHES HOTEL was an elegant Georgian building in a side street off Great Western Road. The taxi left them at the entrance, and Daria started up the three wide steps. She'd been to a wedding reception here a couple of years ago; they'd probably be in the same room tonight – an old-fashioned, wood-panelled ballroom with chandeliers and stucco pillars. An expensive choice for a class reunion, but apparently the manager was someone's father-in-law.

Kit put a hand on Daria's back as they went into the hotel foyer. 'I think we've got it right, coming together. Plus-ones at a do like this can get in the way.'

Daria shrugged. Noah would have headed straight for the bar and left her to as many catch-up conversations as she wanted, if things had been normal. A woman with a list was waiting at the entrance to the ballroom – Ruby Clark, recognisable by her long dark hair.

Kit handed over their tickets. 'Hi, Rubes. Kit Johns and Daria Geddes reporting for duty. You look great!'

Ruby immediately put a hand on Daria's arm. 'Daria, I'm so sorry about your daughter. I don't know what to say. You're very brave.'

No, she wasn't. Daria pressed her lips together. More people arrived, and she and Kit moved on into the ballroom, where – oh, no. Forty people at least were standing around chatting animatedly in groups, clutching glasses, the plus-ones with more distant, polite expressions.

Daria hissed in Kit's ear. 'Does everyone know about Evie?'

'I'm not sure. Ruby and Mhairi organised this, and I told them. I thought it would be easier if you didn't have to tell everyone yourself. But I'm here, my love. I'll help you.'

Small tables were set out along one wall, and they settled down at a corner one before Kit went to fetch drinks. Daria waited, trying to control her breathing and not catch anyone's eye until she was back in control. It was a drinks and canapés do, so a lot of people were going to end up absolutely sloshed. Which of these people had noticed her and were already whispering about how terrible it was and how they'd never be able to cope? That was a killer-remark if ever she'd heard one, a stab in the back every time. If they were in her situation, they would 'cope' too, because what was the alternative? Going mad? She was mad already.

Kit returned with two glasses of Prosecco and a carafe of water. 'Here you go. Let's make a toast – to old friends, huh?'

Daria clinked and sipped. She would hide in this corner for another half hour; that would be enough. She should never have agreed to come, she...

'Kit! And Daria! So sorry, Daria, darling. I heard about your new job, Kit, that must be—'

It was Lisbeth, who'd been hockey captain in their final year and still had the same jolly voice. Daria twitched her lips in the right places – at least the conversation was going on without her. More people were arriving now, and she recognised some of them as teachers – how many were coming, for heaven's sake? A plate of mixed canapés arrived on the table as more people joined them, and Daria sat sipping more water than she wanted because the action gave her an excuse not to talk. Was Liane here yet? She didn't seem to be, but there was another large group at the other end of the room so it was hard to say. It was the kind of party people might well choose to come late to, too.

Lisbeth was passing round photos of her latest holiday, real photos, which almost seemed pretentious. Beautiful beaches followed by perfect sunsets followed by two perfect children beaming behind their sandcastle. To do the woman justice, she whipped that one back before it reached Daria, but a glimpse was enough.

Daria gathered her bag and her crutches and smiled at Kit. 'I'm off to the loo – no, you stay here. I'll be fine.'

Mercifully, she arrived at the cloakroom without having to speak to anyone, and reclaimed her jacket. With any luck she'd be able to grab a taxi on the street. No one was arriving as she left the hotel, and thanks be, now she was outside in the cool air of a Glasgow spring. Daria stood at the bottom of the front steps, and sure enough, here was a taxi. It belched out a family of four, so not reunion guests for her to face, and Daria got in and gave Kit's address to the driver. This was the coward's way out, but oh, how glad she was to be driving away from her classmates. Too much, too soon.

The driver gave her a grin. 'Nice sunset tonight, love.'

Daria ducked her head to see the pink and orange glow shimmering over the buildings to her right. 'Lovely.'

It was, too. And timeless. Like her love for Evie.

CHAPTER 33

Liane kissed Frith goodbye, an odd little lump in her throat. Frithy's first sleepover – or the first that wasn't taking place in hospital, anyway. Frith dived into the garden to join Jon and Ella's two kids on the trampoline, and Liane turned to Ella.

'You will phone straightaway if she has any problems getting off to sleep, won't you?'

'Of course I will. She'll be fine, don't worry.'

Ella saw them to the door, and Liane settled into Steve's car. This was their us-time, but it was still tough, leaving her girl.

The sun was going down as they emerged from the Clyde Tunnel and arrived at the north side of the city.

'We're going to be fashionably late,' said Liane. 'I wonder if Daria decided to go.'

'We'll soon see.'

Steve raised his eyebrows at her and Liane stuck out her tongue. 'Don't worry, I'll be nice.'

Her phone rang in her bag, and she grappled for it. Was Frithy okay? No, bummer, it was Tony. Timing... her ex had it in spades.

'Tony, this isn't a good ti—' Liane broke off. Better not go into detail about where she and Frith were right now.

'Just wanted to give you some news. I have a job, starting next month.'

Liane cast her eyes heavenwards. Whoopee – this would set Frith up for life. Or not.

'Congratulations. You'll want to organise maintenance payments, I expect. What is it – the job, I mean?'

His usual petulant tone was back. 'You can be so mean and stingy. I'll be doing stage-building for the theatre festival this summer, at different venues. If it works out, it could lead to a permanent job.'

He wasn't going to make big bucks, then. 'Call me realistic, Tony, not stingy. I'll take advice about it. Was that what you called to tell me?'

'I've been taking advice too. When I have a regular job, I'll be applying for shared custody. I'll come round and talk to you about it tomorrow.'

The connection broke, and Liane stuffed her phone into her bag. No way, but no way was she going to let him have shared custody of Frith. But could she stop him applying for it?

Steve listened while she told him about Tony's – glory, was it a threat?

'I can't imagine he'd get custody of any kind, but you'll need proper advice. He'd get access, but you give him that already.'

What a mess. 'Let's forget him for tonight. I'll go to Citizens Advice on Monday. Look, it's this street here.'

They slowed down to turn off Great Western Road. Steve drove round the back of the hotel, where the car park was nearly empty. Liane took his arm as they walked into the hotel. Most people would be taking taxis tonight, to let them have a few drinks.

In the foyer, she recognised Ruby Clark and Kit John, who were standing together, Ruby with both hands clasped in front of her mouth and Kit waving her arms around as she spoke.

Kit pounced on Liane. 'Did you see Daria Geddes on your way in? She's disappeared.'

'No. What do you mean, disappeared?' Liane frowned. Kit and Ruby were both wearing very odd expressions – how could anyone disappear?

Kit clasped her hands under her chin. 'She went to the loo but she's not there – she seems to have left. This has been too much for her and it's my fault for encouraging her to come. I thought it might help her to see everyone at once and get it over with.'

Liane stood still. What was the woman talking about? 'Get what over with?'

'Meeting people for the first time after Evie. She's not answering her phone, either. I wish we'd never come!' Kit strode off to the cloakroom, and Liane put out a hand to stop Ruby from following her.

'Ruby – who's Evie?'

Ruby dabbed her eyes with a tissue. 'Daria's little girl – she was killed in a car crash about a month ago. Naturally, Daria's finding things difficult.'

'*What?*' Liane grabbed Steve's arm. 'You're kidding – we saw her last week and she didn't say a word.'

Steve's mouth was a thin slash. 'That's horrendous. How old was Evie?'

'She was four a few weeks ago.' Ruby wrung her hands. 'Daria was—' She broke off as Kit came back, her phone pressed to her ear.

'It's quite all right, my love. As long as you're okay. I'll see you in a bit.' She ended the call and heaved a sigh. 'She went home. Says she's okay, just needs some space. I'll give her half an hour then go back and make sure.' She nodded to Liane and Steve, and wandered off with Ruby.

Liane stood rigid with shock beside Steve. Why hadn't Daria told her about Evie? She had visited Liane at home, been perfectly chummy, and lovely with Frith, she'd babysat – what had been going on in her head all that time?

'Steve, this is – I left Frithy with her, twice, and she must have been – hell's teeth, she wasn't in a fit state to look after a kid, was she?'

Steve hugged her. 'No, she wasn't, but what happened with Frith was as much Tony's fault as Daria's. Poor soul.'

Liane took a shaky breath. 'What should we do? I'm not sure I want to stay here after this.'

'Let's go in and you can say hello to some of them, or they'll be out looking for you in a while. We can get our breath back and see what we want to do later.'

This wasn't how she'd imagined the evening would start, but Liane soon spotted her old clique in the ballroom. In less than ten minutes she was standing with a glass in one hand, catching up with everyone. This was better – they'd have time to think about Daria tomorrow.

. . .

THE MOON WAS CASTING ghostly shadows along the street when Steve pulled up in front of home later that evening – or was it tomorrow morning? The moment he switched off the engine, Liane reached out to grab him for a kiss.

He leaned towards her, then froze. 'Um, Liane, I hate to be a party pooper, but Tony's sitting on your doorstep.'

'You're kidding.' Liane twisted round to see. Not only was Tony on the doorstep, he was out for the count, so he must be drunk.

Steve was laughing. 'One day, we'll be able to do things like normal people.'

Liane wrenched the passenger door open. 'We'll be able to do things like normal people in five seconds flat. Call him a taxi.'

She strode up the path and shook Tony's shoulder, pulling a face when he turned towards her. He smelled like a brewery. 'Tony! What do you think you're doing? Get up!'

His head lolled back, and he half-opened his eyes. 'Wha— Oh, it's you. I came to see my girl.'

'You're not seeing anyone in this state. I mean it, Tony. Go home and we'll talk tomorrow.'

Steve helped her hoist Tony to his feet, and together they marched him back down the path.

'You can't stop me seeing her. I'll have the police on you.' He swayed away from Liane, then spun round and shoved his face in hers. 'Fathers have rights too, you know. And you had no right to speak to me like you did earlier.'

'Drunk fathers have no rights, Tony. You can call me

tomorrow if you want to organise a time for a reasonable discussion.'

Tony glared, but he got into the taxi when it pulled up. Steve handed over a note, and gave the driver Tony's address.

Not knowing whether to laugh or cry, Liane wiped sweating hands down her trousers as the taxi drove off. Was the evening even salvageable now?

Steve offered her his arm. 'Let's try take two, shall we? How about a glass of that nice Prosecco I put in the fridge earlier – or have you had enough already?'

She had, but there was room for a small one without getting legless. Liane blew him a kiss. 'Lead me to it.'

DAY THIRTY – SATURDAY 16TH MAY

CHAPTER 34

It was breakfast time, but Tabitha was nowhere to be found. Evie searched in all the cupboards, and under boxes and behind the chairs in the living room too, but apart from Socks and Daisy, the cats were all in the garden. She opened the back door to see if Tabitha was outside too and straightaway, everyone came running, wanting their breakfast. Everyone except Tabitha.

Evie filled up the bowls with cat food and went to look upstairs. Her room – no Tabitha, and no Tabitha in the bathroom. Evie wrinkled her nose. Mammy had let her have a bath again last night, but the water hadn't drained away properly. It had gone a bit smelly. No Tabitha in the tiny room – she must have gone in with Mammy.

Evie pushed Mammy's door open with one finger and peeked in. Mammy was still asleep, with her mouth open, and she was snoring harder than usual. Evie checked behind the door, and crouched down to see under the bed, but

Tabitha wasn't there – and anyway, if Tabby-puss had been in the house at all, she'd have heard the other cats and run to get her share of breakfast. Evie trailed back downstairs. Had Tabitha got lost? She had a quick look in the cupboard under the stairs, just in case, but Tabitha wasn't there either. She'd have let them know if she'd got shut in somewhere, in any case. Tabitha was a yowler, Mammy said.

There was no milk left, so she'd need to have water with her breakfast today. Should she make toast? The toaster was scary, because sometimes the toast didn't pop up right and then you had to dig it out with a knife and Mammy said that was dangerous. Bread and jam was fine, and afterwards she'd go and see if Frith was out to play yet.

Evie stood on tiptoe to look out of the window. It was a nice sunny day and the way the trees were dancing about was funny. Windy days were lovely – remember when Daddy'd had a kite and they'd gone up the big hill and made it fly? Evie rubbed her eyes. It would be nice when she could go home. But then, they didn't have cats at home. And now she had to look for Tabitha. She might be in the den. They had boxes there, and Tabitha loved boxes.

Evie pushed her way through the jungle, calling for Frith. No answer came, so she squeezed through the bushes to her den. The tiny purple flowers were waving in the wind, but the only cat there was Marmaduke. He miaowed a warning when Evie went in, but she sat down anyway. No Tabitha and no Frith. She could go and ask if Frith was coming out – they could look for Tabitha together.

Eve hurried to squeeze through the back fence. Frith definitely wasn't in her garden, but music from Frith's mummy's radio was coming out of the kitchen window when Evie arrived at the back door. Mummy and Daddy used to put the radio on at breakfast time too. Evie knocked, and Frith's mummy opened the door.

'Hello, Bridie! Have you come for Frith? She's not here this morning, but she'll be home later. I expect she'll be out to play then.'

Oh, no. Evie blinked up at Frith's mummy. She would have to look for Tabitha without Frith.

'I can't find Tabitha – she's the stripy one with kitties in her tummy. Can you send her home if you see her?

Frith's mummy smiled. It was a nice smile. 'Of course I will. I'm sure she's fine, though. Cats are good at looking after themselves. Look – have a biscuit, Bridie, love.'

She handed over a chocolate biscuit in a shiny wrapping, and Evie took it. Ooh, she hadn't had one of these for a long time. She smiled at Frith's mummy and ran back to her den to eat it. She was licking chocolatey fingers when Mammy called her.

'Bridie! Where are you?'

Mammy's face was blotchy red and white, and she was holding onto the back door with both hands.

Evie ran across the grass. 'I can't find Tabitha.'

'Tsk. She'll be fine. Come inside, child, that wind from the sea would take your nose off. No beach for us today, if it carries on like this.'

Evie brightened. Were they going to the beach? That would be fun. 'I like the wind at the seaside.'

'Aye, well, we'll need to see when your daddy and the boys and Maeve are back. Maybe you can go then. Some fish for tea would be nice.'

Mammy closed the door, then walked in a wavy line

through to the living room and plonked herself down on the sofa. Evie went to sit beside her. Mammy's hand was hot when it took hers.

'Dearie me, this is like being on a boat, isn't it? Everything swaying around like a force-nine gale.'

Evie leaned back. 'When will Daddy be here? Where was he?'

'Cork, maid. Best town in Ireland, bar Bantry, and you can't really compare them, can you?'

Mammy coughed hard then, and Evie waited until she'd finished. It was good news Daddy was coming, but why hadn't he been in Spain with Mummy?

'Wasn't Daddy in Spain, too?'

'Spain? Away with you, what would he be doing in Spain? He wouldn't be back for tea if he was in Spain, you know.'

A moment later, Mammy was snoring again. Evie crept back out. Daddy was coming for tea! And surely he'd bring Mummy with him. Would they let her stay to see Tabitha's kitties?

Evie went back to the kitchen. There were still two slices of bread left, so Mammy hadn't had any breakfast yet. She'd make some bread and jam for Mammy too. And water.

It was hard to wake Mammy up for her breakfast. Evie shook hard at Mammy's shoulder, but she still didn't wake up. Oh, well, she would leave the bread and jam here and try again in a minute. On the way out she went past the cupboard under the stairs, and – good idea! She hadn't checked in the cupboard on the upstairs landing. Tabitha might have fallen asleep in the warm in there.

The cupboard was empty of cats but full of old, old

things. Evie pulled at a brown cardboard box. This would be good for the den if there was space under the bushes. It was big enough for her and Frith to get in together. Evie almost fell on her way downstairs with the box but it woke Mammy up, so that was good. She sneaked the box out to the den before Mammy stopped her, then went back to the living room. Good. Mammy was eating her breakfast.

'Ah, that's better. Thank you, maid. Strawberry jam, eh? My favourite.'

'There isn't any milk left.'

'We'll get some later. A sup of pink medicine will set me right.'

Evie fetched the bottle and a spoon, and was about to go outside to play when a knock came at the front door. Mammy stood very still with one finger on her lips. They waited. Another knock came before footsteps walked away again. Evie ran to the living room window. It was the same man she'd seen before, and he was getting into a car. Good, it was driving away. She skipped back to Mammy.

'I'm going to play in the garden.'

She opened the back door to a shriek from across the garden. Frith was back! Evie sped through the jungle to the back fence.

'Bridie! Mummy said I can get a trampoline for my birthday! A great big one for in the garden – you can come and jump on it too!'

'Ooh, yes!' Evie jumped up and down at the fence. But – Daddy was coming for tea. 'Is your birthday soon? My daddy might be back today.'

'Are you going home with him then?'

'I don't know.'

'You're funny.'

'I'm not. I've got a huge box in my den, come and see!'

Tabitha still wasn't anywhere, so they played in the den without her. It was fun in the box, eating the raisins Frith's mummy gave them.

'I hope Tabitha comes home soon.' Evie finished her last raisin and licked her fingers. 'I want a kitty to take home with me when Mummy comes.'

'Isn't your daddy coming?'

That was the silly part. It was always Mummy who took her places and came to get her again, except sometimes when she went to Grandma Millie's. Evie screwed up her face. Mammy might have got it wrong. She'd been talking a bit more funny than usual this morning, hadn't she? So maybe it wasn't Daddy who was coming, maybe it was Mummy. Ooh, it would be so nice to have a proper big cuddle with Mummy. She hadn't had one for ever so long. Or Daddy might be coming tomorrow and not today. Evie pouted. It was horrible when you didn't know what was happening.

She jumped up. 'Let's look for Tabitha again. She might have gone into someone else's garden.'

Frith clambered out of the box too. 'Mummy says it's wrong to go into other people's gardens.'

Evie led the way to the side fence. The lady here didn't have a jungle, so you could see almost the whole garden from the fence. They'd only need to look behind the shed.

Frith pulled at her jumper. 'We can't go in there! That's the nasty lady's garden.'

'We have to find Tabitha!' Evie put one hand on the fence, ready to climb over.

'Bridie! Bridie!'

Oh! Mammy was calling. Was Daddy here?

'I have to go in. I'll be out later.' Evie sped back to the house.

CHAPTER 35

Frith was like a different child here. Gone was the girl who'd agitated to watch Sunday morning cartoons every week; this new Frith couldn't wait to get into the garden every day. Today, she had vanished into the jungle, two packets of raisins clutched in her hand, the moment they'd fetched her home – sitting on her new booster seat in Steve's car – from Jon and Ella's. Happiness bubbled up in Liane. How wonderful to be four years old and well.

Steve was scrolling through the news on his iPad at the kitchen table, and Liane kissed the top of his head as she switched on the coffee machine. Last night had been fabulous, Frithy'd had a great time at Jon and Ella's, all was well with the world. Or it would be if Tony would leave them alone.

Steve accepted his usual black with one sugar. 'I'm on duty this afternoon. Anything you need my muscle-power for before I leave?'

'You've done it all already.' Liane sat down with her mug.

Steve pushed the iPad over the table. 'Look, they've an electric mower on offer at the garden centre this week. You should get one. I'm off all day on Monday – we could go then and you wouldn't have to lug it home on the bus.'

A trip to the garden centre would be an entirely new experience now that she actually had a garden. Liane sipped, gazing at Steve as he scrolled and commented his way around the Saturday morning news. This was the life.

They were still at the table when Frith arrived back, her lips pursed. 'We couldn't find Tabitha. And Bridie has to go in. Her daddy's coming. She might be going home soon.'

Liane's heart sank. Oh, dear, Bridie going home would leave a big hole in poor Frith's life. Come to think of it, where did the family live? There'd been talk of Dublin, but hadn't Margie said her daughter would be back? Liane rushed to comfort Frith. 'If Bridie lives near enough to visit, we can do that, don't worry. And you'll still have the cats, won't you? And Oliver and the others from the library.'

And soon all the other kids at the hospital creche too, but this wasn't the best time to remind Frith about that.

Steve sat back. 'Tell you what, ladies. I'm not on duty until three. How about we go to the garden centre today? We can have lunch, and look at lawnmowers, and trampolines too, of course.'

Frith's face was one big beam again, and Liane mouthed her thanks across the table.

'Upstairs with you and change out of that T-shirt, you manky thing,' she said, pointing Frith towards the hallway. 'We'll leave in quarter of an hour, okay?'

. . .

THE GARDEN CENTRE WAS PACKED, but they found a table in the café and had hot dogs, and chocolate cake as a treat. Afterwards, with the cut-price mower safely in her trolley, Liane followed Frith across the store to look at trampolines. One was set up outside to try, and the little girl showed off the tricks she'd learned at Jon and Ella's. Liane made a note of the price tag. She would manage that in plenty of time for Frith's birthday, now she had a job.

On the way to the cash desk they passed a stand of overalls for kids, and Liane stopped for a look. These were funky – sturdy dungarees with legs you could unzip to turn them into shorts. Garden clothes were a good idea; Frith had already ruined her best jeans.

'Blue or yellow?' She held up two pairs in Frith's size. 'For dirty games in the garden.'

Steve was looking at his watch. 'Why not just let her wear old things? You don't need to keep washing them.'

Liane laughed. 'That's what Bridie does. She looks like a ragamuffin most days. But Frithy's bursting out of all her old clothes this spring.'

Frith pointed to the blue dungarees. 'I like these ones. Bridie's things are all old, Mummy. So is everything in the house.'

'Margie's an old lady, honey pie. Old people have old things. I expect I'll be the same one day.'

Steve took the trolley. 'Ladies, I'm not rushing you, but I have to go.'

Liane thrust the blue dungarees into the trolley beside the mower. 'We're done.'

They were pulling up in front of the house again when a message pinged into Liane's phone. Tony. She slid the phone back into her bag to deal with later, then kissed Steve goodbye.

Frith pulled a face at them. 'Yuk! Can I go and see if Bridie's out?'

Liane waved as Steve drove off, then grasped the lawnmower. 'Don't go into their garden, huh? We don't want to disturb them if Bridie's dad's come back.'

Frith ran off, and Liane took the lawnmower round the back, then sat down on the bench to see what Tony had texted. *Can't manage weekend, will come over to see Frith Tues afternoon.* Liane grimaced. He'd forgotten the 'if that's okay with you' bit. Well, she'd see what Citizens Advice had to say on Monday. It was better to be armed for whatever arguments he was going to produce.

She was about to start the lawnmower when a thought struck. She ought to get in touch with Daria. Whatever was going on in the woman's head, she had lost a child, and after living for years with that same fear at the front of her mind, if anyone could empathise, Liane could. A quick message would be best.

I was so sorry to hear about your daughter last night. Take care of yourself. She hesitated, then added a kiss and tapped send. A few seconds later, her phone rang.

'Thanks for your message, Liane. I'm sorry again about losing Frith that day.'

'Frithy's fine. You must have been under a tremendous strain – you still must be.'

'It's – awful. I think that's why I needed the contact with people who didn't know. Frith's such a lovely girl, and the way she's so enthusiastic about everything – that was Evie all over. But I should have told you.'

Liane's mind raced. 'Would you like to come round for a coffee and a chat sometime? Frith enjoyed being with you too until Tony showed up.'

'I'd like that. Thank you for being so understanding.'

Liane tapped her fingers on the lawnmower. 'How about tomorrow afternoon?'

Daria agreed, and they organised a time. Liane ended the call and went back to the lawnmower. She'd have a quick dash up and down with this and – ah. Now she remembered, Daria wasn't what you'd call mobile at the moment, was she? It might be better if she went to Daria tomorrow. Liane pulled out her phone again. But no, she would leave it up to Daria to suggest a change of venue, if she wanted one. No point in being over-complicated.

DAY THIRTY-ONE – SUNDAY 17TH MAY

CHAPTER 36

It was ridiculous to be so nervous about going for coffee with an old school friend. Daria hopped over to her case and fished for a clean pullover. She'd been at Kit's for almost a week, and Noah was still blaming her for Evie's death. They were going to meet at the flat on Wednesday, with Millie there too, to talk things over again. Daria was still hoping he'd agree to bereavement counselling. Their marriage wasn't going to survive unless Noah came to terms with their loss and 'forgave' her for doing something that was risky, yes, but not illegal. Would she ever forgive herself?

The street was quiet when the taxi pulled up at Liane's a few minutes before half past two. Frith came running down the side of the house as Daria paid and got out.

'You're lucky – I hardly ever get to go in a taxi! Can I try your crutches later?' Frith jumped up and down beside her on the pavement.

Steve joined them. 'Taxis are an overrated pastime, kid.

Hi, Daria – looks like you're walking better. Liane's in the garden, come on round.' He led the way up the side path.

Liane was setting out coffee things on a table on the patio. She pulled out a garden chair at the top of the table. 'Hello! Good to see you, Daria.'

So, they were pretending everything was okay between them – at least while Frith was here. Daria sat, put her leg up on the offered stool and handed the crutches to Frith, who hopped up and down, clutching the handpieces.

'We made lemon drizzle cake. Mummy squeezed the lemons and I made holes in the cake to pour the juice into!'

Daria managed a smile. 'That sounds yummy.' What wouldn't she give to have Evie hopping up and down on crutches right now?

'I wanted my friend Bridie to come for cake too.' Frith handed the crutches back and slid onto the bench.

Liane poured coffee from a thermos jug. 'If Bridie's dad's here, they could have gone out for the day.'

Frith pouted. 'Bridie had a 99 with my daddy and me once.'

Liane ruffled the little girl's hair. 'You see your daddy pretty often, though. Bridie hasn't seen hers for a while, so I expect they want some time together just the two of them.'

Frith heaved a sigh, then came to lean on Daria's chair. 'My daddy plays the guitar, you know. When I'm bigger I can go to his concerts, can't I, Mummy?'

'Yup. You'll be a teenager in no time, don't worry.'

Steve handed round cake, and Daria sat trying to control her breathing as Frith attacked her slice. She cleared her throat and leaned back, searching for something to say. A black cat with white feet was strolling towards them from the bottom of the jungle.

'Is that one of the cats you told me about, Frith?'

Frith bounced in her chair. 'That's Socks!'

The child chattered on, and Daria's discomfort abated. They were making her feel like a normal person – kind of them, when you considered how she'd lost Frith instead of keeping her safe at home that day. Frith ran off to see if her friend was out as soon as she had finished her cake, and Daria gazed after her.

'More coffee?' Liane gave the jug a shake. 'I'll make some fresh.'

She hurried inside, and Steve followed with the milk jug. Were they whispering about her in there? Daria didn't move. They came back seconds later, so maybe they weren't.

Liane perched on the edge of her chair. 'Coffee in two minutes. Daria, were you—'

'Mummy! Bridie has to stay in her garden because her daddy's not there yet. Can I take some milk to put in the den for when Tabitha comes home? We still haven't found her.' Frith tore up the garden and stood bobbing on her toes beside Liane, hands clasped in front of her.

'Cats shouldn't drink milk, honey pie, it isn't good for them. But you can take some leftover chicken from lunchtime. Bring it back if Tabitha hasn't eaten it by tea time, though. It'll go bad, and we don't want to give her a sore tummy, do we?'

The two of them vanished inside, and Steve winked at Daria. 'I have a feeling Tabitha may very sensibly have left the building to have her kittens in peace and quiet, you know.'

Daria laughed aloud – how shocking that she could laugh still and mean it. She relaxed as Frith sped off with some chicken on a saucer.

Liane poured fresh coffee. 'If Tabitha gets to eat that chicken it'll be a miracle. I hope we don't have all the other cats queuing on the doorstep wanting more.' She slid another slice of cake onto Daria's plate. 'No arguments. You need feeding up.'

Daria wielded her fork. The cake was oozing lemony sweetness. Normally she'd have been delighted to have more, but today it was hard to get it past her throat.

Liane lifted her own fork. 'Kit said you were staying with her, Daria? Are you coping okay? Sorry, that's a stupid question.'

Daria fixed her eyes on her plate. 'Noah and I are having – problems. We decided some space was the best way. I'm seeing him on Wednesday.'

Steve gave her arm a squeeze. 'What you're going through is the worst possible thing for a couple. If being apart is right for you now, that's what you should do.'

'Listen to him.' Liane nodded at Daria. 'He knows what he's talking about. He was in charge of the ward when Frithy was so ill – I lost count of the number of stressed-out parents I saw quarrelling because it was all just too hard.'

'I'd never have thought Noah and I would end up like this.' Daria took a sip of coffee.

Steve passed her a tissue. 'Have you done anything about bereavement counselling?'

'We're – I'm thinking about it.'

'Mummy! The cats all want Tabitha's chicken! Bridie's guarding it. I'm going to the loo!' Frith raced straight past.

Liane and Steve were hiding smiles, and Daria slid up her sleeve to see the time. After half past three; she would stay a little longer and then go back to Kit's. This was harder than she'd expected.

Frith returned, and Liane caught the little girl's arm on her way past. 'Are you being good? Is Bridie's dad there yet?'

'No – she says he'll be here soon with her mum. Can I have—'

'No more chicken, Scooby Doo. The cats get plenty of food from Margie, don't they?'

'Bridie fed them today. She gave them water, too.'

'Good that Bridie's big enough to help. I'll call you in a bit, huh?'

Frith vanished into the bushes, and Daria sat forward in her chair. 'I'll order my taxi for four o'clock, if that's okay?'

It was time to leave these kind people in peace to laugh together when they wanted to. Two hours of her company was enough.

'You don't need to rush. Whatever's best for you,' said Liane. 'I know it's hard to get comfy at other people's places when you're on crutches.'

Daria smiled in reply and tapped to connect to the taxi company. Her leg was an excuse, and they all knew that.

Liane pushed her chair back. 'I'll wrap you a couple of slices of cake to take back to Kit's, shall I?' She vanished inside.

Steve gave Daria an encouraging smile. 'Where does Kit live?'

He was good at bridging awkward gaps in the conversation. They chatted about life in the West End in comparison to life south of the Clyde until Liane was back with a package wrapped in tinfoil.

'Excuse the non-environmentally-friendly wrapping. I've run out of greaseproof paper.'

'I can reuse it.' And now it was empty words to fill the time. Daria accepted the cake.

They chatted about nothing for a few minutes, then Daria got to her feet and took hold of her crutches. 'I'd better get round to the front for the taxi. It's been lovely to see you – thank you so much, Liane. And Steve.'

Liane stood up. 'I'll call Frithy to say goodbye before you go.' She took a few steps down the garden. 'Frith!'

Daria limped across the patio to the side path. Sitting in a garden chair for so long hadn't been such a good idea; she had pins and needles in her bad leg.

Liane put a hand on her back as she wobbled. 'Careful.' She looked behind her. '*Frith!*'

No answer came. Liane grimaced.

'I'll leave her, if you don't mind. If Bridie's parents have arrived, they might be in the middle of hellos over there.'

They walked to the front of the house, where Liane gave her a careful hug. 'We'll do this again, Daria. We can take Frithy out sometime too. It won't be long before you're properly mobile.'

'I'd like that. Say goodbye to her from me.'

And here was the taxi. Daria got in, waved as they drove off, then leaned back with her eyes shut. Her friendship with Liane seemed to have survived, but oh, what a tough visit that had been.

CHAPTER 37

Margie stumbled from the living room into the kitchen. Every bone in her body was aching, and her head was throbbing like the engines on a ferry. What had Bridie done with the Calpol? And where was the child? It was almost four o'clock. She'd be wanting her tea soon. Margie pushed the dirty lunch plates to one side and leaned on the table. Oh, this cough was making her so weak. Nice steady breaths, Margie. Take your time.

Ah – there was the Calpol by the sink. A good dose and she'd be better for a while. The kits needed to be fed, too.

Margie swallowed several measures of Calpol then shook cat food into the empty bowls. As much landed on the floor as in the bowls, but the kits would take care of that. She filled a glass with water and took it through to the sofa to drink. The photos of the family were on the coffee table, and she sat leafing through them. Her world. Bridie and Maeve and...

'Aiden? Sam?' Her voice quavered through the empty house. The boys weren't here; they should all be here. But

Daisy was coming to sit beside her, li'l darlin' she was. Margie fussed over the cat, then leaned back, staring at the ceiling. Something was wrong today; her head wasn't working properly. She had to find something. What did she have to find again? Margie tottered through to the kitchen. She'd have more Calpol, that would help.

Five minutes calling round the house and garden was enough to show her that Bridie wasn't at home. Only the kits came running when Margie opened the back door, all except Tabitha. Dear Lord, Bridie must be out looking for Tabby-puss. She'd go and search for the pair of them right now, yes.

Margie swallowed the last aspirin along with some more Calpol. Her head was still swimming, but it was a much more comfortable sensation now, as if she'd been drinking champagne. That Bridie, what a rascal she was! She'd been watching her brothers and copying their wild ways. But they wouldn't be far off; they never were, and it was a lovely afternoon for a walk. She'd find them, Bridie and Maeve and the boys. Down the path, out of the gate. Some seagulls on a roof across the road were crying like they used to in Ireland. She would go to the corner and see if the girls and boys were there.

Margie arrived at the corner then scurried on, and on, searching city street after city street as the afternoon gave way to evening. And on, and on. It seemed so easy today; that would be the Bridie's pink medicine. Bless the child. Remember the summer evenings when the family had played on the beach until all hours? Glasgow was even lighter; at midsummer you could sit out in the daylight until almost midnight. It wasn't daylight now, though, shadows were falling and it was harder to see up the streets she was passing. Margie stopped and leaned on a lamp post. What was she – ah, yes. Bridie, what a li'l rascal she was. Always hiding. Margie drifted along the road, past a pub on the corner and... dear Lord – where was she? Look at these rowdies. Who did they think they were, laughing at her like that? She dodged into a tenement entrance and waited until they'd poured themselves into the pub she'd passed.

Stopping had taken all her energy away, somehow. Margie leaned against the wall. The dim light in the entrance was comforting, and she was tired, so, so tired, and her chest hurt, everything was hurting and Bridie was gone. Margie pushed away from the wall. She had to find Bridie. Two steps and oh, the whole world was swirling around her.

The voice came from far away but it was kindly, a woman's. 'Steady, hen, have a seat here.'

Several firm hands gripped Margie's arms and pushed her down until she was sitting on a step, leaning sideways against a wall. The street had gone all swimmy, and four blurred shadows were bending over her.

A man's voice came. 'Has she been drinking?'

'Can't smell anything – not booze anyway. Where does it hurt, hen?'

Margie gripped her chest. Bridie...

The man again. 'I'll call an ambulance.'

No, no.

'Ambulance... Yes... It's an old woman collapsed in the street outside The Hog in Palace Road... Sort of half-conscious, clutching her chest... She's in a bit of a state, can't stand up... Okay.'

She had to find Bridie. Margie yanked her arm away from

the hand still holding it, but all she managed was a pathetic little flap. What was happening to her?

'An ambulance is on its way, love. They'll have you right in no time.'

Two men's voices started a muttered conversation. Margie strained her ears to hear, but the words meant nothing. The woman beside her patted her shoulder now and again. Margie fought the descending fog. Was this a stroke? No – she could feel her hands and feet. Her heart? But there wasn't any pain, just this fog everywhere.

Sirens swooped up, and new voices were talking over her head. Margie allowed dimness to slide into nothingness.

THE BEEPING WOKE HER, and she reached out – why was it so bright here? They should turn those lights off; she couldn't see a thing.

A girl's voice. 'Hello! You're in hospital, my love, can you tell me your name? Steve – she's awake.'

Someone was wiping her face with a cold cloth. Margie jerked her head away – but this was better. She could see again, though everything was still blurry.

'Where are my girls? Where's Aiden?'

A young man and an even younger woman were bending over her.

The man spoke. 'I'm going to have a quick look in your eyes. What's your name?'

A bright light shone briefly in each eye, and Margie tried to turn her head to the side.

The man clicked off his torch and took her hand. 'You're in the short-term admission ward at A&E. I'm Steve, I'm the head nurse here. Your heart was a bit irregular but we're helping you now. What's your name?'

Margie pressed her lips together. There was no getting away from busybodies today.

The girl was speaking again. 'Is Aiden your son?'

They weren't going to help her here. She would leave the moment she could.

'Her BP's better, Steve.'

'Good. Get her into a gown and I'll call Davie to come and have another look now she's come round. See if you can find any clue as to who she is in her pockets.'

The voices were going over her head. The best thing was to let them get on with it. They'd get tired of her sooner or later and then she'd be able to get on and find Bridie. Margie lay passively as the girl unbuttoned her cardigan. But no, no, she didn't want it off – she needed her things.

'What are you doing? This is mine!' She clutched at the sleeve the girl was pulling down her arm.

'I'll put everything into a bag for you and leave it right here under the bed. Don't worry.'

Margie gave up, and let her arms go limp. She couldn't stop them; she'd have to wait until they'd gone. When the girl had finished, Margie took a quick peek – ah, the man called Steve was coming back.

'The doctor's on his way.' He took her hand in both of his.

Margie sniffed. Her Ned had done that too.

He was smiling into her eyes. A charmer, he was, just like her Ned. 'Tell me your name, my love. We'll be able to help you better if we can look at your records.'

That was what he thought. 'Don't have any.'

'Do you have any in Ireland? Where are you from?'

'Bantry. And soon as I've found my girls, I'll be going back.'

'Can we phone them for you? Who do you live with?'

Ha – he knew nothing. 'My girls and boys.'

'Lovely – are they your grandchildren?'

'Over the sea and far away, they are.'

She was babbling. That wouldn't help her find Bridie. Bridie, who'd gone and come back again and was lost for the second time. Margie screwed up her face, clutching her chest as the beeps from somewhere close by became faster and faster and once again the world faded away.

DAY THIRTY-TWO – MONDAY 18TH MAY (MORNING)

CHAPTER 38

Mammy wasn't here. She hadn't been here last night either, when Evie went to bed. Demelza had come to cuddle her to sleep, not Mammy, and Evie had cried because it wasn't nice here when Mammy wasn't home. And Daddy still hadn't come.

She stood in the kitchen, watching the cats as they rushed around making sure they'd found the last bite of breakfast. Was Mammy cross with her? They'd been naughty yesterday, her and Frith – Frith's mummy had called, and Mammy had called, but they'd stayed quiet as mice in the den, waiting for Tabitha to come and eat the chicken. But then when Frith went home and Evie went back to the house, Mammy wasn't there. She'd waited and waited but Mammy didn't come home. It was lonely when you were all alone. Tabitha was still lost, too.

Evie rubbed two tears away and swallowed hard. This wasn't a nice kitchen, was it, and with Mammy gone it was worse. When was Daddy coming? She went back upstairs to check that Mammy really wasn't there, in her room or in the bathroom, but everywhere was as empty as it had been before breakfast. And the bath still had smelly water in it.

Evie trailed over to her bedroom window. You could see all the bushes in her garden and Frith's from here, but nobody would ever guess there were dens underneath. What was she going to do, here all alone?

It wasn't as sunny today. Evie pulled a jumper over her T-shirt and went outside – Frith might be out playing. Most of the cats were out in the garden too. Evie pushed her way through the bushes to the fence, but there was still no sign of Frith. Would Tabitha be in the den today? Evie ducked back and into the den, but apart from Ermintrude in the big box, it was empty, so she climbed in beside Ermie to wait. She felt all choky and horrible inside.

'Bridie! Are you out?'

Frith! Evie jumped up and rushed through the jungle. Frith was there at the fence with half an apple in each hand. She gave one to Evie and they stood munching.

Frith made a face. 'Mummy was cross yesterday because I didn't come back when she called. I'm not allowed to watch TV today. Was your mammy cross too?'

'I think so. She went away. And my daddy's not here yet, and nor is Tabitha.'

'Where did your mammy go?'

'I don't know. I looked everywhere, but she's not in the house.'

'Did you look in the loft? We have a loft here.'

The loft? Evie wrinkled her nose. 'I don't know.'

'You're so funny – how can you not know? Let's go and look.'

Marmaduke was scratching away in the grass when they ran past to the back door, and Evie pulled Frith well away from him. It didn't do to upset Marmaduke when he was busy.

She stepped up into the kitchen. 'Mammy?'

Nothing, and it was an empty kind of nothing, not like it was when Mammy was sitting quietly in the living room stroking one of the cats. Evie opened the big cupboard, but of course Mammy wasn't in there, and she wasn't in the living room or the hall cupboard either.

Frith started up the stairs. 'Let's look up here, and we can see if you have a loft, too.'

Evie followed, but Mammy wasn't here, was she? And no one had ever said anything about a loft. She didn't even know what that was. She stood on the landing while Frith opened each door in turn then stared up at the ceiling.

'No loft. Your bathroom's yukky.'

Evie didn't know what to say. It was true. You could smell the bathroom as soon as you came up the stairs, but she didn't know what to do about it. 'My other house was much nicer.'

'What other house?'

'Where I lived before, with Mummy and Daddy.'

'Why don't you live there any longer?'

'They went to Spain, I think, or Ireland. I had a bad arm and Mammy was looking after me.' Evie clutched at the one bright thing she knew. 'But Mammy said Daddy's coming home, and he'll bring Mummy with him. They might be back now.'

Mummy and Daddy might be in their lovely kitchen or the living room, drinking coffee and—

Evie sat down on the top stair and buried her head in her knees. Everything was horrible here without Mammy and she was all alone and Frith didn't understand because she had a lovely mummy still with her. Evie glowered at Frith, who was checking in the airing cupboard now. Frith had a yellow T-shirt with a sparkly unicorn on the front, and where were all Evie's own nice clothes and her Pooh bear and her – everything?

Frith came and sat down beside her and put an arm around her. 'Don't be sad. Where is your other house?'

'It's in Albert Drive' Mummy had made her learn that.

'Is that far? Did you come here in the car?'

Evie frowned. How had she come here? There was a car, wasn't there – but then she and Mammy had walked in the rain, but it was a long time ago and she didn't remember exactly.

'I think we walked.'

'Maybe your mammy's gone to see them and then they'll come back and get you?'

Evie sniffed. All, all she wanted was to find Mummy and have a lovely big cuddle on the sofa and hold on tight and never let go again. Mammy said Daddy was coming, and that was yesterday or the day before that, so he must be back by this time. She stood up.

'I'm going to find my other house. Are you coming?'

Frith's eyes were round as saucers. 'That's running away.'

'No, it's not. I'm going home. And we might find Mammy.'

'P'rhaps she's gone to the shops.'

Evie screwed up her face. Mammy might have gone to the shops, she did that quite often. When she did, she went down the path then walked up the hill. It couldn't be far because Mammy didn't walk fast and she was never away for long.

'I'll look there first. Come on!' It was better now she had something to do.

Downstairs, Demelza and Socks were in the kitchen, and oh, she still hadn't found Tabitha. Evie stopped. The little baby kitties were coming soon. But if she found Mammy as well as Mummy and Daddy, that would be all right, wouldn't it?

'Bridie, I don't think we should go away. Mummy'll be cross all over again.'

Evie opened the back door. 'I'm going anyway.'

She stepped past Daisy, stopping to stroke the soft little head. Frith was still rooted in the kitchen.

A voice called from next door. 'Little girl!'

Oh, no, it was the bad cross woman. She was standing in her back garden with her hands on her hips and her mouth was all squashed up and she was frowning. Quick, quick, away!

Evie scurried round to the front of the house, not looking to see if Frith was coming too, and out onto the pavement. There weren't any cars driving on this road, but there was a bigger one up at the top of the hill and some cars were going along there, quite fast, and a bus.

'Bridie! Wait!'

Frith was coming after all! Bridie waited while Frith hurried up the hill. The cross neighbour was nowhere to be seen.

'Is that lady gone?'

Frith stopped beside her. 'She went back inside. Where are you going, 'xactly?'

'Mammy goes up here to the shops. Come on!'

Evie grabbed Frith's hand, and on they went. It was better now she wasn't alone. They were nearly at the top of the hill when she stopped short. Yes! The houses on the other side of the big road they were coming to were different from the houses where Mammy lived, much more like her old house. This must be the right way.

Frith was pulling at her arm again.

'I don't think we should go so far. I'm not allowed to.'

Evie wasn't allowed to go away either, not by Mummy and Daddy or Mammy. But she'd explain when she found Mummy or Mammy again, and it would be all right, wouldn't it? And if Mummy was back, then she could go home properly and they could visit Mammy and the cats and that would be lovely.

'We'll only go a little way along. I'm sure it's here somewhere. It must be.'

Evie grabbed Frith's hand and ran on.

CHAPTER 39

They were kind to her here, but she had to go home. Margie sighed as yet another stranger arrived by the bed – why was she in bed? She wasn't ill, was she? No, a lovely floaty, dreamy feeling was washing all the way through her, like lying on an air mattress bobbing on the ocean in Bantry Bay.

A new nurse was leaning over her. 'Hello, my love. Are you going to tell us your name? Go on, then.'

Aha. An Irish accent, but not the same as Margie's and not to be trusted. She was from the North, this one. Margie closed her mouth stubbornly. The nurse pulled over a trolley and started to wash her.

'Let's get you all nice and clean and ready for a cuppa. Would you like that?'

A cuppa sounded good. Margie peeked through half-closed eyes as the nurse chatted on.

'Will Aiden be in to see you today?'

Ach, her Aiden. Such a long time ago…

'No.'

'Is he your oldest, then? How many do you have?'

'Two boys and two girls, I had.'

'Where are they now, my love?'

Over the sea and far away, and Bridie was gone, was gone. No – that was wrong; she was looking for Bridie, and she had to find her, too, poor maid. Margie jerked upright and tried to swing her legs out of bed.

The nurse laid her back on the pillows. 'You stay right here, my love. We have to take care of you, you know. Where does your Aiden live? What's his other name?'

'Donohoe.' It slipped out before Margie had time to think.

The nurse dabbed her brow with the towel and smoothed the bedclothes over Margie's chest.

'There we are. You have a rest, and I'll bring you a cuppa in a moment. Milk and sugar?'

Margie's eyes followed the nurse as she went over to a desk. She was talking to the young man, the nice one who'd been here before. They were looking over at her. Fear settled heavily in Margie's gut, and she coughed. She shouldn't have told them her name. She shouldn't have told them any names.

But it didn't matter.

They wouldn't find Bridie, would they? Bridie would stay at home where she was safe, and she'd look after the kits, too. She was a good girl, Bridie. And Tabitha. Oh, she wanted her girls. Margie jerked bolt upright in bed, and a beep came from somewhere overhead as her chest tightened. Both nurses rushed over.

'Nice and easy, my love. I'm Steve, I was here last night, remember?' He muttered to the nurse on the other side of the bed. 'Give Davie a call, would you? And see if you can track down her son, now we have a surname too.'

The Irish nurse made a face. 'Long shot.'

'It's the best shot we've got.' He bent over Margie. 'Tell us your first name, love. It would make things easier.'

Oh, no, it wouldn't.

CHAPTER 40

Liane pressed her foot on the vacuum cleaner control, and the cable whirred back in. Monday morning, ten fifteen, housework, box ticked. The weather wasn't being cooperative, though – those clouds were getting ever darker. A rainy-day programme might be the best thing. A visit to the Art Gallery after lunch? Frithy loved the dinosaur skeletons and stuffed animals there. Or the transport museum? She would let her daughter choose. Liane stuffed the vacuum back into the hall cupboard and went through to the kitchen. Coffee time.

The garden was silent, so the girls were either lurking in Frithy's den in the jungle, or at Bridie's. Liane glared at the empty patio and back lawn. It didn't feel comfortable, not being able to see her child, but she'd have to get used to letting go a little. And after yesterday's lecture and TV ban, Miss Frith would come the moment she was called today, you could bet on that. Liane jabbed buttons on the machine and breathed in deeply as the coffee-aroma wafted across the kitchen. Should she take little packets of Smarties out to Frith and Bridie? She pulled a face. Admit it, Liane, that's nothing but an excuse to make sure Frithy was still alive and breathing. And an afternoon out was enough of a treat for her bad daughter today, anyway. She would pop down the garden and have a listen, though. Just to make sure.

The jungle was devoid of little girls, and Frith's den was empty. Liane stood at the fence. Nothing was moving on the other side, and no ghostly giggles from unseen children were echoing around Bridie's jungle. Gawd. Okay, she was being a thoroughly neurotic mother, but so what?

'Frithy! You there?'

Silence.

'Frith! Come here a second, please!'

Silence. And stillness. The hairs on the back of Liane's neck stood to attention.

'*Frith!* Answer me, please. I'm counting to ten!'

Nothing. Liane swung round and ran back to the house. It was possible, yes, it was distinctly possible that Frith had come back in while she'd been vacuuming. It was a chilly day, and if Bridie wasn't out to play there wouldn't be much to keep Frith outside either.

'Frith!' Her yell rang through the house; even old Mr Jenkins next door, who was almost stone deaf, must have heard that. Deep silence was coming from upstairs, but Liane went up anyway and found two empty bedrooms and a deserted loo. Okay. Don't panic. It wasn't a particularly good day out – the girls must have gone into Bridie's house to play. Frithy'd told her they might go into Bridie's garden, hadn't she, so she might not feel she needed to report back because they were going into the house.

Margie's garden was silent as Liane pushed through the gap in the fence and picked her way through the jungle and across the grass on her neighbour's side, seeds from dandelion clocks floating free as she brushed against them. Marmaduke the orange cat was lying on the kitchen window ledge, and three others were sprawled by the door.

A voice came from the left. 'Mrs, ah, Morton, isn't it?'

It was Margie's posh neighbour. Heck, what was her name again? McGarry, that was it. The woman was standing at the fence clutching a large cardboard box, outrage all over her face. Liane swerved over to the fence. Not the moment to point out she was Ms – or Miss – Morton.

Mrs McGarry thrust the box towards Liane. 'Look! This is the last straw. This creature has made the most almighty mess in my shed.'

'Oh! Tabitha – and her kittens! I guess.' Liane gaped at the cat, who was glaring back at her as only a cat could. A wonder she'd stayed in the box to be lugged around like this, but the three tiny kittens – one still wet – would be the reason for that. What a horror this woman was, moving the animal at this time.

Liane didn't stop the chilly tone from entering her voice. 'I thought cats were pretty clean about giving birth? You should have left her where she was. Margie could have collected them later. I'll take them inside.' She grasped the box, and Mrs McG let go like a shot.

The other woman sniffed. 'Mrs Donohoe's – granddaughter, I suppose she is, was running round to the front gate not half an hour ago. You should be more careful who you let your daughter play with.' She about-turned and strode back to her shed, presumably to start deep cleaning it.

Liane murmured soothingly to Tabitha, who was still wearing a scandalised expression, and glided as smoothly as she could to the back door. By the time she got there, four other cats were milling around her feet.

Liane knocked softly, in case a loud thump disturbed poor Tabitha even more than she was already. No answer. Bummer. The niggle of fear was back. Liane tried the door – hallelujah, it wasn't locked. She pushed it open.

'Anyone home?' Liane stepped inside with the box and stood still.

Oh. My. Gosh. The kitchen smelled of cats and to say it was uncared for was the understatement of the century. The floor was filthy, with bowls dotted around, presumably for the cats, and the amount of stuff piled across the work surfaces was incredible. The place looked as if Margie had spent the last month taking things out of cupboards and not putting them back. Empty boxes of cat food were lying around among dirty, empty tins of various things. Bowls, cutlery and cups were spread all over the place, used ones mingling with clean. Liane's shoulders slumped. Her poor neighbour – was all this because Margie wasn't well? Guilt stabbed Liane – she should have checked on the woman again.

'Margie! It's Liane from over the garden. I've got Tabitha here with her kittens. Is Frith with you?' Silence. Liane slid the box with Tabitha and her family into the bottom of the nearest cupboard and left the door open a few centimetres. There. Privacy for Tabitha for as long as she wanted it. Now to find her daughter, and it was sounding mighty quiet in this house.

'Frith! Are you here?'

Nothing. Could Margie have taken the girls to the shops? Without asking, that would be a bit much. The cats had all followed her inside and were milling around her legs and miaowing, so Liane filled one of the bowls with water – the sink was as bad as the floor – and set it down. Several cats pounced on it, so she filled another to stop a riot, then listened again. Still nothing.

Liane came to a decision. She would check the house first, then if she didn't find the girls, she'd run up the road to the shops, and if they weren't there – she didn't know what she would do.

She strode through the kitchen into the hallway, where the carpet was thick with cat hairs and the smell matched the appearance. An ancient wicker cat bed was behind the front door, and a frayed old woollen cardigan was hanging on the stair post, a long tear visible at one shoulder. Horror choked Liane. Poor old Margie; she wasn't taking care of herself, that was clear – why the heck had Bridie's mum left her here? It was incomprehensible. The only piece of furniture in the hallway was a little table, a solitary envelope lying beneath it. Liane squinted down. The back side was uppermost, with the sender's name, but judging by the frayed edges and smudges of dirt, the cats had been playing with it. The only readable letter was a capital A. She stepped past it.

The living room furniture was old and shabby and the television was like something from the 1950s. This room, too, could be in one of those ghastly TV programmes about people deep cleaning houses. Cat hairs were everywhere, and piles of crockery, mostly mugs, lay on every available piece of furniture. Liane moved across to the window, where a knitted blanket was scrunched up, partially covering a lighter-coloured pink garment with a zip. Were all these cat beds?

A dull sound came from upstairs, and Liane's heart leaped. 'Margie? Frith?' She scuttled back to the hallway. Oh, no. Suppose Margie was ill up there, or worse? Liane clenched her fists.

'Margie? I'm coming upstairs. It's Liane, Frith's mum.' Silence from above. Liane held her arms crossed over her front as she walked upstairs and put her head into the main bedroom. An unmade bed, a wooden chair, a thick smell. The grime-covered bathroom had several inches of disgusting dirty water in the bath, which glugged and moved as Liane stood there. That was the sound she'd heard. What was presumably Bridie's room held a chest of drawers and a bed covered with two knitted blankets. There wasn't a toy in sight; oh, this was awful, poor Bridie. But this house was empty, and she had to find her girl. Move, Liane.

Outside, up the hill, fast as she could, and along the road. Heart thumping, Liane jogged towards the shops. Frith... Daria's face slid into her mind, and she moaned inwardly. But here she was at the top already.

The little row of shops only held four possibilities. Liane stuck her head into the chemist's, the minimarket, the post office and the newsagent's in turn. No Margie, no girls. The fifth shop was empty, but a poster on the boarded-up window announced a charity shop was opening there soon. Back home, quick, Liane.

It was faster going downhill. Liane thundered back into Margie's kitchen, where the same silence reigned. She grappled for her phone and called their landline. If Frithy'd gone home in between, she'd answer that. Nothing. Could Margie have taken the girls somewhere else? Surely not.

Or – oh, no. Had the girls gone to the park? Those little toughies were still around. Or – Tony?

Liane ran across the garden, connecting to Tony's phone on the way. For a wonder, he took the call.

'I can't talk now, Liane, we're in the middle of rehearsing. I'll call you back.' The connection broke.

Frith wasn't with him. It was time to get help, proper help. Liane ran across their own garden, but the silence that greeted her at the back door told its own story. She flipped her phone open again. How many times had she called 999 for an ambulance to take a blue and gasping Frith to hospital? This time: 'Police. My daughter's missing. She's four.'

The woman on the phone took details and promised help straightaway. Liane's fingers were shaking so hard she could barely make them do what she needed them to, but eventually she connected to Steve. Voicemail; he was at work. Could nothing go right today? Sobs choking her, she left a garbled message and collapsed onto a hard kitchen chair.

The police were as good as their word. Minutes later, a car drew up outside, and Liane flew to the front door. Two officers, a middle-aged man and a younger woman, were walking up the path.

'Liane Morton? Is it your girl who's missing?' The man flashed his ID at her. Sergeant David Bryson. The woman was PC Jill Summers.

Liane stood back to let them in, then took them into the living room.

'Tell us exactly what happened.'

David Bryson's face grew progressively grimmer as Liane

went through a brief account of that morning. 'Okay. We'll need more detail than that, but we'll get the search started first. I'll need a photo of Frith.'

Liane scrolled through the photos on her phone and tapped on a good one. She passed it to Jill. The sergeant was on his phone, talking to heaven knows who about her child. Liane clasped her hands to her chest, rocking back and forth on the sofa.

There was nothing more she could do now.

CHAPTER 41

The road with the buses was busy. Evie stared along it, first one way, then the other. Some of these houses were like Mummy's and Daddy's – this must be the right way. She started along the road.

Frith was pulling at her arm. 'Bridie, we should go home. My mummy would be cross if she knew I was here.'

'If we find my mummy, she can explain to yours.'

Frith's chin was wobbling. 'It might take a long time to find your mummy. We haven't even found the house yet.'

Evie blinked hard. It was true. The houses here were different nice houses, not the one she and Mummy and Daddy lived in. But she didn't want to go back to Mammy's when Mammy wasn't there.

Frith took two steps back the way they'd come. 'Oh, no! Look! Let's go.'

She pointed along the road, and Evie turned to see what was wrong. A little group of boys was coming their way. They were big boys and they were shouting in a nasty way and kicking a can along the pavement. Evie grabbed Frith's hand and they went quick quick quick back down the hill.

A lady was coming out of a gate as they were running past.

'Careful, girls. Where are you two off to so fast?'

'We're going home. Down there.' Frith pointed, then grabbed Evie's hand again and off they went.

The woman called after them. 'Better stay at home – you're too small to be out alone!'

Evie could hardly breathe for running so fast when they arrived back at Mammy's garden.

Frith made a big 'Uff!' just like Mammy. 'Shall we tell Mummy you can't find your mammy? She'd know what to do.'

Evie pulled her hand away. Mammy wouldn't like that, would she? Remember what she'd said about the shouty old lady who lived next door and was always banging on their door and being nasty. Mammy never talked to other grown-ups.

She shook her head. 'No. Mammy would be cross if we did that – maybe she's home again. I'll go in and look and you can wait in the den.' She pulled Frith up the path and gave her a little push towards the bush with the purple flowers before running to the back door.

'Mammy?' The kitchen was quiet, and Evie stood still. There was no one here, you could tell. And Mammy wasn't in the garden. Evie rushed up to the bathroom, then on the way downstairs again a noise came in from outside – sirens!

She stood still, arms crossed over her front, her eyes scrunched up. The sirens were making her tummy wobble and it was nasty. There'd been sirens before, hadn't there?

She was with Mammy somewhere, and the sirens were behind them in the rain, going to – were they going to Mummy? And her head had hurt and it was all so funny and wrong. Were these sirens going to Mummy too? Evie crouched down, hugging her tummy as huge big waves of wanting to go to Mummy washed over her. It was like jumping into the swimming pool, and all the water went everywhere, but then Mummy would catch her and it was fun again. She had to find Mummy.

Evie ran, quick as she could round the side of the house to the front gate, and peered back up the hill. The sirens were gone, but they'd been going this way, hadn't they? Up to the nice houses? She started up the hill, then stopped. Frith was waiting in the den. But this was more important. She'd go up the hill again and look along the other road, very quickly. The bad boys weren't there any longer, and Mummy would be happy when Evie came home.

Her legs were sore when she got to the top. The big road wasn't as busy now and there weren't any buses coming. Evie stood at the corner and looked downhill. Mammy's house was such a long way away down there, it was hard to see which one it was. She would go along here for two minutes and look at the nice houses to see if Mummy was back yet. Or Daddy. Evie trotted along, keeping to the inside of the pavement because Mummy always made her walk on that side because it was further away from the cars. It would be so nice when she found Mummy again and got a big squishy cuddle and smelled Mummy's lovely perfume. This must be the right way, surely. The houses along here had gardens in front of them and they all had trees and bushes, too, mostly big ones.

Evie ducked into one driveway where you couldn't see the house properly from the pavement. It wasn't her house – she'd known that, hadn't she? She was just being careful.

Was Frith still in the den? Evie crouched down by the garden wall of the house that wasn't her old one. Her legs were too tired to run.

'Hello there! Are you having a rest?'

A lady was standing on the pavement, not as old as Mammy but older than Mummy, and she was smiling.

Evie stood up. 'Yes.'

'Are you all by yourself? Is this your house?'

Evie wound one leg around the other. 'No, I live over there.' She pointed behind the old lady. 'I'm out playing with my friend. She's in our den.'

The lady moved on a step. 'That's nice. You stay in the garden, though, pet, this is a busy road.' She walked away, her shopping bag swinging in one hand. Evie waited a few minutes, then hurried on in the other direction. She was the only person going this way on the whole long pavement. An old man was across the road, walking along the other way and holding a great big grey coat around him in a funny way. He stopped and waved to Evie. And—

Another siren. Evie stood still. It wasn't far away, but it wasn't on this street. She came to another road and checked both ways before running across. It was a little street like Mammy's. And now there was another siren, and – oh! Policemen! They were walking up the other road, quite a long way away but they were coming closer.

Evie ducked into a gate and crouched behind the garden wall to think. This wasn't fun, and she still hadn't found Mummy. It might be better to go back to Mammy's and see what Frith was doing. Frith's mummy would be able to help, even if it did make Mammy cross. Yes.

She left the wall and sped back the way she'd come. Across this road, careful – and on and on and the next road was the big hill down to Mammy's house. Evie came to the corner and stopped, her hands flying to her face. Oh, no. There were policemen down there too – a lot of them, all walking about, and two police cars as well. Policemen were scary. What were they doing? She watched for a moment. They were going in gates and knocking on doors, that was what. Better stay away until they were gone.

Evie scurried across the road. Here were some shops. She stuck her head into a little one with tins and sweeties, but Mammy wasn't there and a lady was looking at her so she ran off again, past the shops and on – there were a lot of trees in the distance, like in a park. She could go there and wait for the policemen to go away again. There might be swings, too.

Three men were coming this way on the pavement, all laughing and pushing each other, so Evie ducked into another garden and hid behind a bush until they were past. The park was after the next lamp post. She slid through the big black iron gate and stood looking around, then walked slowly along the path. This wasn't a park, though. It was the place they brought the dead people to bury them, and then other people brought flowers to remember. They'd gone past in the car one day and Mummy had told her all about it. Evie walked on slowly. She'd been in here once before, hadn't she? With Mammy. There were a lot of flowers, and some big stones standing up with writing on them. Some of the stones weren't standing straight, and the ones over on the other side were very old. She came to a little path between a row of old stones and hesitated. It was better on the big path, but further along there was – oh, no, it was the same old man who'd waved at her before. Evie scuttled into the smaller pathway and walked along looking at the old stones. There weren't many flowers here, so maybe the people buried here had no one to remember them. That was sad. The trees were nice, though, and there was a great big one with floppy branches in the middle. She'd go and look at that in a minute – oh! What was that?

It was like music, except it wasn't. Evie crept further along the pathway.

DAY THIRTY-TWO – MONDAY 18TH MAY (AFTERNOON)

CHAPTER 42

Everything was fuzzy and far, far away. Margie screwed up her eyes – it was still too bright here. The voices around her had gone funny too, sometimes right up in her ear, sometimes so distant she could barely hear them. It wasn't unpleasant, more the sensation of something unravelling. Where was she? Where was Ned? And, oh, her Bridie. Her darlin' girl. This was no use; it was time to go back to Bantry Bay and sit on the beach, yes.

The light and the voices faded as Margie sank into the dream. Looking out over the sea, the wind in her hair and high-pitched small voices all around as happy children splashed and shrieked. Her Ned, his arm slung around her, pulling her close to steal a kiss. This was heaven.

'Hello, my love. Want a drink?' A hand was gripping hers, and Margie opened her eyes, shaking her head slowly. This wasn't heaven; she was in hospital, she remembered now. But why? Everything was fine. Truth to tell, she hadn't felt this good for a long time. The young man was nice; eyes like her Ned's, he had. Was this Aiden? He had his daddy's eyes. But no, Aiden was over the sea and far away. When would she see him again?

But she wouldn't, not in this life.

Stark certainty chilled her to her bones, and Margie's moan came straight from her soul. She wasn't long for the world. Would death come here, in this warm, soft place where the voices around her were kind? She moved her head to see more. The young man called Steve had pulled up a chair by her bed. That was nice. She tried to smile at him.

'What's your name, love? Is there anyone at home we could get in to be with you?'

Home was Ireland. And Bridie, where was she? She'd left Bridie – no, she was looking for Bridie.

'Find my girl.'

'We're trying to find your Aiden. What's your girl called?'

'Daisy. And Ermie. Find all my girls and boys.'

'I'll get someone onto that for you. Are they in Ireland? No? Here in Glasgow? We should be able to find someone, then. You hang on for me.'

A buzzing noise was coming from his pocket. He fumbled with something – and then he was gone again. Like Bridie, he was, here one minute, gone the next.

And the fog was everywhere and the waves were crashing on the beach and her lips were salty from the spray. Her Ned, her Bridie, they were there and they were waiting. And oh, it hurt her cheeks to smile.

The young man was back. He was frowning, but he took her hand in his again.

'We're looking for Daisy now and Nurse Stella's coming to see you too. You know, the one from Ireland.'

Ireland. But Daisy wasn't in Ireland, and neither was—

'Find my li'l baby girl.'

'We're trying to find someone for you, my love. Can you tell me your name?'

Darkness was hovering. 'Margaret. Margaret and Ned.' They'd made their vows to be man and wife, and they had been. He was the only one for her, her Ned.

'Okay, Margaret.'

Her eyes were closing and she couldn't stop them, but the hands enclosing hers were warm. Margie held on for dear life. The world was moving, far away into the distance then swooping up close. The fog lifted for a second.

'Find Bridie. And Daisy and Topsy. And Tabitha and her kits, all my babies.'

'Bridie? Kits?'

The young man was squeezing her hand, just like her Ned had.

'My baby girl.'

He was stroking her head, and the world was leaving her. Or she was leaving the world. Her Ned, her Ned was waiting, with her darlin' li'l Bridie.

'Don't worry, my love. We'll find your girls. I'll look after them for you.'

His voice faded as the rushing in her ears started, the sound of the sea. It was everywhere. Her Ned was holding her hand, so warm and firm. Summer sunshine was chasing the darkness, everything was light and airy and she was floating, away, away into brightness and she'd never be back, she'd never be—

Time of death, 13.47.

CHAPTER 43

Liane banged her phone down on the kitchen table. That was the second time she'd tried to call Steve, but his phone was still off. There had to be a way to contact him in an emergency. Or didn't newish partners count as people who were allowed to interrupt him? If they'd been married it would have been different. Or if he'd been Frith's dad.

There were more police officers here than she could count, and she'd given them every last detail about Frith's short life that might be relevant. 'All' she had to do was wait in the kitchen with PC Jill, who was evidently there to look after her – or perhaps to make sure she didn't do anything dodgy? The police had gone through the entire house looking for God knows what before departing outside. They were going up and down the street now, searching for Frith and Bridie, and Margie too, though whether they were all together was anyone's guess.

Her mobile buzzed on the table, and she scrabbled to connect. Steve, at last.

'I'm sorry, Liane, but I was with an old lady who was dying. I'm wondering—'

'Frith's disappeared. I'm scared, Steve. It isn't Tony this time. She seems to have run off and – can you come?'

'Oh, no. I'll be with you ASAP. Have you called the—'

'They're here now.'

'Hold on, love. I'll be right with you.'

Liane ended the call and sat panting, fighting for control. Having the police here taking everything so seriously made it all so horribly real.

Jill was making tea. 'Here you are. Drink that, it'll help.'

No, it wouldn't, but at least it was hot. Liane sat with icy hands cupped around the mug until Steve arrived. He came straight in without ringing the bell, and she staggered over to him. He smelled of hospitals.

'Oh, Steve. The police are asking round all the houses nearby. If they don't find her, they'll start a larger search.'

He grabbed her, and she held on tightly, the beat of his heart pulsating against her face.

'She must be somewhere, love. We'll get her back. She'll be engrossed in her game again and not listening for shouts.'

Oh, no, she wouldn't. Liane dropped down at the table again, and Steve pulled a chair up close and sat hugging her.

'Again? Has this happened before?' Jill leaned forward.

Liane's hands were in constant motion. 'Once – she didn't come straightaway when I called her. I think she was testing the boundaries after being sickly for so long. She and Bridie, they have dens in the gardens and—' Liane came to a halt. 'I'm babbling.'

Jill reached for her phone. 'I'll pass that on, and about the dens too, but they'll be searching the gardens, don't worry.'

Steve took Liane's hand, gazing up at the police officer. 'Wait, this might need passing on too. Liane, the old lady who died in the A&E short-term ward today – she was brought in yesterday, but she wouldn't give a name right up until the last moment when she said Margaret. I'm wondering if she might have been Margie. She talked about an Aiden, and her kits, and just at the end she mentioned Bridie and Daisy. If it was Margie, then no one's living over there now. Frith and Bridie would be out alone.'

Jill got to her feet. 'Can you find out if your old lady's been identified yet, please?' She moved out to the hall and started calling in the new information.

Liane held Steve's hand while he had a short conversation with someone at the hospital before ending the call. Apparently, the old woman's identity still wasn't clear.

He put his phone on the table. 'They're going to send a pic of her clothes – we'll see if you recognise them.'

Liane frowned. It seemed unnecessarily complicated. 'Can't they send a photo of her?'

'They might to the police, but not to me. She still has patient confidentiality.'

Did it matter, when the woman was dead? Liane jumped as another call came into her phone. Daria. This wasn't what she needed.

'Hi, Liane, I'm wondering if you've found a gold chain bracelet? I lost one yesterday but – what's wrong?'

A sob escaped as Liane tried to control her breathing. 'Frith's gone missing. Bridie too. And Margie might be dead.'

'Oh, no. You must be out of your mind. Let me know if I can do anything. I'll call you another time.'

Liane was left listening to a silent phone. What if she never saw Frith again? How did Daria cope?

Jill came back in. 'Our officers have spoken to some people who noticed the girls on the street this morning, heading up the hill, and someone else saw a dark-haired child alone later on. It's looking hopeful they're in the area.'

Liane forced back a sob. She needed more than 'hopeful'. A few minutes later Steve's phone vibrated. He seized it and tapped, then held it out to Liane.

'Here you go. Do you think these could be Margie's?'

The pair of trousers could have been anyone's. It was impossible to see details on the photo. Steve swiped to the next image, and Liane grabbed his arm.

'Yes! That's her pullover – she was wearing it the other day. I remember the baggy neckline. And—' She used her thumb and finger to enlarge the image. 'Look how frayed it is, too. Oh, no – she's dead?'

Liane leaned against Steve. How unreal this all was; her whole body was raw with pain. In the course of an hour, her life had morphed from Frith hiding, to her little girl being lost or abducted. A shiver ran straight through Liane's gut – there'd been those young hooligans in the park recently. Okay, there was a difference between pinching a little kid's skateboard and physically harming her, but if some idiot scared Frith even a tiny bit... Shuddering, Liane pressed the heels of her hands on her eyes. She was one of those mothers you saw on the news on TV, with shiny, blotchy faces, grief and horror etched in every pore and wearing God knows what. She was a member of the sisterhood no one wanted to join, condemned because she hadn't watched her child every second of every hour. Her stomach heaved and she fled from the room, hearing Steve tell Jill to leave her for a moment. Bless him.

Liane vomited into the downstairs loo, then leaned against the basin, panting. A knock on the door, and Steve was behind her. He filled a glass with water and handed it over.

'Hold on, Liane. It's all we can do.'

She stood there, rinsing and spitting while he leaned against the wall, one hand on her back. For four years, she'd been there for Frith, through three ops and countless procedures, with loving, reassuring words on her lips and terror in her heart. She'd managed that, but this was so much harder. It wasn't true that watching someone you loved go through hell was the most difficult thing you'd ever do. Not being able to watch was ten times worse, a million times worse, and where was her baby?

Steve passed her a towel, and Liane pressed it to her cheeks.

'I'm all right.' She wasn't, but he'd know what she meant.

The back door crashed open. 'Mummy!'

Oh, my days. Liane raced out and Frith flew into her arms, panic streaming from every cell in her body.

'Mummy! Bridie went away and she didn't come back to the den and Margie's got lost too and there are policemen in all the gardens and I'm scared, Mummy, what's happening?'

Liane sank to her knees in the middle of the kitchen with Frith in her arms. Her baby. She had her girl back and whatever had happened, Frith was okay. Shaking, agitated, but she was here and no one had hurt her… and oh, thank you, thank you. She cradled the little girl, inhaling deeply. Frith was panting against her chest, her hot little head pressed into Liane's neck.

'Frithy, where did Bridie go? It's important we find her because, um, Margie's in hospital. That's why the police are here, we need to find Bridie to help her.'

'Margie's in hospital?' Frith's mouth and eyes were round Os of astonishment and dismay. 'Who's going to look after Bridie? And the cats?'

Jill pulled a chair up beside them. 'That's what we have to organise.'

In two minutes, Jill had the story from Frith – the trip up to the main road and back, and Bridie going inside and not coming back – then went out to the hall to call the news in. Liane stroked Frith's back; the poor kid was trembling. And, oh, heck, poor Bridie. Looking for her mammy, and all the time Margie was dying in hospital.

Twenty minutes later, Sergeant Bryson knocked on the back door and came in holding three clear plastic bags containing what might be grimy rags from Margie's house. His expression was grim – what did that mean?

He came inside and sat down. 'We've been in Margie Donohoe's. Did you know it's in a state?'

'Yes. I went in this morning to look for Frith.'

'We've found several things that could be Bridie's – we need something for the dogs to scent. Can you tell me if she's worn any of these clothes recently?'

Liane kept hold of Frith's arm. 'Look, but don't touch, sweetie. Did Bridie have anything here on this weekend?'

Frith leaned over, and together they stared at the bags. One held a truly ancient pair of cotton trousers and a T-shirt, another a filthy pink jacket. Liane peered at the washing label on the jacket: *Lavado a máquina 30°.*

Sergeant Bryson was looking too. 'Does the family have any connection to Spain, do you know?'

Liane and Frith both spoke at once.

'I don't think—'

'Bridie's mummy goes to Spain a lot. And Bridie was wearing that T-shirt yesterday.'

The sergeant smiled. 'Good girl. That's what we need to know.'

CHAPTER 44

Daria slid her glass into the dishwasher and swung through to Kit's living room, where her phone was on the coffee table. Everything was so hard, so impossible. Thinking over and over about Evie and her death and what life would be without her – she would go mad if she went on like this.

So, this was the end of the road. She would make today the first day of the rest of this new life she'd never wished for, and it was up to her to make it a success. She lifted her phone and connected to the GP surgery.

'It's Daria Geddes here. My little girl died in a road accident a few weeks ago, and I'd like to organise bereavement counselling. How should I go about it?'

'Mrs Geddes, yes.' Keyboard sounds punctuated the woman's voice. 'I can give you an appointment to see the nurse here, and she'll go over your options with you. Would Wednesday at ten o'clock suit you?'

Daria accepted. There. She had taken a step towards

facing tomorrow. She lifted a magazine and leafed through it, then flung it back on the coffee table, the brief burst of positivity over.

It didn't matter what she did, the constant Evie-ache was still pulling at her heart – and now there was Frith, too. Frith's smiling face slid into her mind, and Daria reached for her crutches. It was awful when you were het up and worried, and couldn't pace around the room like you were itching to. Would Liane let her know if Frith was found? She got up and went to the window overlooking the botanic gardens. A young family with two little boys on scooters were heading for the park gates. Daria swallowed hard. She and Noah would have brought Evie here too, if things had been different.

It was nearly an hour since she'd called Liane. A quick text to find out how the search was going; she could do that. Now she knew how people had felt about calling her after Evie's death. It was hard to find the right line between being concerned and being too familiar.

She sat down again with her phone, her heart beating faster – but it had beaten faster still for Evie, hadn't it? *Any news yet? xx*

The phone rang almost before Daria had drawn breath. 'Sorry, Daria – she's found. I should have let you know.'

Liane's voice was brittle – something still wasn't right.

'Is she hurt?'

'No, she's fine. She and Bridie went walkabout, then came back to their den, but Bridie's gone missing again. And it seems that Margie who she was living with, her grandmother…'

Liane's voice dropped on the next few words, and Daria pressed her phone to her ear.

'… passed away today, in hospital.'

'Oh, no. Liane, I know you have lots of closer friends, but – I mean – can I do anything?'

There was silence for a few seconds, and Daria flinched. The two of them were more acquaintances than friends nowadays, and Liane had Steve there to help; he and Frith were talking in the background.

Liane's voice was still low. 'If you could come round, it might be helpful, thanks, Daria. Most people are at work, and they – the police – are looking for Margie's relatives, but I may have to go to the hospital later, you know, for, um, Margie, and I'd like Steve with me if I do.'

Daria flinched. Identifying your dead neighbour, how terrible. 'Of course I can come and stay with Frith. I'll be with you in quarter of an hour.'

Daria rang off and ordered a taxi. Rain was spotting the windows as they drove across the city. She gazed out glumly. That poor little girl, out all alone, lost and maybe panicking. It was an odd story about the grandmother in hospital, though. Why had nobody helped the child?

Steve opened the door when Daria arrived at Liane's. 'Good to see you, Daria. Come in.'

He ushered her into the living room, where a young woman in police uniform was sitting on an armchair while Liane and Frith were on the sofa, Liane with a white face and Frith absorbed in an iPad.

Daria sat down carefully in the other armchair and laid her crutches on the floor. Liane grimaced at her. 'Still no Bridie. Coffee?'

Steve was on his feet already. 'I'll make it. Milk and sugar, Jill?'

The police officer got up too. 'I'll give you a hand.'

'Can I have an ice lolly? Please?' Frith put the iPad on the arm of the sofa, then rushed out when Liane nodded.

Daria stretched out her legs. 'Have you heard from the hospital yet?'

'No. I'm really hoping I won't have to identify poor Margie. Her house is in a dreadful state, you know, she obviously hasn't cleaned it properly for months and there are cats every— oh, my gosh, I'd forgotten about Tabitha. I left her in a cupboard with a boxful of brand-new kittens.' Liane passed her hand over her eyes. 'Don't say anything to Frith, huh?'

Daria nodded. 'We always had cats when I was little. A nice peaceful cupboard sounds about right for new kittens. I wouldn't worry.'

Frith arrived back with a lurid green ice lolly, followed by Jill carrying a tray. Daria sipped her coffee, then admired Frith's prowess shooting beans on the iPad. It was bittersweet, having a child leaning on the arm of her chair, showing her something and chatting away solemnly. A lump came to Daria's throat when Frith broke off in the middle to ask Liane when they'd find Bridie. The little frown on her face was so like Evie's expression when she'd been worried about something. Deep breath, Daria.

The sound of the doorbell made them all jump. Jill went to answer it, and returned with a tall police officer.

Frith whispered in Daria's ear, her eyes wide. 'That's Sergeant Bryson. He's looking for Bridie.'

Daria rubbed the child's skinny shoulders.

'And I hope we'll find her soon.' Sergeant Bryson was

staring meaningfully at Steve. 'Could someone take Frith through to the kitchen for a while?'

Steve and Frith trooped out, and Daria turned her attention to the police officer beside Liane on the sofa. He'd have said if he'd wanted her out too, so presumably this was something general, just not for Frith's ears. He was holding a clear plastic bag which he deposited on the floor by his feet, and—

Daria's body froze, then she lurched up and took two painful steps across the room. She swept the plastic bag into her arms, a silent scream tearing from her throat. This was – but it couldn't be – how was this possible? Shaking all over, she stretched out one hand to Liane, her mouth working.

Liane was beside her in a second. 'Daria?'

The world swam, then everything went black.

A VOICE WAS TALKING in the distance. Daria moved her head – something rough was scratching her cheek. She opened her eyes and blinked. She was lying on the floor, Steve's concerned face only a foot from hers.

His fingers were on her wrist. 'You're okay. You passed out. Lie still for a bit, huh?'

Daria lay until he let go her wrist, then she struggled to sit up. Still on the floor, she leaned back against the sofa, breathing raggedly. Liane and Frith were nowhere to be seen, but the police officer was perching on the armchair, the plastic bag on his lap.

Daria pointed at it. 'That's – that's Evie's jacket.'

'Evie?' Sergeant Bryson frowned at her.

Daria opened her mouth to explain, but this scowling

policeman – how could she tell him about the devastation in her life when his mind was firmly focussed on another child? She motioned to Steve, who summarised the accident and Evie's death into one sentence while Daria sat limply, fighting to get her head back together. With an effort, she pulled herself up onto the sofa.

Sergeant Bryson was making notes. Daria couldn't take her eyes from the jacket. Ice chilled around her soul as shivers vibrated through her body. It was Evie's, definitely Evie's. The last time she'd seen this was moments before the accident. Daria's stomach cramped, and she choked back the bile that rose in her throat.

Sergeant Bryson glared at the jacket. 'And Evie was wearing this? How can you tell it's hers and not another the same style?'

Daria stammered in her haste to get the words out. 'My parents live in Spain, they sent this last year.'

Sergeant Bryson shook the bag around, peering into it. Daria needed all her self-restraint not to grab the jacket and hug it to her heart. This was madness. Evie'd been wearing that jacket in the minicab. Or – had she? Daria bent double over her knees, her body shaking. How impossible it was to find even a microsecond of the crash in her memory. Had Evie been wearing the jacket, or had she taken it off during the drive to the airport? Daria pressed her hands together. Suppose she'd been holding the jacket – it could have been thrown out along with her and picked up by anyone. Daria's mind sharpened. Think, woman. It was perfectly possible Margie had walked past sometime on her way to the main road, seen the abandoned jacket and taken it for her granddaughter. Another little girl had worn Evie's jacket.

'Right.' Sergeant Bryson poked at the bag. 'That's not enough for us to be sure this was Evie's jacket, and even if it is, we still have to find out how it got here.'

Was he doubting the jacket was Evie's? Daria grappled for her phone. 'I have a photo of her wearing it. There's a mark on one sleeve.' She scrolled though photos; Evie laughing over a game, Evie in the bath, Evie blowing out birthday candles. Here it was, Evie in the park with her pink jacket. The usual agony poured into Daria's heart. She might get Evie's jacket back, but what did a scrap of material matter when her child was gone forever?

Liane came running downstairs. 'Frith's playing in her room. What's happening? Are you okay, Daria?' She sat down heavily on the sofa, glancing at the photo on Daria's phone.

'Is that…? But – oh my *God*!'

Daria jumped in fright as Liane clapped one hand over her mouth and stretched her other hand out to Steve.

'Steve, oh, no – look.'

Daria almost dropped her mobile. 'Liane? What are you—'

Liane's hand was shaking as she pointed to the photo on the phone. 'That's Bridie. Isn't it, Steve? I don't understand.'

Daria clasped her hands together. The world was revolving around her and she was deadly still and quiet in the centre of it all. Her breathing was calm now, calm as death. The accident. The forgotten crash. And then… she'd heard a child cry; she'd been so sure it was Evie. If Margie was passing and saw Evie on the ground…

Was it even remotely possible that Bridie was Evie?

Daria moaned, pressing both hands against her chest, oh,

she was so full here; she was bursting with the hope and the horror of it all. Her wonderful, sweet Evie with a frail, sick old lady in a house that was 'in a state', for weeks and weeks? No, no, please, that mustn't be. But what was she *talking* about, of course she hoped with all her heart that Evie'd been there in filth and squalor all this time because that would mean Evie was Bridie, and Bridie was alive.

But where was she?

Liane was crying quietly, and Steve put his arm around her. 'Daria – do you want to call Noah?' His eyes met hers over the top of Liane's head.

Noah? No, no. Not yet, not until there was definite news. 'Later.'

Sergeant Bryson plucked the phone from Daria's hand. 'We'll need that photo.' He strode out to the hallway to talk on his own phone, his deep voice droning as he paced up and down, but Daria couldn't make out what he was saying. She leaned forward, her elbows on her thighs and her head resting in her hands. Upstairs, Frith shrieked for her mother, and Liane ran, leaving Daria alone with Steve and Jill. Her stomach was churning furiously.

Frith's high-pitched voice floated downstairs, saying something about Daddy, and Daria's throat closed in grief and frustration. Her child had been here in this district, in Liane's garden, all this time, and no one had known.

What would have been going through her girl's head all these weeks? Daria bit down on her lower lip and tasted blood. A month was an eternity at that age. Evie might have been concussed, confused, she might think she *was* Bridie, she might think Margie was her true family. Perhaps she didn't remember her real home. And that was before you even began to think about how she might have been injured in the accident. All these unknowns, too many of them. And where *was* she?

Panic rose in a huge wave and broke over Daria. If she didn't get her Evie back, her life would be destroyed for the second time.

CHAPTER 45

It was as if she had taken root in Liane's sofa. Daria pressed her phone, now returned to her, against her heart, her eyes following Frith as the little girl followed Liane into the room. Both of them sat down in the armchair vacated by Sergeant Bryson, Frith cuddled on Liane's lap. Daria's throat closed.

'Mummy, when will the police find Bridie?'

Liane stroked the little girl's head. 'Soon, I hope, sweetie.'

Steve appeared with a tray of mugs and handed them round. 'Drink, Daria. You've had a shock.'

Daria accepted a mug of sweet tea and sipped. She didn't even have the strength to find it disgusting, she cared about nothing except her girl. Bitterness rose in her throat as Frith nestled further into Liane. Some people had all the luck. Oh, that wasn't fair, Frith's little life had been full of bad luck as well as good, but at least Liane had her child to cuddle. What if the police didn't find Evie? What if the worst happened and her daughter vanished all over again, this time for ever?

'Mummy? I want Bridie to come home.'

Frith's lips were trembling, and Daria winced. The child wasn't stupid, she knew something was wrong here. How to start explaining to her that Bridie wasn't Bridie?

'Policemen are good at finding people, Frith.'

Reassuring, nursey tones from Steve.

The little girl pouted. 'O–kay. And when Bridie comes back very soon, can she stay for tea? And cake?'

Liane kissed the worried little face. 'We'll see.'

And all the time they were waiting, waiting. Daria thumped her mug down on the coffee table. This was wrong, she should be out there, doing something, looking for her girl. She half-stood up, then dropped back onto the sofa as Jill came into the room.

'We've got dozens if not hundreds of officers out combing the streets, Daria, and Evie's photo's being distributed everywhere.'

What did 'everywhere' mean? Anger hardened Daria's voice. 'It might not be enough. She's only four years old – suppose she's been taken again?'

'That's what we're trying to prevent. Is there anyone we can contact for you? Evie's father?'

'We're separated. I should – I'd better give you his number.' Daria passed her phone to Jill to note the number, then jerked round to stare into Liane's face. 'Can you drive?'

'Yes, but—'

'I want to go out looking too. Can you take me?'

Jill was shaking her head. 'That's not a good idea, Daria, you're distraught and—'

'I'll be more than distraught if my daughter isn't found! There can't be too many people out looking, can there?'

Daria pushed herself to her feet and stepped over to her crutches, lying abandoned beside the sofa.

Jill put a hand on her shoulder. 'We can go in a police car if you—'

'No. A police car might scare Evie off. I want to go alone with Liane.'

She grabbed her crutches and stood straight.

Liane shrugged at Jill. 'I can take you in Steve's car, I guess. Are you insured for me driving it?'

He was shaking his head. 'Sorry. It's insured for me and Jon only. I'll take you, Daria. Liane should stay with Frith anyway.'

Frith was wide-eyed on her mother's lap. 'Why's Daria looking like that? Is she cross with Bridie?'

Liane kissed her. 'No, baby. She's just worried. We'll stay here in case Bridie comes back by herself, huh? We'll make some strawberry milk while Steve and Daria are out looking for her.'

'Ooh, yes!' Frith vanished into the kitchen.

Liane hugged Daria tightly. 'They'll find her, Daria. They have to.'

Jill sat down again. 'I'll contact you straightaway if anything happens here, then.'

Daria looped her bag over her head and followed Steve outside. Last time she'd been in this car was the day she'd lost Frith and Liane had been so angry with her. Now it was Evie who was lost, lost once after the accident and lost again before she'd ever been found. Dear God.

Steve jabbed the key into the ignition. 'Where do you want to go?'

'You know the area better than I do. Where would a little girl run off to?'

'Frith told Jill they'd gone up the hill and seen some houses that Br— Evie said were like your place. Let's see if we can find those.'

Daria gave him a brief nod. But the police were already doing this, weren't they?

Steve drove up the hill and along Montgomery Road, passing some fabulous old detached houses with large gardens. These hadn't been split into flats, but she could see why Evie'd thought they were like home.

They came to a mini roundabout, and Steve steered the car right round it. 'Evie wouldn't have come this far, would she? Let's go back and try the other direction.'

Daria couldn't speak. If someone had bundled Evie into a car, she could be anywhere by now. Her heart thudded painfully as they passed a couple of police cars. Several officers were out on foot too; they'd be talking to the people who lived in the houses. Had anyone seen Evie? But they'd let her know, if anyone had. Wouldn't they? The traffic was moving faster here; they'd left the residential area and were passing the cemetery and—

'Stop! Please. I want to get out for a moment.'

Steve shot her an uneasy glance and pulled over into a narrow parking space beside a row of shops. He switched off the engine. 'Is this…?'

Daria pushed her door open and got out, not speaking. Steve came round to help her. Rain was falling now, fat drops plopping onto her jacket, turning the pale blue several shades darker. Dark to match her life. Daria stood with her back to the car, staring down the road, her mouth working.

'That's where it happened. The accident.' She swung forward on her crutches and Steve followed. Daria limped on, away from the shops, past an empty building and – here. She stopped, rain mingling with the tears on her face. Across the road was the cemetery, further on was the college and the burned tree, blackened further now by rain.

Steve put a hand on her shoulder and rubbed. 'Do you remember being here?'

'Vaguely. I remember lying on the ground and hearing Evie crying. Everything hurt. Next thing I knew I was in the hospital. By that time, it was the Saturday and they'd operated on my leg. Oh, why can't I remember more, Steve?'

He put an arm across her shoulders, hugging tightly without knocking her off balance; Christ, he was too good to be true, this bloke. Despair washed over Daria along with the rain. Margie had somehow taken Evie away, and no one had seen it. And even that didn't matter because Margie was dead now and Evie was who knew where. There was no comfort in all the world that anyone could give her. Daria whimpered.

'Daria, do you want to go back? We could drive round the park near Liane's.'

Daria wriggled her shoulders away and started up the road, her face grim. 'I want to go into those shops first, and show them Evie's photo.'

Her crutches slid on the wet pavement, but she didn't stop walking.

CHAPTER 46

The funny music was in the far corner. Evie trotted along to where the sound was coming from, but a row of bushes at the end of the path was hiding whatever was behind them. She came to the end of the row and peeked round the bushes and – how lovely! It was like a little fairy garden here, with much smaller stones, and most of them were white, not grey or black like the big ones, and as well as flowers they had toys here, too, and stone angels and windmills, and – a windchime was stuck in the ground beside one of the white stones and it was making the tinkly music. Evie crouched down to look at it. It was a bit like the one a friend of Grandma Millie's had hanging up in her window, one day when Grandma Millie had taken Evie there to visit. This one was nicer, it had silver tubes hanging from a round silver circle, and it was making lovely fairy music.

She stood up again and moved to the next stone. This one was shaped like a heart, and there was only one word on it.

When she was bigger, she'd learn to read, but she knew the first letter already; it was a D like Mummy had in her name.

A cold wet splash hit her hand, and Evie turned her face up to the sky. Dark grey clouds were pushing against each other and big fat raindrops were pattering down faster and faster. The stone angels were getting wet. She should go back to Mammy's, and if Mammy still wasn't there she could go and find – oh, no! Evie pressed her hand against her mouth. She'd forgotten all about Frith, waiting in the den. Back around the hedge, quick, onto the bigger path, along to the gates, out onto the street, and it was this way now. Or that way? No, this way.

Evie started along the pavement, then her tummy went all tight and sore. The funny old man was there. He was limping along, coming closer and closer. Better go the other way after all; she didn't want to have to run past him. Quick!

The road was busier again. Cars were swishing along fast and nobody else was out in the rain. A car skidded just ahead, tyres screeching before it caught its balance and went on. Evie stopped, her hands pressed to her cheeks. That screech – it was making her tummy all funny and scared. She pressed back against the wall and looked across the road at a big building. What had happened to the tree over there? It was all sad and burned and this wasn't a nice place, look, no no no – big boys were shouting at each other, further along the road. Run, Evie, quick, away.

Evie ducked back in through the cemetery gates and ran past the first few rows of stones. She'd go back to the wind-chimes and the angels. It was safe there. Where was the little path going to the stone angels? It wasn't here, and the fairy music was gone too; all you could hear was rain pattering on the path and people shouting in the distance. The big tree wasn't far away, though. It would be dry under there.

Evie pushed past the thin branches that were almost down to the ground, and yes, it was almost dry under the tree. This was like a tree house. She would sit here with her back against the tree trunk and wait until the rain stopped and then she'd go home to Mammy's. The tree was making a whooshing sound in the wind. She and Mammy had been here once, hadn't they? Maybe Mammy was back now, wondering where Bridie was. And Tabitha might be, too, maybe she'd had her kitties and they were all waiting. And Mammy would make beans on toast for tea, and they'd sit on the sofa with the cats and tell stories about Ireland. Oh, she wanted to go back there, back to Mammy and Tallulah and Tabitha and everyone, and be safe. Mammy was happy when they were all home together. Evie pulled her knees up to her chest and leaned her head on damp blue trousers. She didn't want to cry here, all alone.

'Room for another one?'

Evie jerked up, pressing back against the tree. Oh, no. It was the old man with the big coat. Her throat was stuck; she couldn't say a word to stop him coming right in under the tree and sitting down almost beside her. He pulled a can of beer from under his coat and popped it open.

He winked at her. 'Good day for the ducks, eh?'

His voice was fuzzy like cotton wool. Evie gaped. 'Why?'

'They like the wet, don't they? It's fair pi— pouring down out there. You've found the best place, hen. What's your name?'

Evie wrinkled her nose as he leaned his head back and had a long drink from his can. Daddy had beer sometimes too and it smelled yukky. The old man smelled too, worse than the beer. She inched away.

'Sometimes I'm Bridie and sometimes I'm Evie.'

'And who are you today?'

He was chuckling into his can, then he coughed like Mammy.

'Bridie.' But was she? She'd been looking for Mummy, hadn't she, and at Mummy's she was Evie. But that was such a long time ago. A drip landed on Evie's hand, and she wiped it off. It was sad when you wanted to be in two places and you didn't know how to get to either of them.

'Well, Bridie, when this rain stops, we should go home. Where do you live? You're very small to be out all by yourself.'

The old man rummaged around under his coat. His hand came out with a scrunched-up paper bag. He opened it out and offered it to Evie.

'Reckon you'll feel better after a sweetie, hen. Go on, take one. They're magic sweeties. They make the rain go off.'

Evie stood up. There was something wrong about the man, and Mummy had always said, never take sweeties from strangers because they would make you ill. That would be nasty and she'd been ill once when she was at Mammy's so she didn't want to be ill again. Anyway, Mammy had drunk all the pink medicine.

'Go on, hen. Take one.'

He was standing up – he was coming after her! Evie ran, fast as she could, back towards the big black iron gates. Quick, quick, home to Mammy.

CHAPTER 47

They walked along the narrow pavement, side by side but without speaking. A food bank was first in the row of half a dozen shops, and Daria turned in. It was well populated; dear heavens, what had the world come to? Steve stood by as she showed Evie's photo around amongst a warm wave of Glasgow concern. But no one had seen Evie, and they returned to the street. No one in the bookmaker's had seen the little girl, and neither had the assistant in the newsagent's.

'I don't think so, but we get so many kids coming in and out here.'

'But you definitely didn't see this child today?'

Righteous indignation filled the woman's voice. 'If she'd come in alone, I'd have called the police. Kids that size shouldn't be out on their own. Unbelievable what some parents allow their kids to do these days.'

As if she was to blame for small children going into the shop alone. All Daria could do was thank the woman and swing out of the shop again, Steve holding the door for her. On the pavement they stood still and looked at each other.

'Daria, we shouldn't be doing this. You could end up getting an earful of abuse. This is a job for the police.'

Raindrops were splashing ever faster onto their heads, and Daria's heart sank in defeat. The odds of finding anyone who'd seen Evie today were minute. She shivered. On a sunny day, there'd be more chance of people being out and about for the joy of it, with time to notice a small girl out on her own, but not today.

Steve gripped her arm. 'You're cold. Come on, let's go back to the car and see what you want to do next.'

Daria swung her crutches forward, and Steve put a hand on her arm, steering her back along the pavement. The crutches clicked every time they struck against the pavement, over and over, and the rain was falling ever faster. But here was the car. Steve opened the door, and Daria collapsed into the passenger seat, breathing heavily.

'Wait. Give me a minute.'

He sat back, and Daria dabbed her wet cheeks with a tissue. A minute to do what? She stared back towards the shops, seeing nothing. The cloudburst was coming to an end, and the sudden flash of light as the sun emerged from behind the clouds was hard to bear. Rain suited this day so much better.

Uncertainty and helplessness were wafting across from Steve, and anyone would understand why. Poor guy – he was probably scared he was out with a poor crazy woman who was going to lose it any moment. A police car sped past, lights flashing, and skidded into the alleyway behind the row of shops. Daria's gut tightened. Were they looking for Evie too? But there were no sirens, and surely that must mean they hadn't found her.

Her phone buzzed in her pocket. Noah.

'Daria – why the shit didn't you tell me? I've just had the police on the phone. This is crazy. Unimaginable. Where are you?'

He was right, of course she should have called him. 'I'm with a friend. There's nothing we can do except let the police get on with the search.'

Heavy breathing sounded in her ear. When he spoke again his voice was lower than usual, and uncertain. 'Shall I come? Are you all right?'

A confrontation with him would be the last straw. 'Of course I'm not all right. Wait at home, Noah. Call your mother, but leave my parents alone. I'll be in touch soon, okay?'

Daria ended the call and squinted at Steve. 'Can we go back to Liane's, please?'

He jabbed the key into the ignition and the engine leaped into life. 'Hang on, Daria. You'll get through this. They must find her.'

Steve reached out and gave her hand a squeeze, and Daria sat silently while they waited for a gap in the rush-hour traffic. The sun was glistening ever brighter on the wet road. Was Evie still outside? Had she sheltered somewhere, or was she wet, desolate, lost, afraid? Or worse. Don't think it, Daria. Leave the blackest thoughts until you know for sure.

Hopelessness was pinning her down; city streets even in sunshine were no place for Evie all alone. And the 'golden hour' was long gone. The likelihood of finding her girl was shrinking with every minute, every second that passed. All she could do now was go back to Liane's home, to be close to the place where Evie had spent the past four weeks. More than four weeks.

A gap appeared in the traffic, and Steve swung out, grabbing the sun visor to shield his eyes against blinding sunlight. Daria grappled for her sunglasses and jammed them on, staring straight ahead. Ten minutes and they'd be back at—

A horn blared, and a scream – hers? – rang through the car as a small figure pelted out of the cemetery gates, straight into the path of the car in front, which swerved violently. *No no no no no.*

Steve yanked the car to the side and they screeched to a halt by the burned tree. Daria had the door open before the car had stopped and tumbled out, forgetting her crutches, limping across the street to a growing crowd gathered around a small figure sprawled over the road.

'Evie!' Daria dropped to her knees on wet tarmac, bending over her child, fighting off the hands trying to stop her. Evie wasn't moving.

CHAPTER 48

The police had left them alone. Jill had given Liane a card with a number to call 'if you need me', and she tucked it into her handbag where it wouldn't get lost, but really, it wasn't likely she'd need the police when she was here at home with Frith. Unless Bridie – Evie – came back under her own steam, and after all this time, that did seem unlikely.

Frith trailed into the living room, baby doll under one arm. 'When's Bridie coming back? And why's Margie in hospital? Can we take Bridie to visit her? I want Bridie to be here again.' She flung the doll onto the sofa and folded her arms.

Liane patted her knee, but Frith wasn't in the mood for cuddles. The little girl perched on the sofa, her chin jutting stubbornly forward. Liane's heart ached for her. There were no reassurances she could give her poor girl. Was this the time to tell her that Bridie wasn't Bridie and Margie was dead? Liane gazed into the middle distance. No. Not yet. Better to wait until Evie was found, then at least there'd be good news to mix in with the bad.

'We'll ask Steve about Margie when he comes home. She was on his ward, so he'll know all about it.' Cripes, that past tense had slipped out.

Fortunately, Frith didn't notice. 'And Bridie?'

'The police are working as hard as they can to find her, don't worry.' Inspiration struck, and Liane stood up and held out her hand. 'But there is one thing we can do to help. I think I know where Tabitha's hiding.'

Frith's petulance disappeared as if by magic. She jumped up and took Liane's hand. 'Ooh! Can we go and look?'

'We might need to ask a policeman if we can go into Margie's house to find Tabitha, but I'm sure they'll say yes.'

Fingers crossed they would, because there was no saying Tabitha was coping with her new family, was there? Surely no policeman would deny them permission for a quick check.

Margie's garden was empty of police officers as they crossed the scrubby grass, though several cats appeared and wound their way around Frith and Liane, miaowing loudly.

'I think it might be dinner time, you know.' Liane put on her best cheerful voice. Her job was to keep Frithy occupied and as happy as possible, in the circs, and she would give it her best go.

'Can we feed them?'

The back door was closed, and Liane hesitated. Was this breaking and entering? There was no police seal, though, and when she scooted round the front to look, a solitary officer was on the other side of the road beside his car, talking into his phone. He glanced up as Liane approached Margie's front gate.

She gestured at the house. 'Is it okay if I go in to feed the cats?'

He gave her a thumbs-up. Liane swivelled round and trotted back the way she'd come. Frith was sitting on the step trying to stroke about six cats who were clearly queuing up for one thing only, and it wasn't cuddles.

Inside, the house was eerily quiet – or did it just seem that way because she knew that Margie was gone forever? There wasn't a sound to be heard from Tabitha's cupboard, and the door was as she'd left it. Liane scrutinised the messy kitchen. A packet of cat food was leaning crazily against the toaster, and she set Frith to filling food bowls while she did the same with water. When the cats were all occupied, she beckoned to Frith.

'Don't make a sound. I think Tabitha's in here. We'll have a quick look and if she's okay, we'll leave her alone. And, um, any kittens she might have had.'

Margie and Bridie were forgotten as Liane eased the cupboard door open and they peeked in. Tabitha was stretched out in the box, four kittens suckling vigorously. Frith's face was a picture of awe. Tabitha glared and hissed.

'She's fine. We'll leave her alone, love bug.' Liane pulled Frith away and pushed the cupboard door to again.

'When will they come out of the box? Can we have one? Mummy, Tabitha hasn't had any dinner yet!'

Frith's anguished whisper filled the kitchen. Liane opened the back door. 'As soon as the other cats have gone back out, we'll put some grub down for Tabitha.' She whipped up both water bowls as an inducement and placed them on the cracked concrete slabs behind the house. Marmaduke and Socks followed her out, but the others were still chomping away and Liane didn't like to pull food bowls out from under hungry chins. They could wait five more minutes.

Frith was crouched by the cupboard, squinting in through the centimetre-wide gap Liane had left, but at least she wasn't fretting about Bridie. Liane pulled out her phone – no messages. Bummer.

The front door rattled as someone knocked vigorously on the other side, and Liane nearly died of shock. Good grief – was that the police officer? Why didn't he come straight in? Frith sticking close behind her, she strode down the hallway and yanked the door open.

A man in a dapper grey suit stood there, a shock of salt and pepper hair falling over his brow. He stepped back, eyes widening as they went from Liane to Frith.

'Can I help you?' Liane took in the cut of the suit and the shine of the black leather briefcase the man was holding. He'd be more at home in a swanky bank, this bloke. What was he doing at Margie's?

'I'm sorry – do you live here? I'm looking for Margaret Donohoe?'

What an odd accent he had – guttural Glaswegian with a lilt, somehow, and a hint of something foreign, too.

'I'm her neighbour. Who are you, please?'

'I'm her son.' He slid a hand inside his jacket and presented her with a business card. Liane stared at the name, her heart sinking to her boots. Aiden Donohoe. Oh, my gosh, no. She found her voice and gave Frith a little push towards the kitchen.

'Just check on Tabitha, would you, baby?'

When the kitchen door swung shut behind Frith, Liane held out a hand to the man. 'I'm Liane Morton. Aiden, I'm so very sorry...'

CHAPTER 49

Daria knelt beside Evie, thankfulness flooding her soul. She had her daughter back she had her daughter back she had her daughter back. Evie lay on the wet road, eyes unfocussed, oblivious to her mother by her side, but she was breathing, she was alive. Daria laid a gentle hand on the child's chest. Evie's hair was filthy, her little face was pale and she was wearing the same jumper she'd had on the day of the accident, though her trousers were different.

Steve, crouched above Evie, was holding the little girl's head still. Sirens swooped towards them, their shriek niggling through the haziness in Daria's mind. She'd heard that swoop of sirens before, right here, lying on the wet road by a tree that would soon be scorched and maimed. But she should focus on here and now.

'It's all right, Evie. Mummy's here. You're going to be all right.' Please let that be true.

Two green-clad paramedics arrived, and after checking Evie and talking to Steve, they loaded Evie, now immobilised with a neck collar, into the ambulance. Daria was ushered in too.

Steve called after her. 'I'll follow on in the car.'

He was smiling, so Evie couldn't be badly injured, could she? Daria leaned over and stroked the grubby hair from Evie's forehead.

'We'll soon be at the hospital, darling, and the doctors will put everything right. Mummy's here.'

'Mummy?'

A breathy little croak of a voice. Oh, how she'd dreamed of this. Evie was talking to her again. Too choked to speak, Daria squeezed Evie's hand, and the answering squeeze came. The ambulance moved off, and Daria glanced out. Steve's car was already gone.

In just ten minutes, her crutches were clacking over the floor of the Children's Hospital as she walked beside Evie on her trolley. The ache of loss was gone, replaced by apprehension. What if Evie was horribly changed? What if there was something they didn't know about yet? What if they didn't let Evie come home to her broken family and her mother who hadn't insisted on a car seat?

Steve joined them as they were going into A&E. 'Breathe, Daria. Not long now.'

He was greeted by several people as they went – of course, he'd worked in Children's before moving on to his current job. Evie was taken into Paediatric Trauma, an echoing chasm of a room with six generous treatment bays. Steve pulled Daria back a few steps as the team of doctors and nurses descended on the trolley. Evie was definitely awake now, and definitely not too horribly injured because she was answering yes and no to the questions they were asking her and moving her arms and legs as directed. Daria's tears were flowing freely, but these were healing tears. Two nurses moved away, and Evie looked straight at her.

A young doctor stepped over to Daria. 'She has no obvious injuries apart from grazed knees and a scrape on the head. I'll talk to the consultant and we'll do a scan to see if it shows anything. We'll keep her still for the moment, but I'd say she's got away with it.'

Daria staggered backwards, and Steve gave her a little push. 'Evie's waiting. On you go, Mrs.'

Dark blue eyes widened as Daria arrived at the trolley – something solid to hold on to – and she stretched out her hand to touch Evie's head. Take it slowly, Daria. Oh, my, in four short weeks her child had shot up. All the baby chubbiness was gone. Daria bent her head and held her face next to Evie's. She was floating on air, she was delirious with elation, but deep inside she was raging too, wasn't she? Raging at the taxi driver, at Margie, at herself and Noah for not being better parents while Evie was gone. No one could say if this oddly silent little girl would ever be the same Evie again – in fact, she wouldn't be. None of them would come back unchanged from what had happened.

There was a commotion outside, and voices, then a nurse ushered Noah in. He crept up to the trolley and put a trembling hand on Evie's head, stretching his other arm towards Daria. Daria stood frozen to the spot, then grasped the offered hand. Evie needed her family.

. . .

It took an hour, but by the time Evie returned from her scan, she was talking again and her eyes were shining in almost the old way.

'She's a trouper,' said the nurse who arrived with the scan results. 'We don't often have kids that age who cooperate so well, and it speeds things up no end.'

Evie pulled herself up to sit cross-legged on the trolley. A tiny smile flickered over her face. 'I was looking and looking for you, Mummy. I couldn't find the right house.' She frowned, peering at Daria's crutches. 'Why have you got those?'

Daria bent her head and kissed Evie's forehead. Nothing, nothing else mattered. 'I broke my leg. I was looking for you, too, all this time. Can I give you a big hug?'

Evie stretched out both arms, and Daria pressed the child to her heart. The consultant arrived and reached for Evie's arm, bending her wrist this way and that and feeling up and down the length of the bones before pressing around on her hand.

His eyes crinkled at Daria. 'Her head's fine, and we only found one other injury, which I'd guess was from the accident four weeks ago. She had a greenstick fracture here below her elbow, but it's healed beautifully. We'll keep her in tonight as she was pretty dazed when she came in, but all being well, she can go home tomorrow.'

'Mummy, I want to see Frith. And Mammy. And Tabitha and the cats.'

Her heart breaking, Daria reached out and stroked Evie's grubby hair. 'We'll see Frith very soon, I promise. And Liane.'

Evie nodded solemnly. 'And Mammy.'

Steve came up to the trolley. 'Mammy's in another hospital, Evie. She's – sick, I'm afraid. Don't worry, Liane and Frith are going to feed the cats.'

'I want to see Tabitha's kitties, too, when she has them.'

Pleading eyes were staring at her, and Daria managed a smile.

'I think we'll manage that.' She would manage anything now.

Steve put a hand on her shoulder and murmured in her ear. 'Liane's next door with someone you'll want to talk to later. He'll be able to give you more insight into Margie.'

Evie pulled at Daria's sleeve. 'Is Frith there too?'

Steve shook his head. 'She's at Oliver's. She'll see you tomorrow, huh?' He bent his head closer to Daria's ear and murmured, and Daria breathed out through pursed lips. Oh, my. Margie's son was here. How horribly tragic.

If Aiden Donohoe had come just a day earlier… Daria dabbed her eyes. It was too late for Margie and Aiden, but not for her and Evie. She would grab this chance she'd been given to be Evie's mum again. Life was for living, and she would live every minute to the full.

DAY THIRTY-FOUR – WEDNESDAY 20TH MAY

CHAPTER 50

'I liked it better when Bridie lived with Margie. And I don't want all the cats to go to a nice new home.'

Frith stomped across the kitchen, scowling at the toast and chocolate spread Liane had waiting for her. Liane pulled up a chair too. The news that her little friend was going to live with Daria, and the looming loss of the cats – the RSPCA were picking them up tomorrow morning – had hit poor Frithy hard, harder even than the news that Margie was dead.

'We'll go over when the cat people come. You can help them check they've got everyone, and say goodbye. And we'll ask about a kitten for us, too, shall we?'

Frith's scowl lifted marginally. 'One of Tabitha's?'

'We'll see. But kittens stay with their mums for a few weeks, remember.'

Frith's lips were trembling, and Liane nearly dropped her coffee mug as inspiration zinged into her head.

'Which is your favourite cat, love bug? Apart from Tabitha?'

Frith cocked her head. 'Socks, because he plays a lot and he has nice feet.'

'Mm. I think so too.' Say no more, Liane. No point making promises you don't know you'll be able to keep, but if they were having one cat, they might as well have two... Her mobile buzzed in her pocket, and she slid it out to read the message from Daria. *All good for this afternoon. See you in the car park at two? Coffee at The Swan Hotel afterwards.*

Liane sent a text to confirm and sat back with her toast. A child-friendly memorial for Margie was a brilliant idea. Aiden was taking the ashes back to New Zealand, where he and his brother would have a ceremony of their own, but he'd been touchingly pleased to join in with Daria's idea too. And this afternoon would bring closure for Evie.

THE PARK where Daria and Noah had planted their tree was north of the city. Liane hadn't been there since she was a child, but it was a lovely area. They went in Steve's car, and pulled into the car park to see Daria, Noah and Evie there already, with Kit Johns and an older couple who must be Noah's parents. Frith rushed over to Evie, her face alight.

Apart from being better-dressed and several shades cleaner, Evie/Bridie looked the same child she'd been the last time Liane had seen her in the garden – and thank goodness for that. It showed the poor kid hadn't been desperately unhappy all the time she'd been at Margie's. Liane did a round of hellos, then hugged Daria.

'Are you okay? You must be shattered.'

Daria, who was walking with sticks today, pulled a face. 'I slept better last night, in my own bed again. Those beds for parents at the hospital don't exactly give you a good night's sleep, do they?'

'Tell me about it.'

Liane turned round as Aiden Donohoe arrived in a black Volvo.

He was wearing blue trousers and a white cotton shirt today, and the bags under his eyes were telling. Poor guy. Imagine coming on a business trip from New Zealand, hoping to persuade your mother to return there with you, only to find her dead.

Noah led the way along by the river, and everyone trooped after him. Liane took Steve's hand. Noah's mother was carrying a bunch of what were surely home-grown roses, what a nice touch, and they were beautiful. They stopped by a little lilac tree, planted near the water and bloomless, though the trees around it were heavily laden with violet-hued flowers that were just past their best.

Daria's hands moved restlessly as soon as she laid her sticks on the ground, and Liane winced in sympathy. This might be tricky for Evie. Daria had decided that Margie's death was enough for Evie to cope with the day after she'd been found, so neither little girl knew yet that Aiden was Margie's son.

Daria took Evie's hand. 'Daddy and I planted this tree while you were staying with Margie. Now we want it to be a place we can come to remember her.'

Evie nodded, and Aiden stepped forward and crouched down beside the little girl.

'Evie, do you know where Aiden lives?'

Liane held her breath as Evie's blue eyes locked with Aiden's. 'Bantry Bay?'

'He used to live there. Who else did?'

'Sammy and Maeve... and Bridie. And Mammy and her Ned.'

'And what did they do there?'

'We went fishing and swimming and Mammy sometimes bought ice cream. And we ate prawns. And it was the best place ever, but I don't remember that.'

Liane forced back tears. Evie's little face was lit up. Look at the way she'd gelled straightaway with Aiden. How amazing.

'Mammy was nice, wasn't she? Evie, do you know who I am?'

A shake.

'I'm Aiden. Sammy's my brother and Maeve and Bridie are my sisters, but it was a long, long time ago that we all lived in Bantry Bay with Mammy. Poor Mammy couldn't think properly when she got old, you see. She thought you were her Bridie. But she saved you when your taxi crashed, didn't she?'

A solemn nod.

Aiden put his hand on the little girl's arm. 'We're all sad that Mammy's gone to stay with the angels in heaven. But she was very, very happy to have her Bridie to look after for a little while.'

Liane mopped her eyes as Evie turned to Daria for a cuddle. What a sad story it was, but Aiden had told it so well. Maeve was 'with the angels' now too, and poor little Bridie hadn't seen her fifth birthday, but no need to mention that today.

Daria's eyes were glistening as she wiped Evie's face with a tissue, and Liane hugged Frith against her side.

Millie unwrapped her roses. 'Evie, would you like to help me leave the flowers here for Mammy?'

Noah's dad produced a small plastic vase, the kind you can leave on a grave, and went to fill it in the river. He stuck it into the ground, and Millie handed the roses one by one to Evie.

Evie placed the last one in the vase and went back to Daria and Noah. The couple were standing slightly apart, but they each took one of Evie's hands, and gladness warmed through Liane. Who knew what the future held for these three, but surely they had a chance of being a family again?

Daria lifted her sticks. 'We'll bring flowers here for Mammy as often as you want to, Evie. We won't forget her, will we?'

'Or the cats.' Evie's face lit up and she ran across to Frith. 'Tabitha's coming to live with us! And the kitties! And Mummy says you can have one, and Grandma Millie's having one too!'

Aiden's deep laugh rang through the woodland. 'Ach, Mammy'll bless you all from heaven for looking after her kits so well. Evie-Bridie, we'll stay in touch. I can't lose my little sister now, can I?'

Liane walked back to the car with Steve, her heart full. Hopefully, they would all stay in touch. Something was telling her Margie would have approved…

ACKNOWLEDGMENTS

Thank you, so much, to everyone who helped in the creation of this book.

To Debi Alper for her insight, advice and editing, and to Alison Baillie for reading early versions and making so many valid comments.

To my sons, Matthias for reading and checking the manuscript, and Pascal for IT help and work on my website.

To my writing 'family', especially Louise Mangos, Cass Grafton, Alison Baillie, Mandy James and Jill Marsh, for their encouragement and support – 2020 has not been an easy year.

Very special thanks go to the team at Hobeck Books, to Rebecca and Adrian for taking on *Daria's Daughter*, and working so hard to turn a story on a word document into a beautiful book, to Lynn Curtis for editing and to Jayne Mapp for the amazing cover image, and to everyone who works behind the scenes.

Last but definitely not least, to everyone on social media – I'm not naming anyone here as there are so many of you, but you know who you are – thank you SO MUCH.

LINDA HUBER

AUTHOR'S NOTE

Daria's Daughter is set in Glasgow, my old home town and the place where I grew up. Some of the places named in the book are fictional, but most are real. The hospitals where Daria and Frith are treated are based on the Queen Elizabeth University Hospital and the Royal Hospital for Children, which were opened in 2015 on the site of the old Southern General Hospital, where both my mother and I used to work. Writing this book brought back so many memories, and I'd like to thank staff of the SGH and the QEUH for looking after both my parents in the last years of their lives.

LINDA HUBER

ABOUT THE AUTHOR

Linda grew up in Glasgow, Scotland, but went to work in Switzerland for a year aged twenty-two, and she has lived there ever since. Her day jobs have included working as a physiotherapist in hospitals and schools for handicapped children, teaching English in a medieval castle, and several extremely strenuous years as a full-time mum to two boys, a dog and a rapidly expanding number of guinea pigs, most of whom have now fortunately left home. After spending large chunks of the last few years moving house, she has now settled in a beautiful flat on the banks of Lake Constance in north-east Switzerland.

Her writing career began in the nineties, when she had over fifty short stories published in women's magazines before finding the love of her writing life, psychological suspense fiction. Her first book was published in 2013 and followed by eight others, all standalone novels set in the UK.

Linda says she finds her plot ideas in little incidents and moments in daily life – talking to a fellow wedding guest about adoptions, a Swiss documentary about fraudsters, a BBC TV programme about family trees.

For Linda it is when you start to think 'what if…', that is when the story really starts.

ALSO BY LINDA HUBER

The Runaway

Stolen Sister

Death Wish

Baby Dear

Ward Zero

Chosen Child

The Attic Room

The Cold Cold Sea

The Paradise Trees

HOBECK BOOKS – THE HOME OF GREAT STORIES

We hope you've enjoyed reading this novel by the brilliant Linda Huber. To find out more about Linda and her work please visit her website: **https://lindahuber.net**.

If you enjoyed this book, you may be interested to know that if you subscribe to Hobeck Books you can download a free novella *The Clarice Cliff Vase* by Linda, exclusive only to subscribers. There are many more short stories and novellas available for free too.

- *Echo Rock* by Robert Daws
- *Old Dogs, Old Tricks* by A B Morgan
- *The Silence of the Rabbit* by Wendy Turbin
- *Never Mind the Baubles: An Anthology of Twisted Winter Tales* by the Hobeck Team (including all the current Hobeck authors and Hobeck's two publishers)
- *Here She Lies* by Kerena Swan

Also please visit the Hobeck Books website for details of our other superb authors and their books, and if you would like to get in touch, we would love to hear from you.

Hobeck Books also presents a weekly podcast, the Hobcast, where founders Adrian Hobart and Rebecca Collins discuss all things book related, key issues from each week, including the ups and downs of running a creative business. Each episode includes an interview with one of the people who make Hobeck possible: the editors, the authors, the cover designers. These are the people who help Hobeck bring great stories to life. Without them, Hobeck wouldn't exist. The Hobcast can be listened to from all the usual platforms but it can also be found on the Hobeck website: **www.hobeck.net/hobcast**.

Finally, if you enjoyed this book, please also leave a review on the site you bought it from and spread the word. Reviews are hugely important to writers and they help other readers also.

Printed in Great Britain
by Amazon

62930955R00224